Darren Coleman

author of the Smash Hits
'Before I Let Go' & Do or Die

Presents:

I Shoulda' Seen It Comin'

Tasha,
It was nice to meet you!
Danette Majette

by Danette Majette

I Shoulda' Seen It Comin'

a novel

by **Danette Majette**

P. O. box 274, Lanham Severn Road, Lanham, MD 20703

Power Play Books and the above portrayal log are trademarks of **Power Play Media Incorporated.**

This novel is a work of fiction. Any references to real people, events, establishments, or locales are intended only to give the fiction a sense of reality and authenticity. Other names, characters, and incidents occurring in the work are either the product of the author's imagination or are used fictitiously, as are those fictionalized events and incidents that involve real persons. Any character that happens to share the name of a person who is an acquaintance of the author, past or present, is purely coincidental and is in no way intended to be an actual account involving that person.

Cover design by Darren Coleman & Azarel
Cover Art by Anthony Carr
Graphic photography by Edward "Outback" Walker
Cover layout and graphic design by Les Green

Library of Congress Cataloging-in-Publication Data;

Majette, Danette
  I Shoulda' Seen it Comin': a novel/ by Danette Majette
  For complete Library of Congress Copyright info visit;
  www.powerplaybooks.com

ISBN 0-9724003-5-4
Copyright © 2005
All rights reserved, including the rights to reproduce this book or portions there of in any form whatsoever.

I Shoulda' Seen It Comin'

by Danette Majette

www.powerplaybooks.com

In Memory Of:

Grady T. Majette

&

Sean Sessoms
(of the Blue Light)

Acknowledgements

To my mother, Nellie M. Best I cannot thank you enough for all your love and support over the years. I'm truly blessed to have someone who loves me unconditional as you do.

To my father Melvin Hester, Stepmother Patricia Jennings and brothers Ronald and Pookie thank you for your support. To my children, Bryan Majette and Marketa Salley you guys are my life. I know you get tired of me preaching, but it's only because I want the best for you. Love You!

To the Matriarch of the Majette family, Verdell Majette thank you for holding our family together and teaching us that there is nothing more important than blood.

To my uncles and aunts, Stanley, Johnny, Wendell, Wilma, and Lucy I love you all and thanks for the support. To my cousins, I'm sorry I didn't name you all but let's face it, that's a lot of ink. I love you and I thank you all for your support.

To my cousin Shelly Carrington, thanks for all the advice and always listening with an objective mind.

To my ex-husband, Marc Salley we haven't always seen things eye to eye. Hell back in the day, we couldn't even be in the same room together. Who would have ever guessed we would turn out to be the best of friends? Thanks for being such a great father and friend.

To Harold (Smax) Morning, over the years I have learned a lot about myself because of you. I think the most important thing I've learned is that I can do anything I put my mind to. Know that no matter where I go or who I'm with we will always be friends.

My extended family, Betty Hamilton, Karen Gordon, Fannie Gordon, Tamika Gordon, Ebony Dudley, Colleen Jennings and Nicole Jennings thank you for treating me like part of the family.

To the best friend anyone could ever ask for Erika Arndt, let me just tell you something. (Ha Ha) If it were not for you I wouldn't have even considered writing this book. Your encouragement and support have meant the world to me. Thank you for listening to me whine and letting me cry on your shoulder. Hopefully I've cried my last cry!

To Anita Belachew, I don't know what I would do without you and I didn't realize it until I almost lost you. Remember God tests us to show us who's real and who's fake. Always know you can count on me. Sista's for life.

I want to send a special shout out to my girl Tiffany Atkins, you have been there for me through the good times and the bad. I am truly blessed to have you as a friend. Thanks for being a real sista! Reggie I didn't forget about you. Know that dreams do come true. I don't have to tell you that though. You're almost there!

To my girls, Angie Wagon and Karina Slota, thank you for always having a listening ear.

To Darren Coleman, you are truly in a class by yourself and those that don't know it, need to recognize. Thanks for believing in my work as much as I do and giving me the chance of a lifetime. I know I've been a pain sometimes - so thanks for not holding it against me. You're one and a million!!

To Tressa Smallwood, I can't thank you enough for not only being a great publisher, but also a great friend. You have no idea how much our little talks mean to me. When I'm having a bad day, I can always count on you to lift my spirits and give me that extra push. I know it hasn't been easy working on my book along with handling your own projects, just know relief is near.

To Leslie German, when I think of all the times you've sat beside me at my computer helping me make this book the "Beast", I can't help but think how blessed I am. Our author/editor relationship has turned into a friendship that I will value for the rest of my life. I also want to thank Lisa Richardson and Angela Oates, you came highly recommended and you lived up to the billing. I realize it takes a lot of eyes to churn out a great book.

To Kwan, thanks for taking time out of your busy schedule to talk to me and lend your support.

A special thank you to my god brothers Kevin Levy, and Equan for always keeping my lights on and refrigerator full!! I miss you both and hollar at a sista.

To my boy Terrance McKinley thanks for always holding a sista down. You've been a true friend and I appreciate that. To Earl Taylor, I can't thank you enough for looking out for me over the years. You kindness will not be forgotten.

I would also like to thank my Nordstrom family, Frank Androski, Gerren Logan, Caroline Rogers, Dottie Minton, Courtney Caughy, Dontrae Neal, Denise Payne, Norene Wilson, Karen Schriver, Kim Butler, Lori Tamulovich, Alena Gasperick, Dan Grossman, Jared Avery, Mike Miranda, Keisha Poole, Claudia Korrot, Lisa Lilly, Samatha Beard, Lucia D'Avella, Brenda Banneker, and the BP&TBD girls (Oh you too Daryl Johnson) at 626. To Amelia Lechter and Delana Sunday thank you for inspiring me to make it against the odds.

To my friends, Audrey Thomas, Pastor and Mrs. Frank Askew, Chink Santana and Marquise, Willie Savage, Nicole Wiggins, Sabrina, Janette, and Annette Wright, Cheryl Vance, Pamela Chase, Sheena Johnson, Jodie Adams, Angie Whitaker, Andre Tibbs, Marcus Gates (of the Critical Condition Band), Michael (Putt)Turner, Dave Taylor, Gary Stewart, Barbara and Lindsey Love.
Thank you all!

To the following artists Mary J Blige, Karen Clark-Sheard, and Donnie McClurkin your music as inspired me to keep living when I wanted to give up. Thank You!

To the staff at All Daz and Shooters, and Michunu, thank you for your support and putting the word out about the book. Thanks to everyone at Karibu Books in DC for the support in advance, and to Rico Douglass for sending me to Darren. Thanks so much to Karen, Kevon, Karen and Erik, and everyone at A&B. Thanks to Natti at Afrikan World Books. Much love to Massamba, the King of Jamaica Ave, keep pushing brother.

To everyone who said I couldn't do it and for those who rooted against me, I have to thank you for the extra motivation to get here you might as well quit hating and enjoy. God willing, this is only the beginning.

I Shoulda' Seen It Comin'

a novel

by **Danette Majette**

"If you want to know the end, look at the beginning."

— African Proverb

Chapter One

I was so tired of being married to this motherfucker. He acted like a bitch every time I wanted to go out.

"Shut the fuck up, Deonte! Maybe if yo ass had some damn friends to hang out with, you wouldn't always be trippin off me and my friends." I was screaming at the top of my lungs. Deonte looked as if that was the last straw. More than anything else, he hated when I talked shit to him. We had been arguing since Brina called and asked me to go to a party up in Richmond with her, Sheba and Nicole. Deonte started coming towards me. I wasn't really scared but I ain't crazy. Deonte was a big nigga. At 6'3" he towered over my 5'4" frame. His muscular arms could send me flying to the other side of the room. Up to this point, Deonte had only man-handled me. He hadn't actually hit me, but he had a new look on his face, so I grabbed my 5lb weight off the floor by my bed. When I thought Deonte was in striking distance, I swung with all I had, missed, and sent my body spinning. Deonte took the opportunity to grab me by my hair and yank me in close to him. Out of the corner of my eye, I saw Zeta standing in the bedroom doorway holding her Barney doll. I figured Ryan was pretending to still be asleep. He hated it when we fought.

As he tightened his grip on my hair, he barked, "Zsaset, your trifling ass can't ever act like a wife and mother. My mother said your ass was trash. Look at your daughter standing over there – you think she proud of your trifling ass, Zsaset?"

Deonte said that same shit every time we argued. His grip on my hair was causing my head to throb in pain, but I managed to say, "Do you think I give a fuck what your mother thinks?" He had me in an awkward position, but I twisted and managed to kick him in his sack. He doubled over in pain, releasing my hair. I screamed down at Deonte as he squirmed on the floor, "You ain't my fucking father – get over it!"

It wasn't uncommon for Deonte and I to fight about me going out, especially since I was liable to hang out Sunday through Saturday. The only reason that I had been in the house the last couple of weeks was because I'd been sick as hell and my mother, who was my steady sitter, had been out of town visiting my uncle in North Carolina.

Marriage hadn't slowed me down one bit and as a matter of fact, it sped me up. I got married too young and I wasn't happy. I ran the streets to avoid Deonte. Our relationship was falling apart. It was no surprise considering we had only dated three months before I got pregnant and we tied the knot. Deonte was a romantic and I got caught up in the fairytale. He had pretty chocolate skin and a smile to die for. His muscular body was fresh out of a three year stint in the Marines when we met. But a few weeks after we were married, we were at each others' necks because we never got to know one another. He was a Marine for sure. Everything had to be in order and on time. That shit drove me crazy. By the time we realized that we weren't in love, it was too late. He was controlling and boring and I wasn't *Holly the Homemaker*. Hell, I didn't even like his sex that much, which drove him crazy. That's when I started hanging out with my girls every chance I got, which was almost every day.

Zeta was crying at the doorway. I felt a twinge of guilt about leaving her upset. I consoled her by promising to take her to see Grandma tomorrow. I quickly gathered my party gear and rolled out before Deonte regained his composure. I could still hear him moaning in the bedroom as I left out the door.

I pulled into Brina's complex and up to her building. Brina was my girl from way back. We'd been tight from the days of Tidewater Park Elementary and Mr. Smith's fourth grade. She was

I Shoulda Seen It Comin'

the prettiest girl in our neighborhood and her mother always bought her designer clothes from New York that no one else in our neighborhood had. This made her the target of jealousy. Those that didn't hate her, hated me because she liked me so much.

"Why do you hang out with Zsaset? She's ugly and she can't dress," some of them would say when I wasn't around. Some of them would try to break our friendship up by telling us that the other one was talking about her, but we never fell for their games. In fact it made us closer.

I threw my car in park and blew the horn. I looked out the passenger side window and noticed Nicole standing outside talking to this guy who was wearing a Cross Colours jacket. It was the same guy she had met in the Blue Light, a club we frequented around the corner from Brina's apartment. We made eye contact and she put her finger up to me. I blew the horn so Sheba and Brina would come down. I sat in the car for about ten minutes putting on my make-up before I yelled, "C'mon y'all, let's go." Patience was never one of my strong suits. Not to mention, I was ready to get my groove on. After a few minutes Brina and Sheba ran down the stairs and piled into the car.

Before I could even drive two blocks Sheba, who we called Rumpshaker, lit up a blunt.

"Bitch, can't you at least wait until we get on the bridge," I yelled, rolling down the windows.

In between long puffs on the blunt, Sheba slowly said, "Oh, I thought we were already on the bridge."

I laughed so hard, I had to pull over and get out of the car. When the four of us got together, it was always one big comedy show.

After we drove across the Hampton Roads Bridge, Sheba rolled down the window and yelled, "Richmond, the Norfolk Divas are on their way. So get your money right, and make sure ya'll clothes are tight."

Sheba was a piece of work. For her, it was all about money, and men with money. She was the type of scandalous bitch you would have to sleep with one eye open around. She would fuck your man and smile in your face like it was nothing. I met Sheba through Brina about two years ago. We probably wouldn't have liked each other except for the fact that we were both tight with Brina. Just looking at Sheba, she wasn't cute. On a scale of one to ten, on raw looks alone, she was probably a six. She is busty with broad shoulders and not much ass. She has the classic V-shaped body. Her dark pie shaped face sports thin lips and a flat wide nose. But Sheba dresses her ass off and walks with confidence. If Sheba sees a dude she wants, she approaches him without hesitation. Most guys seem turned on by her aggressiveness.

"So Brina, who are these niggas we're going out with?" I asked.

"You remember K-Dog and his friends who came down a week ago?"

"Oh, the guys who went with us to the club."

"Yeah, Boy, that's them," Brina said. For some crazy reason, Brina called everyone Boy.

"They look like ballers," Sheba said. "Although some niggas can fake it if you don't pay close attention."

"You would know best," I teased.

"Anyway," Brina interrupted. "They said if we came up they would take us out and show us a good time. All the Moet and food we want. Of course, everything's on them."

"That's my girl," Sheba said.

"Yeah, that's cool, as long as they ain't looking for no ass," I said. Sheba rolled her eyes.

"Speak for yourself, Zsaset."

"Look, just because you're known to "fuck for a buck" doesn't mean we will," I snapped.

"Look, Boys, we ain't come up here for all that. We're here to fun in '91. We just gonna go to the club, get our drink on and then bring our black asses back home," Brina said. After a few seconds of silence Brina added, "And we ain't looking for no drama tonight." We all looked at Nicole.

"What! Why ya'll looking at me?" Nicole was notorious for starting shit. She took a long puff on the joint. In a low voice muffled by the joint's smoke, Nicole said, "I'm chillin', I'm chillin' as usual."

Chapter Two

By the time we got to Richmond, Sheba and Nicole were high as shit and me and Brina had a nice contact high. We met K-Dog and his friends at the McDonald's on Broad Street.

We drove into the parking lot and couldn't believe our eyes. There were niggas all over the place. If you wanted a man this was the place to be.

"Oh my God. I'm in heaven," Sheba said.

"It's more like hell for your devilish ass," I snarled.

As we circled the parking lot blasting reggae, Brina spotted K-Dog's truck. "Pull in between the black Cherokee and the white BMW," she said.

Brina stepped out the car and put on her sexy strut as she went over to greet K-Dog with a hug. The next thing I knew, guys were peeling out of cars one by one. We looked at each other like we had just hit the jackpot, and gave each other high-fives. "Girl, I'm waiting for the ugly one to peel out. You know there's always that one ugly guy," I said.

"Not tonight. I guess they told his ass to stay home," Nicole said. "Ain't that the truth?"

We waited a few minutes, and then got out of my car. Brina introduced everyone except me. I knew it was her way of letting them know that I was "off limits". I cut in and cut my eyes at Brina, "And she forgot me–my name is Zsaset."

I heard one of the guys say under his breath, "Don't forget Zsaset."

"So, you ladies ready to go clubbing?" K-Dog asked.

"Hell yeah," Sheba said.

K-Dog put his hands up and yelled, "Let's do it." We got in the car and headed towards the club.

I Shoulda Seen It Comin'

We drove about a mile before we reached the club. The line was wrapped around the corner. Ivory's was the hottest club in Richmond and with DJ Kool on the turntables it was almost impossible to get inside on a Saturday. "I'm not standing in that long ass line to get into a club. It's too damn cold out here," I yelled.

"Don't worry, K-Dog has connections here," Brina said.

"I hope so or I'll see ya'll back in Norfolk."

We parked about a block from the club and started walking to the door. I guess people could tell we weren't from Richmond because all eyes were on us. And they had a reason to be, because our clothes were tight and we were all sexy as hell. Being the Divas we were, we started sashaying like it was all about us. And you know what, it was.

But as usual, Nicole started getting irate when she saw these girls looking at us and whispering to each other.

"What the fuck ya'll bitches lookin' at? Ya'll must wanna get fucked up or somethin'."

Of course, I started laughing. I knew it was only a matter of time before she blew up. More than anything else, she hated people staring at her. Nicole had a terrible attitude and the ability to fight like a heavyweight champ. She was a time bomb waiting to blow. To make matters worse, Nicole was your classic pretty girl. She had light golden brown flawless skin, with light brown eyes to match. Nicole had that "I got Indian in my family" hair. It was long, wavy and cold black. She had an hour glass shape with a flat stomach and an ass like a shelf. Niggas loved her, though she didn't trip off of them too much. The average bitch disliked Nicole before she ever opened her mouth. Females wanted to whoop her ass just on G.P., but Nicole's shit talkin' always fueled the fire.

Brina put her arms around Nicole's shoulders and said, "Don't forget, Boy, we in these bitches backyard."

"I don't give a fuck," Nicole shot back. But she must have thought about it because she wasn't that loud.

I looked back at the girls standing in line. Just as I did, the little short fat one of the group said to her friends, "That's OK, we'll see that bitch inside."

We got to the front of the club, and security let us right in. "I told you he got connections," Brina said. I guess he did. We got in for free, and we didn't even have to show our ID's.

In the club, K-Dog and his friends ordered about ten bottles of Moet. DJ Kool was jammin'. He was playing a mix version of LL Cool J's, *Mama Said Knock You Out.* I noticed K-Dog's friend named O.B. staring at me. I had actually scoped him out from the moment he got out of K-Dog's car. He was about 6'1, slim with a rock hard body, and a fashion sense that made him even more appealing to the eye. He was dressed in a pair of Armani jeans, a Coogi sweater and some ostrich boots.

After staring for a moment, he walked over and very abruptly said, "So, why did your girl try to skip you on the introductions?"

"I guess she considers me "off limits."

"Oh, are you?"

I toyed with him, "It depends."

"On what," O.B. said.

"Um...a lot of things." I wanted to skip the subject so even though I knew it, I said, "Tell me your name again?"

"O.B.," he yelled over the music.

"That's unique."

"You think so?"

"Yes," I replied, sipping on my drink.

"Does your friend always act like that?"

"Who?" I asked.

"That one," he said, pointing to Nicole.

With a sarcastic tone I said, "Yeah, but it usually doesn't take her so long to make a scene. I guess she's losing her touch."

I don't think he found my joke amusing because he turned around and walked away from me.

I Shoulda Seen It Comin'

We made our way around the club to check everyone out. The place was pure heaven. All the guys were cute and dressed real fly.

"Do these mothafuckers know how to party or what," Sheba said.

"Hell yeah," Nicole said in agreement.

DJ Kool put on Naughty By Nature's, *O.P.P.* and we all started screaming, slapped each other five and hurried to the dance floor. Sheba yelled, "Let's show these bammas how it's done."

After Naughty By Nature, DJ Kool put on Shabba Ranks. Now reggae was our shit, and we got down right nasty when we danced to it. We were out on the dance floor winding our bodies to the sounds of Shabba when I looked up briefly and noticed one of the girls that Nicole was talking shit to outside in line, standing behind her. The girl was dancing but barely moving. Her eyes were fixed on Nicole. Nicole was so high and into the baller she was pressing her body up against, she didn't notice anything. I kept winding but slower as I scanned the dance floor. Several of the girls were positioned around us on the floor.

I danced in towards Brina, "Bri, keep dancing but listen– some shit 'bout to go down. Them bitches from outside got us surrounded. I think it's 'bout seven or eight of them."

Brina breathed deeply. She tried to be calm, but she wasn't a fighter. "Shit, Nicole always running her fucking mouth," Brina said.

"Yeah, I know. You tell Nicole what's up. I'ma get Sheba's attention."

"Alright," Brina nervously squeaked out.

Just as I turned towards Sheba, out of the corner of my eye, I saw the girl behind Nicole push her in the back of her head. Nicole swung around with a vengeance. "Bitch, watch what the fuck…"

The short fat girl cut Nicole's words mid stream as she swung and hit Nicole hard in the side of the face just to the left of her mouth.

Danette Majette

"Naw, bitch, you watch what the fuck you doing," the girl yelled as she put on a show for her crew. Nicole, a bit dizzy, tried to swing back but before she could another girl had grabbed her from the back. Nicole's arms were locked in the girl's embrace while the short fat one combo'd on Nicole's face. The crowd on the floor dispersed. I ran towards the action but was tripped up by one of the crew. I jumped back up and noticed Brina running in the other direction as I jumped on the fat girl's back. I put my arm around her neck and choked her with all I had. One of the crew had apparently grabbed my hair and was pulling me back, but I didn't let go even though it felt like my hair was being detached from my scalp. I am not sure if it was the same one or a different one that sent a fist crashing into my jaw. I still didn't let go of that fat heifer. I had no idea where Nicole was now.

I heard one of the girls scream, "Bitch, let her go. She can't breathe. Let her the fuck go."

"Fuck you," I screamed as I tightened my hold. I tasted the blood in my mouth. I didn't even realize that I had been hit in the mouth.

The next thing I know, Brina, K-Dog and his crew were on the floor with security breaking everything up. DJ Kool had stopped playing music. I was sort of in a daze as one of the security guards pried my arm from around that fat bitch's neck.

I could hear DJ Kool admonishing us. "C'mon ladies, leave that mess outside. We're here to have a good time tonight."

Because K-Dog was cool with security, they let K-Dog, O.B., Quan and the rest of their crew walk us outside. I could hear DJ Kool starting the music back up as we got out the door.

"Where them bitches at? Fuck this shit–where them bitches at!" Nicole demanded. Her face looked bad. Nicole wasn't used to losing a fight. But the appearance of her face said that we had lost this one.

"Security put them out the back door," Brina said. "C'mon let's go back to the car. We don't need no more drama tonight."

I Shoulda Seen It Comin'

We all started heading back to the cars. Everyone began talking and laughing about the situation with the exception of O.B. He walked behind us like a spoiled brat who couldn't have his way. And I think I was the only one who noticed it. Maybe they noticed it too, but just didn't care. This led me to wondering why I cared. If he didn't want to go out with us, he should've stayed home. All the pouting and frowning was unnecessary.

When we reached my car, K-Dog suggested we stay the night. "Ya'll too fucked up to drive back to Norfolk. Plus Sugar Ray here needs to hurry up and get some ice on that face." He motioned towards Nicole. "Why don't ya'll stay with us? I promise you we'll all behave like perfect gentlemen. You ladies can have the bedrooms and we'll sleep in the living room."

"Oh hell no. I ain't giving my room up. Speak for yourself, man," O.B. blurted out.

"Well you have no choice if we decide to stay," I said.

"Who the fuck are you?"

"Who the fuck are you?" I yelled back. "We don't need your funky ass room. C'mon ya'll I can drive back."

"Boy, you ain't gonna kill me," Brina yelled.

"Naw, I can't let you drive back like this. Don't worry, he'll give up his room," K-Dog insisted.

"Let's just stay here tonight. I'm tired," Sheba begged.

"Alright, but keep him away from me, I don't like him. He has a serious attitude problem."

"Deal. Ya'll follow us," K-Dog said.

Chapter Three

We drove through the heart of Richmond. I had only driven maybe ten minutes when I felt my eyes starting to grow weary. We ended up a few miles outside of the city. The area where K-Dog and his friends lived was a quiet, resort-like, peaceful community, unlike the city where everyone looked suspect. It was a good thing I didn't try to drive back because we all would have been on the morning news.

"Wake up, sleepy heads. We're here," I yelled.

"Why you yelling, Boy? We hear you," Brina yawned.

"Well then get the fuck up. I ain't taking nobody in the house tonight, so you better get up or you'll be sleeping out here with Big Foot."

"Where the hell are we at?" Nicole mumbled through her swollen lips.

"We're in the suburbs of Richmond. Don't it look spooky? Ain't nothin' out here but trees and they don't even have street lights," I said as I looked around.

We gathered our belongings and followed the guys into the house. "Well, you ladies can make yourselves at home," K-Dog said.

Being the nosy person I am, I headed upstairs to case the joint. A few minutes later, Nicole came up holding ice to her face. Now that everything had a chance to swell, she was looking like she was wearing a monster mask. I tried not to stare but I could barely see her pretty little face through the heep of swollen flesh.

"Zsaset, what you doing up here?" she asked.

I Shoulda Seen It Comin'

"Hell, he told us to make ourselves at home. So that's what I'm doing. Besides, I wanted to make sure there weren't any dead bodies up in here."

"Girl, it's not that big of a deal," Nicole said in disgust as I looked underneath the bed.

"Hell, we don't even know their real names. All we know is a bunch of nicknames. If we get raped by these guys, all we can tell the police is a bunch of fucked up nicknames," I yelled.

"Shhh, I hear somethin'," Nicole said.

O.B.'s mean ass walked up. "Is everything up to your standards, detective Zsaset?"

"Yes everything is okay so far," I said getting up from the floor. "What is your name again?" I faked.

"It's O.B."

"Where'd you get the nickname O.B.?"

"My friends, why?"

"Nothing just asking."

I laughed to myself thinking, how fitting, his friends named him after a tampon. It was probably because he acted like a woman on her period. O.B. must have noticed the smirk on my face because he said, "Yeah whatever."

O.B. and Nicole went back downstairs. I checked the remaining rooms. Everything was cool so I went back downstairs only to find everyone asleep. I mean everyone. They were all laying on the floor over top of each other. They were so fucked up, they couldn't even make it up the stairs. I wasn't sure about sleeping on the floor with a bunch of strangers, but I was too scared to sleep upstairs alone. So I squeezed in between Sheba and Brina, and dozed off. That was the first time I had slept on a floor, and I was going to make sure it was the last.

I awoke the next morning in a panic. "What's wrong Zsaset?" Brina asked.

"I forgot to call Deonte and let him know I wasn't comin' home last night."

"Ooh, he's gonna fuck you up. I thought you called him before you went to sleep."

"Well, you thought wrong."

"Bitch, don't get smart with me, 'cause you gonna get your ass kicked."

I wasn't even worried about that happening. If he even thought about hitting me, I would fuck his ass up. I may be a lot of things but a punk wasn't one of them. I would go round for round with anyone that put their hands on me, with the exception of my momma.

"Hello," Deonte said in a groggy voice. Shit, I was hoping the answering machine would pick up.

"Hi, it's me. I forgot to call and let you know I wasn't coming home."

"Where are you?"

"I'm in Richmond."

"What the hell are you doing in Richmond?" Deonte didn't hide the disgust in his voice.

"We went to a club and we were too dru... I mean tired to drive back."

"So Zsaset, where the hell you at?"

I stumbled over my words but finally got out, "We at the Days Inn in Richmond." I couldn't tell him we were staying with a bunch of dudes.

Deonte wasn't buying it. "Yeah whatever, Zsaset." He paused for a moment. I prayed he was going to let it go there but of course he didn't. "You know what Zsaset – you and your friends are some hoes. Zeta wants to talk to you."

Shit. Why did he have to put the baby on the phone? "Mommy, you comin' home now?"

Zeta's voice was so sweet. I was irritated with Deonte for using her the way he did. I heard him in the background saying, "Ask her where she is Zeta?"

I Shoulda Seen It Comin'

I put on my sweet mommy voice, "Hey Zeta, mommy will be there in a little while, OK sweetie. I'll make sure to bring you something."

"Mommy, Barney wants to talk to you." Shit. I wasn't in the mood for this.

"OK baby but first put Daddy back on the phone."

A second later Deonte got back on the phone. "You're pathetic," he yelled. He kept yelling as I held the receiver away from my ear. I gave him about a minute to vent before I hung up. I was not trying to hear that shit. I was tired and I had a headache and this mothafucker wanted to yell. Oh hell no.

After I hung up, my friends started cracking jokes. Everyone thought it was funny except me.

"If you were my wife, I would black both yo eyes as soon as you walked in the house."

I turned to see who was talking and it was that smart-ass O.B.

"Is that so?" I replied. "Well, if you were my husband and you gave me two black eyes you'd be walkin' around dick-less fuckin' with me."

I usually don't talk to people like that, but he pissed me off. I guess I pissed him off too because he stormed up the stairs and slammed his door. *Why did he feel like he had to say something anyway? This was between my husband and me. He was not in the equation,* I thought to myself.

Since Deonte was already mad there was no need for me to rush home, so I fell back to sleep. I awoke later to the smell of pancakes and turkey bacon. I followed the smell to the kitchen. K-Dog was at the stove and everyone else played Spades at the table.

"What...you can cook? I'm impressed," I said to K-Dog. He smiled. I could tell he must've come from a good family or either he was the oldest sibling, because any other man would have just made himself breakfast.

Danette Majette

I looked up from my plate and noticed O.B. staring at me. He looked as if he wanted to cut my head off. So I frowned back at him. Truly, I would have preferred to cut something else off of him. It was obvious he had a problem with me but at the same time it seemed to be his weird way of showing that he was digging me. He was sending mixed signals and it was driving me crazy.

"O.B. did you take care of that thang?" K-Dog asked.
"Naw, I'll go take care of it now."
He quickly ran upstairs to get dressed and when he came back down, he began pacing around the house like he was looking for something. Quan got irritated and yelled, "What the hell you lookin' for, man?"
He kept fumbling around as if he didn't hear him. "I was lookin' for these, is that alright with you," he said grabbing his keys.
"Yeah, now get the hell out."
Quan seemed really laid back. But I could tell O.B. got on his nerves because they argued the whole time we were there.
Quan was called the Don of the crew. He looked half-black and half Chinese. Sheba was on him hard and he seemed to be on her too. She had walked up to him in the club from behind and put her arms around him and put her hands under his shirt on his stomach. In her best Chinese accent she'd said, "You so fine–me love you long time." Quan turned around grinning from ear to ear. When I woke up this morning I noticed the two of them were nowhere around. Sheba's such a damn freak.

O.B. seemed to be stalling. "You wanna go?" he asked looking at me.
I faked. "Hell no, so you can kill me and leave me on the side of the road somewhere. I don't think so," I said.
"Ain't nobody gonna do nothin' to you, girl."
"Zsa get your shit and ride with the man. You know you want to go," Sheba said. She was right, I did want to go.

I Shoulda Seen It Comin'

"Are you sure you want me to ride with you? I mean you have been pretty nasty to me."

"If I didn't want you to go I wouldn't have asked."

When we got outside, I slid in the car and looked over at O.B. He glanced at me from head to toe and at that very moment, I was digging him. I was trying not to be obvious in checking him out. I couldn't help but notice how large his hands were as he gripped the steering wheel.

O.B. was leaned way back in his seat. "Can you see where you're going?" I said seductively.

"I can see just fine thank you," he snapped.

"Sorry. I just don't want to lose a limb 'cause you wanna take a nap in your seat."

O.B. smiled. I guess he found my comment humorous. His entire face lit up. His thick sexy lips spread neatly across his face. Everything about his face was dark and smooth except his brown eyes. He had a scar to the left of his nose that gave his face a cute rugged look. I wondered what had happened to cause the scar but dare not ask him. At least not yet.

"You should smile more often, it looks good on you."

"You think so?" he asked stroking his goatee.

"Yeah, I do."

"So if I do, does that mean you won't be *off limits* to me?" I smiled at him and buckled my seatbelt but I didn't say anything.

The drive was crazy. It was like taking a field trip from *The Jefferson's to Good Times*. I couldn't believe all the buildings that were surrounded with police tape. Seeing all the crackheads made me check my door, but nothing beats what I saw when we drove past a sign that read *Mosby Court*. It was a project on the east side of Richmond. There were apartment buildings with boarded up windows, men pissing outside in broad daylight, and used needles on the ground.

We parked on the main strip and O.B. rolled down his window. A rotten-mouthed crackhead approached the car. The other smokers that stood on my side scared the wits out of me.

"What's up, O.B.," one of them yelled.

"What's up, Pipe?"

"These people are pathetic," I mumbled under my breath.

O.B. told the crackhead to step back for a minute. He turned back to me. "What do you mean these people? They're just like you and me."

I had obviously offended him which seemed to be easy to do, of course. What did he mean they were just like me? The last time I checked, I was drug free. I frowned at O.B.

"Oh, I guess you grew up privileged, huh Zsaset?"

"Look O.B., I did grow up in the projects. But it didn't look anything like this. My family had pride and we tried harder to keep ourselves together because we knew people were already going to look down on us for living in government paid housing. These people look like they don't care about shit. We made it our business to get out of the projects as soon as we could."

"Well some people don't have that choice," he said cutting the conversation short. He grabbed the keys from the ignition and opened the door.

"Maybe I used a poor choice of words when I said these people, but I was referring to the drug addicts anyway. Now where are you going?"

"I have to pick up something," he said. Before I could say another word, he slammed the car door. "Curiosity killed the cat," he said, as he walked away with a pipe-head named Gums.

I had suspected that K-Dog, O.B., Quan and the rest of their crew were drug dealers. This trip confirmed it for me.

Just great. Not only did he bring me to the projects, he left me in the car. I slumped down in my seat and began to observe the people outside the car. Crackheads were searching the ground as if a magic self-generating crack rock was going to appear. The female crackheads were dressed in dingy tattered short skirts and ripped nylons with lipstick smeared across their faces. They peered into cars that passed by looking for potential johns. There

I Shoulda Seen It Comin'

were kids playing in the street without shoes. Where were their damn parents? I wanted to dig in my purse and give them money because they reminded me of the Somalian kids I see on PBS. I always thought the place I grew up was bad. But compared to this place it was Beverly Hills. *I am definitely blessed,* I thought to myself. I'll never take a nice home, healthy children and a refrigerator full of food for granted. It saddened me to see so much poverty. I mean here I was looking down on people and I could easily be one of them.

The sound of shattering glass interrupted my thoughts. I jumped and screamed at the same time. I turned to see that the back windshield of the car had been smashed out. A cinder block rested on the back seat. Without even knowing what I was doing, I jumped over to the driver's seat. My hand was trembling so bad I couldn't get the car started. Of course, I couldn't think straight enough to remember that O.B. took the keys with him. I didn't even realize that the driver's side door was open until I heard the voice.

"Tell O.B. he better leave my li'l brother alone. He might run these projects but he don't run my family!" I couldn't tell you what this nigga looked like 'cause I didn't dare look at him. I could just feel that he was big as shit. I leaned my face forward on the steering wheel and didn't respond. I was too scared to say anything. "You hear what the fuck I'm saying? Let that motherfucka know that the next time it ain't gonna be his car – it's gonna be him."

When O.B. returned a few minutes later I was still in the same position with the door open. "Zsaset, what happened? You OK? What happened?"

I glanced at O.B. and started laughing a bit hysterically. "I don't fucking know what just happened. You tell me O.B. A nigga smashes out your window and then starts screaming at me about you and his li'l brother – I don't know what the fuck is going on."

Danette Majette

Something must have clicked for O.B. "Oh, OK, I'm gonna fuck that nigga up." He threw a large duffel bag in the car and told me to move over. He quickly jumped in, started the car and peeled out.

"How could you leave me set up like that? That was fucked up O.B.," I shouted. He didn't respond. I positioned myself in my seat so that I was facing the opposite direction from O.B.. I gazed out of the window thinking *how do I get hooked up with niggas like this?*

O.B. pulled over once we got in the suburbs. "Zsaset, I'm sorry about what happened over at Mosby Court. I swear nothing like that has ever happened to me over there. I wouldn't have left you there if I thought for one minute something like that was going to happen."

It was very interesting watching this side of O.B. He was actually being sweet and he sounded sincere.

"It's cool. I guess there was no harm done," I said.

I thought I would take advantage of this opportunity to pry into some of O.B.'s business. "What's that in the bag?" I asked.

"There you go again with the questions. Can you please just sit back and shut up?" O.B.'s sweet demeanor was gone just as fast as it came.

"Don't tell me to shut up. My husband don't even tell me to shut up." "That's because he's a punk."

"You don't know anything about my husband, so don't talk about him." Pissed off, I twiddled my thumbs and tried to remain calm. It was one thing for me to put my husband down, but I'll be damned if he was going to.

After that, the remainder of the drive back was quiet and the tension between O.B. and me was so thick you could cut it with a knife. I decided to try to break the ice. "Do you have a girlfriend?" I asked.

"No, I don't. I have a wife."

"A wife," I said, flaring my nostrils. "Who the hell married your mean ass?"

"My wife," he said without expression.
"Do you have any kids?"
"Yes, I have a son. Now stop asking me so many questions. I'm not going to tell you that shit again."
Here we go again, I thought. "If you can't talk to me with respect, then don't talk to me at all," I said. He must have known I meant business, so he apologized.

O.B. pulled up to K-Dog's and parked. I quickly grabbed O.B.'s arm when he went to open the car door. I leaned over in my seat and looked him in the eyes. "You like me don't you?"
O.B. smiled. "There you go with the questions again."
I was extremely irritated by his response. "Nigga plea..." O.B. put his index finger over my lips.
"Yes, I do. Is that straight enough for you?"
"Yes, it is. So where do we go from. ..." Before I could finish my sentence he pulled me closer and kissed my lips. His lips were soft and his kiss was nice. When O.B. pulled back I said, "You kiss good to be so mean."
"Maybe I'm not mean. Maybe you just been pushing all the wrong buttons," O.B. said.
"Well you got to show me the right buttons," I said as I got out the car. O.B followed me out the car.
"Well that definitely can be worked out," O.B. slowly said as he studied my body from head to toe. I got to K-Dog's door first and rang the bell. O.B. came up behind me very close as I stood at the door. He was so close that I just slightly felt his jeans rub against my ass and I felt his breath on my ear. I pretended he wasn't so close and like he wasn't making me hot.
I turned just slightly. "Dag, nigga give me some space."
O.B. backed up just a little. "Yeah, I'ma give you some space for now, Zsaset," O.B. confidently whispered.
Brina, Sheba and Nicole all eyed me suspiciously when O.B. and I walked in. I didn't realize it, but we had been gone for a

while. "It's about to get dark so we better go," I said. "You guys ready, right?"

"We been ready!" Nicole said.

As we all stood in the driveway, I couldn't help but squirm in my jeans thinking about kissing O.B.'s juicy lips again. He ignited something in me that I lacked in my marriage. I didn't want everyone to know what was going on, so I sat in my car while they said their good-byes. Brina and K-Dog were all hugged up leaning against K-Dog's car. Quan and Sheba were the last ones to finally come out of the house. I don't even want to know what Sheba may have been doing to him in there.

O.B. finally walked right over to me and asked if I was going to call him. I thought everyone was watching us, so I tried to act like I wasn't interested in what he was saying. "Look, I don't want my friends to know about this. Is there anyway you could sneak me your number?"

"Yeah, just take this pager and I'll page you and put my number in." I quickly grabbed the pager and slid it in my purse.

"Alright O.B., work on being nicer to me the next time we talk," I whispered.

O.B. smirked. "Yeah O.K," he said as he walked back towards the house. "OK, Zsaset."

Chapter Four

No one said anything about O.B. for about the first thirty minutes of our drive home. I knew they were dying to know. Then out of the blue Nicole hit me in the back of my neck.

"Zsaset, since you ain't gonna bring it up on your own, what happened? Girl give us the low down."

"What?" I asked playing dumb.

"Bitch, don't play-you know who I'm talkin' 'bout."

"Who, O.B.?" I said pretending to be bewildered.

"Who, O.B.?" Sheba imitated me in a cartoon-like voice. Everyone laughed.

"Oh, I mean nothing really," I said nonchalantly.

"Stop lying Zsaset. Do you think anyone in this car is gonna tell Deonte? Stop trippin' – what happened?" Sheba said, showing her impatience with my reluctance to talk.

I wasn't giving up any information, so they started assuming shit. "Ya'll were looking kinda hot and heavy to me," Nicole said determined to get all up in my business.

"That's 'cause you can't see too well right now." I tried to make a joke and shift the conversation to Nicole and the fight. It didn't work. Sheba and Nicole continued with their line of questioning. Brina was mostly quiet. She already knew that I was gonna tell her everything once Nicole and Sheba weren't around.

Nicole smirked, "Ya'll were gone quite a while today and the look on your face when ya'll walked in K-Dog's house said, I'm guilty."

"Who asked you?" I said irritated.

Danette Majette

"Don't get mad at me 'cause you cheatin' on your husband. Yo ass should've never got married in the first place. You know you still got the hoe up in ya real thick."

"What? Where does she get this shit from?" I turned to Brina and Sheba. There was a moment of silence and then we all burst out laughing.

After dropping everyone off, I thought of a plan for handling Deonte. I knew he was going to be pissed. He probably has his bags packed again. He always did that when he got mad, of course he never went anywhere. We would just fight and then make up as usual. In a weird sort of way I think Deonte was obsessed with transforming me into the perfect little housewife. I think he looked at it as some sort of competition or challenge that he didn't want to lose at.

Turning the doorknob slowly, I braced myself for Deonte's wrath, but he was cool and collected. *What the hell is that all about? Why isn't he mad?* I wasn't about to go looking for trouble. Instead, I took my clothes off and jumped in the shower. By the time I was finished, Deonte was sitting in the living room watching television. I cautiously sat on the couch next to him.

"Zsa, I just want to let you know you ain't doing nothing slick. I called the Days Inn in Richmond. They didn't have you, Brina, Nicole or Sheba as a guest there."

I played it off. "For your information, Deonte, the room was in Sheba's cousin's name. Damn, you always trying to check up on somebody." I pretended to be pissed by the fact that he was doubting my word. "You need to work on that shit." It was quiet for a moment. "Where are the kids?" I quickly tried to skip the subject.

"I fed them and put them to bed," he said, flipping through the pages of the T.V. guide. "Someone had to do it."

"What's that suppose to mean?"

"It means you weren't here as usual, so I had to do it."

I Shoulda Seen It Comin'

I knew Deonte wouldn't be able to maintain his calm demeanor much longer so I decided to go off before he did. I got up and walked to the kitchen and got a cup of water.
"Well, what about all the times I've had to do it. What, I don't deserve a break sometimes." I slung the cup of water on the floor. "I work and take care of the kids just like you do, probably more. So don't give me that bullshit about somebody had to do it." I stormed out of the room.

The next morning I got Ryan off to school and Zeta to the babysitter's. I was on time for work, I entered the store and walked pass my manager's office quickly in an effort to avoid talking to her. She was 65 years old and looked every day of it. She had worked at the Marine Corp Exchange for 30 years. For at least fifteen years before she started working at the Exchange, she had worked every other job on the Norfolk Naval base. Everyone including the Commanding Officer of the base wished her ass would retire. There wasn't one person on the base who liked her. I personally wanted to choke the shit out of her for some of the stunts she pulled.
"Good morning, Zsaset," she said in her usual smart-ass tone.
Damn she saw me. I doubled back and poked my head in. "Good morning, Mrs. Bea."
"How was your weekend?" she asked.
"It was great," I said imitating her wickedness. She didn't care how my weekend was. She was just trying to be funny with her phony ass.
I counted my drawer and before I could open my department, an elderly white lady stood in my line. I imagined myself telling her, "Get the fuck away. I ain't open yet, bitch," but instead I said, "Give me a moment please, ma'am."
I had worked in the shoe department at the Exchange for about a year and half. I didn't have any friends there. A few girls were phony with me, but I truly didn't like most of the girls in

Danette Majette

there, and they didn't like me either. But everyone knew I used to be in the Marines, so they didn't bother me too much. Of course, there's always that one person who likes to push the envelope. Her name was Mindy and she worked in Cosmetics. Mindy was a skinny little white chick that looked like she threw up after every meal. We were in orientation and training together when we were both new to the Exchange. On the third day of training I told her to, shut the fuck up, after she kept asking stupid questions. Everyone was ready to go home at the end of each day's training session but she asked so many damn questions that she ended up keeping us there for an extra hour. The other people in the class and the trainer all appreciated me checking Mindy. Anyway, from that point on Mindy made it her business to get under my skin. Whenever I was on smoke break or away from my register, somehow Mrs. Bea always found out. I know it was Mindy's ass. Cosmetics was up on a platform and from her post, she could see me and my entire department. I would have long since whooped her ass if I could afford to lose my job.

At lunch time I went into the cafeteria and Mindy's was the first face I saw. She was seated with two other girls that worked in Cosmetics. I got my food and sat at the only open table which happened to be right behind the table Mindy was sitting at. She kept giving me dirty looks and she was shit talking loud enough so that I could hear her.

"What's her name, Zsashit?" The other girls cracked up. "No seriously, that's not it? Oh my God – I was getting ready to invite her to eat with us. I was going to say, Zsashit, come join us." Mindy and the other two were almost hysterical now. "Oh my God and you mean that's not her fucking name. What's her fucking name? Damn her mother should have given her a fucking normal name. Maybe that's why she always has an attitude, 'cause her name is all fucked up. Damn, she probably just wants to be called Mary or Jane or some shit like that." Mindy and her friends were in tears now.

I Shoulda Seen It Comin'

I tried to ignore her but it became clear that I wasn't going to be able to. She kept running her mouth. I slowly stood. I walked over to her. At that moment I didn't care about losing my job. Mindy's eyes got big when I bent down and put my face in hers. Her friends instantly stopped laughing. I took my hand and smooched her in the face. I knew her skinny ass wouldn't do anything back so I wasn't too worried about a fight breaking out. When her head snapped back and we were face to face again I said, "Honey, you don't know me like you think you do. So stop running your mouth before I beat your ass like you stole something from me."

I was waiting for her to say something back, but she didn't. Feeling my job was done I cleared my table and left. I should've waited until we got off of work to confront her, but I just had to say something to her right then and there. I had to let these bitches know I was not to be fucked with.

All morning, I fantasized about O.B.'s kisses. He had paged me with the number to call him at last night, so during my lunch break I gave him a call. The phone rang several times before someone answered.
"Hi. Is O.B. home?" I asked.
"Naw," the voice on the other end replied.
"Okay, could you tell him Zsaset called?"
"Yeah, I'll tell him."

On Thursday while I was preparing to open my department, my phone rang. "Marine Corp Exchange, Women's Shoes," I said.
"May I please speak with Zsaset?"
"O.B.," I said.
"Yeah, girl – what's up?"
"Nothing – It took you long enough to call me."
"My fault – I been thinking about you though."
"I can't tell," I said seductively.
"When am I gonna see you again?" O.B. cut to the chase.

"Soon, I hope," I said.

I wasn't sure what I was doing with O.B., but I knew I needed to see him again. We talked a little while longer until I had to go because the Exchange was opening. Before we got off the phone we made plans to see each other again. I felt heat rush through my body as I hung up the receiver. This man turned me on in a way I never imagined. I definitely had a weakness for evasive men with a rough exterior. The problem was O.B. was married and so was I. I had no idea what the situation was with O.B.'s marriage. I had to consider the fact that maybe he was happily married and just wanted me as a side chick. I knew if I tried to ask him too many questions he would tell me to mind my business. I wanted to believe that O.B.'s marriage was falling apart like mine. Maybe he was even in the middle of a divorce. I knew we had chemistry though. I figured I would work hard on getting him to tell me about his situation the next time I saw him.

And while I didn't know the details of O.B.'s marriage, I knew my own disastrous situation. I was really just trying to make it work for Ryan and Zeta at this point. Deonte is Zeta's daddy and he is the only daddy Ryan has ever known. Even though Deonte was cold to Ryan whenever he was mad at me, Ryan somehow still adored him.

Other than the kids there was one other reason I stayed married to Deonte. I didn't want to seem like a failure to my family. I was putting up a facade for my mother and my brother, Frankie. My brother always did everything perfect. He was happily married to little miss perfect. They had three little perfect kids and lived in the perfect little house in the perfect little neighborhood. They got on my nerves and I often avoided family functions so I wouldn't have to see them. Anyway, for a long time Deonte and I pretended to be the Brady Bunch. However, it wasn't long before we were found out.

One day back in the summer I was cooking spaghetti and meatballs for dinner. Deonte and I got into an argument about a

VIP pass he found in my purse. A guy at the club had given it to me the weekend before.

"Who did you have to fuck to get a VIP pass?" Deonte scoffed.

"Deonte, I told you before – Don't go in my purse!"

"I didn't touch your purse. Zeta went in your purse," Deonte yelled.

"Yeah whatever, Deonte. You're always snooping and looking for something. You act like such a little bitch. I don't go through your shit. Remember Deonte, I am supposed to be the bitch in this relationship!"

Deonte became enraged. He glared at me with his fist clenched. He drew back his right fist and punched a hole in the dining room wall. His fist went clear through to the other side of the wall. "Zsaset you gonna fucking learn how to talk to me with respect. You ain't gonna keep disrespecting me!"

Deonte and I continued to yell obscenities back and forth at one another. Meanwhile Ryan came over to attempt to mediate. Ryan put his hand on Deonte's side to get his attention. "Daddy," Ryan said. Deonte paid Ryan no mind. He was in the process of picking up a kitchen chair to throw and ended up elbowing Ryan in the chest.

The blow knocked Ryan out. He fell to the floor and I franticly yelled, "Call 911, call 911, Deonte."

Deonte wouldn't budge. He was still in a blind rage. He even pulled the phone cords out of the wall. *Has this mothafucka lost his mind?* I looked around the house for something to throw at his ass, but I had to take care of my child first. I ran to the patio door and yelled across the street for my girlfriend Karla to call the police.

The ambulance pulled up after what seemed like forever. Ryan laid in my arms as I rocked him in the middle of the kitchen floor. Deonte let the paramedics in and sat on the couch like nothing happened. On the way to Bayside Memorial Hospital I thought to myself, if something is wrong with my baby I'm gonna kill Deonte's ass. If his real father was any good, he'd kill his ass too.

The doctor examined Ryan and ran some tests. After a few hours they said he would be fine. He went on to tell me that a social worker was on her way to speak with me.

"To talk to me about what?" I asked.

"Well, ma'am when I asked your son what happened, he told me your husband hit him."

"Yeah, that's right. We were arguing."

"I know, ma'am. When there is a case of suspected child abuse I am required by law to inform Child Protective Services," the doctor said in a solemn tone.

"Child abuse," I said in a state of shock.

What if they tried to take Ryan from me and place him in a foster home? What am I going to do? I paced for about an hour before a tall black woman in a gray Liz Claiborne suit appeared. "Good afternoon are you Mrs. Jones?" she said extending her hand.

"Yes."

"I'm Mrs. Smith from Child..."

"I already know who you are," I said cutting her short.

She explained to me that she had to talk to Ryan before her final decision was made. She left me standing in the hallway. I was mad as hell at Deonte's ass.

The look on the social worker's face when she walked out of Ryan's room scared me. She informed me that based on what he told her, it was her decision to put him in the care of someone else.

"Someone else like who?" I said.

"Mrs. Jones we have foster parents who are ready to provide care and shelter to children who need it."

I started to cry. "Please, is there anything else we can do? Please."

"The only thing I can tell you is that if you have a relative that Ryan can stay with, we will talk to them and visit the home to see if it is safe for Ryan. If we determine that the home is safe for

Ryan, then he would be able to stay with that relative until Child Protective Services determines that your home is suitable for Ryan to return."

I swear I didn't want to, but I called my mother. I knew she would agree to keep him. Ryan was without a doubt her favorite grandchild. But now the cat was out of the bag that we weren't the Brady Bunch. My brother's wife called to offer her help with the situation, but I know she just wanted to gloat.

Before we could get Ryan back, I had to take parenting classes and Deonte had to take anger management classes. I completed my classes immediately. Deonte never did take his classes. We broke Child Protective Services' rules. Ryan ended up spending half his time with us and half his time with my mother. Ryan is still in the custody of my mother.

That incident was the last straw for me. I knew I had to leave Deonte. My job at the Exchange simply wasn't enough to afford an apartment. The rest of the summer and through September I looked for a part-time job but I wasn't able to find one. It killed me to admit it, but for now I knew I had to stay put.

Chapter Five

I decided to stay in and relax the next Saturday night. After dinner, I flopped on the couch and opened a Heineken beer. The phone rang. I grabbed it figuring it was Brina or Sheba. I was prepared to tell them I was chillin' tonight.

"Oh, hey, Ma," I was surprised to hear my mother's voice this late on a Saturday night. Ma went to church at the crack of dawn on Sunday.

"You busy, Zsa? Where the kids?" I sensed an uneasiness in my mother's voice.

"No, the kids are asleep. What's going on, Ma? Is something wrong?"

Ma hesitated, "Oh, well, ah, kinda."

"Ma, just spit it out." I hated when she beat around the bush.

"Alright, Zsa. Is ah, is Deonte there?"

"Yeah, Ma, he's sleep though. Why, is this about him?"

"Yeah, Zsa. It's about Deonte." I was quiet and Ma was quiet. If she didn't say another word at that moment I knew what she was telling me. Ma's voice cracked, "I been trying to get up the nerve to tell you for the last three days, Zsa."

I didn't say anything. It's not like I didn't see the signs a long time ago, but I didn't take heed to them--coming in the house late claiming he was out with his friends, concerned about his appearance all the time, and too tired to make love to me. That fool thought he was really doing something.

Ma went on to tell me that while visiting her best friend Ida, she noticed a picture of her daughter, Rhonda, with a familiar man.

"Zsa, I asked Ida about the photo and she said that it was her daughter's boyfriend. When she said that, I got up real close on the photo and just about fainted. Ida asked me what was wrong and I had to explain that Deonte was my son-in-law. It was awful, Zsa. Ida was just as shocked as I was. Ida told me that Deonte and Rhonda had been dating for about six months and were talking about marriage. We both blamed ourselves for not seeing Deonte for the scum he really was."

Mom and I talked for a while longer. I actually ended up feeling pretty sorry for Rhonda. She thought Deonte was her knight-in-shining- armor. At least I knew he wasn't shit. After we hung up, I filled up a large pitcher with ice cubes and cold water. I went into the bedroom where Deonte was sleeping and poured the entire pitcher on him. Deonte jumped up screaming.

"What the fuck, Zsaset?"

"That's for Rhonda, motherfucker." Deonte's angry expression turned to one of shock. "Nigger, I know you ain't think you was slick."

Over the next week, we walked around the house like we were strangers. The nights were even worse because we both refused to sleep on the couch. I despised Deonte. All I could think about were the lies he'd told and him making love to someone else. Several nights I woke up wanting to kill him in his sleep. I tried to keep it together, but it got harder every day. We talked about one of us moving out. Deonte reminded me that neither of us could afford to and I hated to admit it, but he was right. So we decided we would both stay at the apartment, until he could afford to take care of himself and pay me child support.

I was so excited when I finally got a call from O.B. asking me to visit him. I made the necessary arrangements and asked my mother to watch Zeta. She questioned me about my trip, but of course I didn't tell her anything. How could I tell her I was going to see another man? And no matter how crazy my marriage was, I was still married. I could hear my mother, the devout Christian, preaching, "Thou shalt not commit adultery." I knew she was right, but I was tired of being miserable. Not even God could get me out of this. I wanted a real relationship and I was hoping O.B. was the man who could give it to me.

Before I left for Richmond, I called O.B.. The anticipation of being with him made me pause briefly and take a deep breath. After the fourth ring he answered.

"Hi," I said trying to sound as sexy as possible. "I am on my way and I just wanted to make sure you're gonna be there when I get there."

"No doubt, baby," he said making me wet between my thighs.

"Alright, I should be there in about thirty minutes. Have my bubble bath ready."

"Okay. I'll see you when you get here," he said.

I must have arrived in record time. Hearing O.B.'s sexy voice made me do 90mph all the way to Richmond. With my MCM purse thrown across my shoulders, I walked into the bachelor's pad. O.B. strolled over to me and grabbed my bags. I spoke to Quan as I followed him up to his room. I almost stepped on his five rows of sneakers that took up most of the floor. I sat on the bed and before I knew it, he was on top of me giving me CPR. O.B. must have sensed my hesitation. He lifted off of me and said, "I missed you, girl."

"Oh, did you now?"

"Yeah, Zsaset, I did."

As we lay across his bed, we talked and got to know each other a little. I was amazed to find out we had so many things in common. We both liked karate flicks and were exceptional bowlers. More importantly, we both wanted to be rich by the time we were thirty. He said the money wasn't so much for himself, but for his family. He wanted to buy his mother a house in North Carolina so she could be near her family. He also wanted to have a college fund set up for his son so he wouldn't have to work while getting his degree.

I Shoulda Seen It Comin'

After pouring me another glass of champagne, O.B. looked at me with those sexy eyes and I felt my panties moisten at that very moment. I tried not to show my excitement, because I wanted him to work for this pussy. I needed him to lick me up and down and to feel his tongue flick across my clit a few times before I let him get all up in it. I tried to excuse myself to go to the bathroom. "Remember my bubble bath?" I reminded him, trying to sound real sexy.

"Later," he said while kissing me hungrily and pushing me back down on the bed. As soon as I felt the size and hardness of his dick, I couldn't even fake. My body temperature shot up and I wanted him bad. I tugged on his zipper so I could get my hands on that thing. He grinned at me and slipped off his pants. Damn, his dick was pretty! I pulled off my jeans, exposing my red lace thong. I could tell he liked what he saw. He slid my thong down my thighs with his teeth. Then he slowly licked me from my ankles all the way back up to my inner thighs, while gently massaging on my breasts. He teased the shit out of me, letting his tongue dance all over my booty before plunging it deep inside my middle. That was it for me; I was in love with this pussy-eating mother fucker.

"Fuck me now, O.B.," I moaned over and over again, getting louder each time. I held on to his head tightly. Purring like a kitty, my hips rose mid-air and I came harder than I thought I could.

"Oh, I see this is a first come, first served basis," he said showing no signs of being through with my ass. Before I knew it, he flipped me over on my stomach to go in for the kill. He put his tip in and stopped. I turned around and looked at him over my shoulder like he was crazy. "Beg for it," he commanded. I did just that. I lost my breath when he pushed all 10 inches of it inside me. In. Out. In. Out. Faster. Faster. His jewels made a slapping sound hitting against my ass. O.B.'s stamina was off the hook. Although I had already come again, I tried to keep up, but he just kept going and going, like the Energizer Bunny. If it had been the Olympics, he would definitely have won the gold for the shot put. I knew my shit was going to be sore for days, but I loved every minute of that good pain—it had been way too long since I had felt that good.   His sex reminded me of some New Edition lyrics: *"slap it up, flip it, rub it down, oh nooo, this dick is POISIN..."* And I was ready to die for it.

Finally he reached his climax when we heard a knock at the door.

"Who is it," O.B. yelled pulling out.

"It's me, Quan. It's time to go, man."

"Time to go where?" I asked.

"Oh shit, I forgot. I have to go take care of some business."

"Business, uh?" I said with a smirk. O.B. shot me a quick glance.

"Yeah, it's nothing. Look there's a mall on Midlothian Turnpike. He dug in his pockets and threw a wad of money on the bed.

"Why don't you go do some shopping?   By the time you finish, I'll be back," he said walking out the room.

I was so pissed off, I couldn't think straight. *Who does he think I am? A trick or something,* I thought to myself. After I counted the money, I didn't care what he thought I was. If tricks got paid like this, then I'll be his trick for the day. So off to the mall I went.

My first stop was Up Against the Wall. Browsing through the store I noticed the new DKNY collection. I held a handful of outfits and I strutted towards the dressing room. The black spandex cat suit fit me like a glove. But the rest looked equally as good. I couldn't decide so I bought them all.

After spending almost every dime he gave me I headed back to the house. I walked into the room and O.B. was on the phone. Anxious to show him what I bought, I emptied the bag of clothes on the bed. I could tell something serious was going on by the way he hit his fist on the bed. O.B. began yelling at the top of his lungs. I couldn't tell what it was about but it was clear he wasn't happy. I stood there being nosy. Trying to divert my attention, he asked what I bought.

"Something I think you'll love to take off me later," I said holding my slinky bed time special.

"Umm, I can't wait. Let me just finish up with my man then I'll get up witcha."

"Okay." I kissed him on his cheek.

I unraveled myself from his arms, and went to prepare for round two. I took my bubble bath and pampered myself for a while. When I came out of the tub O.B. was no longer in the bedroom. Once I was in my Victoria's Secret sheer Barbie doll teddy, I yelled for O.B.. He walked in the room speechless.

"So what do you think of the color red."

"It became my favorite color after this afternoon," he said licking his lips. Needless to say, that time around was better than the first.

On my last night in Richmond O.B. and I took in a movie and then had a quiet dinner. We talked for hours about our families, lives, and plans for the future. I was enjoying myself, but in the back of mind I wondered about O.B.'s wife.

"So what's the deal with you and your wife?"

"She does her thing and I do my mine," he said sipping on his Corona.

"How long has it been that way?" I asked digging deeper.

"About two years."

"Oh."

"Yeah, but we're getting divorced. We got married after we found out she was pregnant. At the time, I thought it was the right thing to do. But it's not working out. We fight all the time and it is starting to affect my son, so we're just gonna call it quits."

"What about you?" he asked.

"Ditto," I said. O.B. laughed.

Danette Majette

"What you mean, girl?" O.B. said with a confused smile.

"I mean we're getting divorced too... we got married after I got pregnant ... its not working out ... we're fighting in front of the children, etc. etc."

We both cracked up at the irony of how similar our situations were. We talked a little more and then we left to go back to his place.

It was time for me to go home and I was dreading it. It felt good to be away from Deonte and all the drama in my home life. With O.B. I could breathe again. Sensing my hesitation to leave, O.B. assured me we would do it again real soon. Before I left, he planted a kiss on my lips and told me to drive safe. I winked and headed home.

Chapter Six

I spent the next weekend and almost every weekend with O.B. in Richmond. I was having the time of my life. One Sunday all hell broke loose when I returned home. Deonte and I got into our biggest fight ever. But this time it was physical.

When I walked in the house that Sunday I could tell something wasn't right. Shit was all over the floor. I slowly walked in and stopped in the middle of the living room trying to take inventory. For a moment it looked as if someone had broken in, but I quickly noticed that the television and stereo were still there. Deonte walked from the back bedroom in a pair of boxers. He looked as if he had been crying. He threw something at me that turned out to be a picture.

Deonte had found a picture that O.B. and I had taken hugged up together in a picture booth. I don't think Deonte would have been so angry except for the fact that Zeta was in the picture asleep. It was a night when O.B and I had met at a strip mall halfway between Richmond and Norfolk just to see each other and talk for a while. I didn't have a babysitter so I bathed Zeta, put her in her pajamas and after she fell asleep, put her in the car. She didn't wake up until the next morning in her bed. She never knew she had been out of the house. Anyway, Deonte didn't know any of these details. He was rabid with anger.

"Bitch, how you gone have my baby girl around some bitch-ass nigga just 'cause you fuckin' him?"

I wanted to cuss Deonte out but something inside me told me not to. He seemed almost deranged with anger so I attempted to reason with him. "Deonte, it ain't what you think."

These were apparently the wrong words to say to him because he lost any remaining composure that he had.

39

"What? What the fuck you mean it ain't what I think?" He picked up the picture from by my foot and smushed it into my face and yelled, "Zsa, look at the fucking picture. Pictures don't lie, it is exactly what I think." Deonte pushed my head back. I fell back and tripped over my purse. I fell to the floor and hit the lower part of my back on the side of the couch. I jumped up in spite of the pain. Deonte started swinging and even though he stood a foot over me, his hits didn't faze me. I started swinging on his ass. He threw me down on the floor a couple times, but I kept getting up. The last time he knocked me down I came back up swinging so hard, I left my mark on him. With a piece of broken glass I put a two-inch gash in his chest. He looked down at the cut in shock then looked back at me. "Yeah, that's right. Hit me again, bitch. The next time it's gonna be your throat that gets slashed," I said.

I was just about to pounce on his ass again when I heard Zeta cry out. "Daddy. Daddy." I was so mad at him for hitting me I didn't even think what a scene like that would do to her. After calming her down, I assured her that he was all right. He thought I was just going to roll over and cry. He had it all wrong. That shit was not happening. I was not about to let him put his hands on me. It was either him or me.

The next morning, I called O.B. and told him what happened the night before. He immediately went into a frenzy.

"Pack yo shit and just leave him," he said.
"And just where am I suppose to go."
"Move up here with me."
"What about my kids?"
"What about them? Bring them with you. We have enough room."
"I don't know. I have to think about it."
"What is there to think about? Do you want to stay with a man who hits you?"

It took me two days to make up my mind. I agreed to go. Usually, decisions like this took a lot of planning. But I figured what the hell, things couldn't get any worse than they already were.

    My mother was the first on my list to call. We had the kind of relationship that my girlfriends only dreamed of having with their mothers. We were like two peas in a pod. So I knew this sudden move was going to be very upsetting for her. But never the less I told her that I was leaving Deonte and moving to Richmond. It didn't surprise me that she supported my decision even though she knew it was a mistake.

    "I can't tell you what to do, but I don't think you should take both of the kids. You're gonna be in a new city and it's gonna take time to settle down. You can't do that with both of them kids. Let Ryan stay here with me, I could use the company."

    What she said made sense, so I accepted her offer. "Where ya'll gonna live?" she asked.

    "I have some friends who live there. They said I could stay with them for a while. At least until I get a job and find a place of my own."

    In an uneasy tone she said, "Well, that's nice of them." My mother was no dummy. She knew me real well.

    "I'm just gonna put my trust in God that you'll be okay up there," she said.

    Now that I had my mother's blessing, I started packing my things. I was excited and scared at the same time. What if things didn't work out the way I thought they would? After all, I had only known O.B. for a short period of time. That seemed to be a growing trend with the men in my life. But I came to the conclusion that I had to stop dwelling on the negative and try to think of it as a new beginning.

    I called Brina and filled her in. She knew that O.B. and I had been hanging out but she was shocked when I told her that Zeta and I were moving in with O.B. and the other guys.

    "Zsa, you sure that is a good idea. O.B. is like a Dr. Jekyll and Mr. Hyde. One minute, he all nice and the next minute he's trippin' on your ass."

"Brina, O.B. has been nothing but nice to me for a good while now."

"I don't know, Zsa, you sure you know what you're doing?"

"No, I don't. But I am sure I can't stay with Deonte any longer."

"Yeah – I feel you on that 'cause that nigga's crazy." We both laughed and then Brina got serious. "Zsa, I can ask my mother if you and Zeta can come over here for a while."

"Nah, Brina. But I love you for saying that. Look, I got to get packed. I'm gonna call you later on."

"Alright, girl."

By the time Deonte got home, most of my things were packed. He looked surprised. I don't know why. Did he really think I was going to stay with him after last week?

"Where are you going?"

"Take a wild guess, Einstein," I said in a taunting voice.

"Are you going to your mother's house?"

"No, I'm moving to Richmond."

"You just gonna pack up and take my daughter to Richmond?"

"Um, let me see. Yeah."

"Zsaset, she's only two years old. Why would you do that to her?" "Do what to her?"

"Fuck this shit. You can take *your* son, but Zeta is staying here. I'll take you to court if I have to," he said, walking towards me.

"Really. Did you forget about the incident with Ryan? There isn't a court in Virginia that would give you custody. You're a registered child abuser and you're taking anger management classes."

"I'll take my chances," he said.

"Go ahead and I'll make sure you never see her again."

It frustrated me that he was trying to make me out to be the bad guy. If anything I was trying to protect her from living in a home where her parents hated each other.

Seeing that there was no changing my mind Deonte's face grew hot with anger. "Well leave then, bitch," he said, throwing my clothes.

"I ain't gonna be too many more bitches," I yelled back. Just when I was about to explode on him a cool sensation ran through my body. *Why am I even wastin' my time.* I was about to leave his miserable ass and that's all that mattered.

It was late evening when I peered out to my car. It was packed with our clothes and a few toys for Zeta. I told Deonte he could keep the furniture until I got a place of my own. Before we left, Deonte kissed Zeta and told her he would be in Richmond to see her soon.

"I need you to sign these papers before you leave," he said, handing me a manila folder.

"What is this?" I asked.

"Just sign it."

He must be out of his mind, I thought to myself.

"I know you don't expect me to sign this without reading it first," I said in anger, shoving the papers in his chest.

"They're just legal separation papers."

"I know what the fuck they are. But I ain't signin' them."

He stood there for a minute with the papers in his hand. "If you don't sign them and you leave, I won't have to give you shit. I'm trying to help you."

"Naw, you're trying to help yourself. 'Cause trust me, I'm gonna get mine."

I was so tired of dealing with his shit, I signed the papers and threw them in his face. I didn't care if he didn't give me one red cent. All I cared about was getting away from his dumb ass and moving on with O.B.

I took one last look at the place I use to call home as I put my seat belt across my chest. The thought of leaving everyone I knew and loved saddened me. So I took a deep breath, prayed to God to give me strength, and drove off.

"Mommy, we goin' bye-bye?"

"Yeah, baby, we going bye-bye."

"Daddy not goin'?" she asked looking back at Deonte.

"No daddy has to work, but he's gonna come and see you real soon okay."

"O-tay," she said, playing with her doll.

The forty-five minute trip took nearly an hour and a half. It was my first road trip with Zeta and I had to stop several times for her to use the potty, as she liked to refer to it. We got to O.B.'s place and there were several cars in the driveway. "Must be a full house," I said, turning to Zeta. She nodded her head yes as if she knew what I was talking about. Nervous, I walked up and rang the bell. A voice filtered from the other side of the door. "Who is it?"

"It's Zsaset," I replied.

The door swung open and I was greeted by O.B. with a big hug. "So who do we have here?" he asked kneeling down on one leg.

"This is my daughter, Zeta. Zeta this is mommy's friend O.B. Can you say hello?"

"Hi," she said shyly with her fingers in her mouth.

"She's a little cutie, just like her mother," he said with a smile.

"Thanks," I said, twirling her ponytail.

"We'll get your bags later," he said.

In the house, I found K-Dog doing what he did best, talking on the phone. I waved to him and Quan from the living room. Zeta must have been taken back by so many men because she gripped my jacket tightly. "It'll be okay. Mommy's here."

O.B. told us to come into the kitchen to get her some juice. K-Dog stood with a doo-rag on at the breakfast counter.

"Hi, K-Dog."

"Hey, Zsaset." K-Dog gave me a bear hug.
"K, I told you Zsaset gonna be staying with us for a while," O.B. said.
"What's a while, nigga?"
"As long as she needs, mothafucka."
"Nigga don't get smart with me. This is my damn house. Ya'll just freeloaders," K-Dog taunted.
They all laughed and then went back to their business. O.B. took a few bags from my car so we could prepare for bed. By the end of the night we kicked it watching television like we had known each other all our lives. It meant a lot to know they trusted me enough to give me a key to the house.
The day's events had taken its toll on both Zeta and me. She was out like a light. I picked her up and we headed for bed.
"You comin'," I said, looking back at O.B.
"Naw. Ya'll take the bed. I'ma sleep down here." O.B. felt it was best if we slept in separate bedrooms for Zeta's sake.

I awoke to find Zeta was missing the next morning. I grabbed my robe and ran down the stairs. I walked in the kitchen and saw her sitting at the table with the guys eating breakfast. They were spoiling her rotten and she loved every minute of it. It was a relief for me to see them getting along with her. I wasn't sure how they were going to react to a baby being in the house. From the sign of things everything was going to be all right.
I cleaned the kitchen after breakfast. It was the least I could do since they were letting me stay rent-free. I wiped the table and took Zeta upstairs to give her a bath. Zeta already settled in the tub, I turned and noticed O.B. on the phone. Men don't know how to cover their tracks. He was whispering so low I knew he was talking to some other chick. Not wanting any drama in front of Zeta, I ignored him.
I let Zeta play in the tub a while before I wrapped her in a towel and carried her in the bedroom. I couldn't believe O.B. was gone. He left without saying a word. *I'm gonna kill him,* I thought

as I stormed down the stairs. He was nowhere to be found. To calm my nerves, I lit a cigarette. I threw on my clothes and took Zeta for a walk.

It was around 6:00 p.m. when O.B. came home. He slammed the car door and ran up on the porch where I was sitting. Kneeling down he kissed me with a nonchalant attitude.

"Why didn't you tell me you were leaving," I said still fuming.

"I told Quan to tell you," he said pointing.

"Why didn't you tell me?"

"What difference does it make who told you?"

"That's not the point," I yelled standing up.

"Look, I'm not a kid. I don't have to check in and out with you," he said. His tone and attitude totally surprised me. I wasn't ready for that. I knew this was a sure sign of trouble on the horizon.

It took me some time to calm down. He totally made me rethink this whole thing. I went in the house to start dinner. Observing the sad look on my face, K-Dog asked if everything was okay. He told me that he had overheard my argument with O.B. and for me not to worry about it. "He acts like that all the time. We just ignore him. For your sake you better learn to do the same thing," he said.

By the time I finished marinating the T-bone steaks everyone was gone. *What was the point of cooking if no one was going to eat,* I thought to myself. Disappointed, I fixed Zeta and me a plate. We ate, cleaned up and went upstairs to get settled in for the evening.

Later that night, I heard O.B. creep in the room. He took his clothes off and slid in the bed. Neither one of us spoke a word. *I can't believe I'm going through this shit with another man. I should'a stayed my ass at home.*

I turned on my side to signal that I was still awake. "What you still doin' up?" he asked.

I Shoulda Seen It Comin'

"I couldn't sleep."

"I know somethin' that will help you sleep," he said, throwing his legs over me.

"I would prefer an apology," I said sitting up.

"Okay, I'm sorry," he said kissing me. "Now let me show you."

He could tell I was still upset. "Look, Boo, I'm just under a lot of stress. My wife is nagging me and these stupid ass niggas keep fucking up."

"What niggas?"

"I don't want to talk about that shit right now. All I want to do is make love to you," he said, leaving me naked after lifting my nightgown over my head.

O.B. wasted no time handling me. He caressed my lower lips long enough to get me moist. I gazed hungrily into his eyes wanting more. He had a way of making me forget about all my worries. Before I realized, I was screaming, "Go ahead, O.B. taste me, don't hold back a thing." Let's just say that by the time the night was over, my lips swelled so big, I had to soak in a tub of warm water.

He was truly the best. He was my new addiction.

Chapter Seven

The next couple of days with O.B. were like a fairytale. It was lovemaking by morning and fancy dinners by night. We were like a little family-me, him, and Zeta.

One Saturday afternoon, Quan watched Zeta so we could spend some quality time together. Halfway into our day he got an urgent call. "I gotta take care of somethin'," he said.

"Are you gonna take me back to the house?" I asked.

"Naw, I don't have time."

This was very unusual. He never took me with him when he did business. This was one part of his life that was "off limits". Deep down I knew what he did but I closed my eyes to it.

We drove up to the Mosby Court project. "You remember this place don't you?" he said, putting the car in park.

"Yeah, how can I forget," I said. He chuckled and motioned me to follow him. I was so scared I walked on O.B.'s heels. The group of men by the dumpster gave me the creeps. Children with snotty noses and tacky heads hung from the tree like little monkeys. The row of low brick homes reminded me of someplace out of a horror movie.

He led me down a short path that took us to a gray steel door. He pushed open the door and went in. "Wait here I'll be back," O.B. said. He disappeared into a back room.

It may have been the projects on the outside, but not on the inside. A big screen television swallowed up the entire wall. Someone definitely had good taste by the looks of the fine Italian leather sofa.

Moments later a girl who looked like a light skinned Beverly Johnson walked out.

I Shoulda Seen It Comin'

"Hi, I'm Lina," she said as she sat crossing her legs on the arm of the couch.

"Hi, I'm Zsaset."

"Nice to finally meet you, Zsaset. I was beginning to think you were ugly or somethin'," she said with a smile.

Of course, I didn't think it was funny. So I gave her my infamous I'm not amused look.

"Just kidding, girl. Just kidding," she said quickly. "I always mess with O.B. about not bringin' you around here to meet us. I told him he must be trying to keep you a secret. Anyway, O.B. will be out in a minute."

Just as I was about to sit down, O.B. emerged from the back room with a scruffy short guy.

"Zsaset, this is Coley."

"Coley this is my shorty, Zsaset."

We exchanged greetings. O.B. pulled me down a narrow hallway into a small bedroom. I couldn't believe my eyes. Money machines were lined everywhere. The cash was stacked neatly like money in a bank vault.

"Where did all this money come from?" I asked.

"You know exactly where it came from." I tried to act like I didn't know what he was talking about. But it was evident he was on to me.

"So I guess I was right about you."

"I guess you were," he said.

"I know you probably don't approve of my methods, but I have a kid to feed. I gotta do what I gotta do."

"I understand what you're saying, but why don't you just get a job?"

He laughed, "Who's gonna give me a job with my wrap sheet."

"Driving without a license is not that serious," I said, referring to the reason he told me he spent a little time in jail.

Danette Majette

"Either you are really naive or you are a good faker. You know that? Driving without a license is the least of my crimes. But we won't get into that."

What the hell did he mean by that? Right at that moment I knew my fairytale was coming to an end. "Look, I just wanted to come clean. I'm tired of trying to hide this shit from you. I'm tired of getting into fights because I can't tell you where I'm going in the middle of the night. It was really starting to get to me, Boo."

After listening to him, I kissed his lips and promised to love him no matter what. It wasn't true though. As soon as we got back home I began to feel differently around him-scared even. The thought of him selling drugs to his own people turned my stomach. But was it really his fault? Or was he a victim caught up in the game? There wouldn't be any drugs if the government didn't allow them in the country. And the dealers wouldn't be in business if there weren't addicts. That's how I started to rationalize his lifestyle. But truly there were no excuses. None.

Chapter Eight

It wasn't long at all before my fears turned into nightmares. It all started with late night calls that had O.B. running in and out of the house. Some days I didn't see him at all. Talking about it always led to big blowouts. So I let him do his thang. I filled my time spending his cash. People said I had nothing to trip about, but to me happiness reigns over money any day.

Spring brought out the best in me. My spirits were high. I slid on a pair of daisy dukes, hopped in my car and cruised down to the projects to surprise my man. As I pulled up on the opposite side of the street, I saw O.B.'s car parked by the *Wack Crack* bench. This was the hang out spot for dirty ass crack-heads. I pulled down my Chanel sunshades not believing what I saw. My first reaction was to jump out the car. That was my heart talking. My mind said chill for a minute. I saw a female shadow lean in to kiss my man. "Oh no the fuck he ain't," I said, hitting the steering wheel. "This nigga cheatin' on me." I snatched the car door handle ready to whoop some ass. Before I got out the car good, Lina jumped in. She was watching the whole thing from her window.

"Girl, let's get the fuck out of here."

"Oh no, I'm getting ready to kick his ass," I said, tugging away from her.

"Look...just drive off."

I was about to curse her out, but I noticed tears running down her face. "What the fuck is wrong with you? I should be the one crying. I just saw my man kissing another woman," I screeched.

"Well, at least he was just kissing her." Steaming, I slammed on the gas pedal and drove off right past O.B. and that hoe. "I just found out Coley got some chick across the street pregnant," Lina yelled when we got to the light.

My heart sank for Lina. "Damn, Lina, I'm sorry. What's wrong with them?"

"I guess it's to be expected. Bitches want that money and they'll do whatever it takes to get it. They don't care if these niggas got somebody or not."

I was beside myself.

"I should have known something was wrong. Lately, every time I asked him to make love to me, it was like asking him to give me a damn kidney. I guess he was too busy screwin' that bitch," I yelled. "That's fine though, his ass is grass."

"Zsaset, look you don't know O.B. and Coley like I do."

"What's that suppose to mean?"

"If I were you I would just forget you even saw that shit."

"Excuse me?" I slammed on the brakes dead in the middle of Hull Street. I didn't even care that I could've caused a five-car pile up. I gazed at her like she had three heads. "You done lost your mind, Lina?"

Every since I had first met Lina, she seemed a little off but now she seemed straight up crazy.

"If you press this issue, it could get really ugly for you and your daughter," she said in a terrified tone.

"Are you saying he might try to do something to me or my daughter?" I asked.

"Look, that's all I can say."

I could tell from the look on her face that she was scared. I think she regretted saying anything.

"So are you gonna stay with Coley?"

"Yeah, I have to," she said with an outer space look.

"Why?"

"I have my reasons."

"What possible reason could you have for staying with a guy that treats you like shit?" Lina just sat there quietly. "Yeah well, O.B. can kiss my ass." We drove back in silence.

I Shoulda Seen It Comin'

I was so confused I drove around for hours. What was I suppose to do? I didn't have a place to stay and I damn sure wasn't going back home. I needed a plan and quick.

I went home and Zeta and K-Dog were in the living room. "So was O.B. surprised to see you?" K-Dog asked.

"That's an understatement," I said.

"What happened?"

"If you don't mind I don't want to talk about it."

I grabbed a beer and went upstairs with tears in my eyes. I had to make a decision about what I was going to do. O.B. humiliated me and all the money in the world wasn't worth that.

O.B. came in the house trying to kiss me like nothing was wrong. I knew Lina told him I saw him. I guess he thought he could kiss me and I would forget it ever happened. That bastard had his lips plastered on some other chick just hours earlier and he expected me to let him touch me. Fat chance.

"What's wrong with you?" he said.

"What's wrong? I'll tell you what's wrong. I saw yo no good ass kissing that tramp."

His face showed a flicker of surprise. "Look, before you start going crazy, she's just a girl I've been using."

"Whatever."

"I'm serious. She's just a trick I use for business. In the game it's never about pleasure. We need her crib that's all."

Now I've been fed some bullshit lines in my time, but this one took the cake. "So you tryna tell me, you willing to jeopardize what we have for business," I yelled.

"You acting like a spoiled fucking brat. You know that."

I looked him straight in the eyes. "I'm not about to stay with a man who doesn't respect me or our relationship. So do what you do, baby. But you gonna do it without me."

I was so proud of myself for standing my ground with him. It hurt like hell, but I had no choice. I couldn't let him think he could play with my heart. But then again what did I expect would happen. After all, he was cheating on his wife with me. That's what happens when you lie down with dogs.

I cried for what seemed like hours. I needed to clear my head. I decided to go for a walk. I figured the fresh air would do me some good. Here I was again getting my child in some ole stupid shit. I wondered how all this turmoil would affect her. By the time I reached the playground, I had smoked five cigarettes. I sat on the swing like a mental basket case. *"Zsaset get your stuff together,"* I repeated to myself. After the fiftieth time, I felt strong enough to go back home.

I twisted the knob and the first person I saw was O.B. *Damn, just what I needed.* I rolled my eyes and stormed into the kitchen. He followed me.

"Can we talk please?" he said sincerely.

"There is nothing to talk about. It's obvious you love your business more than you love me." I said, slamming the refrigerator door.

He lowered his head not able to look me in the face. "Zsaset, I made a mistake."

"Yeah, you made a big mistake." I lifted his chin with my index finger. "Look O.B. after all the promises you made to me about never treating me like Deonte, and you turn around and do the same thing? You killed that trust." A tear fell from my eye. "Looking at you is like looking at my husband. Any feelings I had for you are tainted with hatred and disgust."

"So what you gonna leave and go back home to your wife beating husband?" He just had to hit below the belt. That was his only recourse.

"You know what—don't worry about me. I'll be just fine."

Tired of talking, I ran up the stairs yelling, "I'll be out of your house tomorrow." Gathering my belongings, I stuffed my last pair of jeans in the bag with nowhere to go. I crawled in the bed with my baby and cried myself to sleep.

Zeta woke me up the next morning with kisses. It was just what I needed. She dragged me downstairs for breakfast. As soon

I Shoulda Seen It Comin'

as my foot hit the first step I heard O.B. snapping at K-Dog and Quan like a madman. He gave me a look that almost made my heart stop when I sat at the table. That nigga had kill in his eyes. I didn't understand it. He was the one cheating, not me.

"What the fuck you looking at?" he asked.

I looked behind me to see if there was someone else there, but there wasn't.

"Are you talking to me?" I said getting pumped.

"Who do you think I'm talking to?"

K-Dog warned me about his attitude but I wasn't prepared for this.

"Wait a minute, why do you have an attitude with me," I said with my hands on my hips.

"'Cause I told your stupid ass it was just business, but you don't believe me. So fuck you," he said and walked out the door.

I stood motionless a few seconds before I sat back down. I tried to block the whole ugly scene out of my head, but it was useless. It replayed in my head like a scratched CD.

K-Dog sat down to comfort me. He tried telling me corny jokes but it didn't work. My emotions got the best of me. Before I knew it, I was balling.

"It's gonna be alright, Zsa Zsa."

"What did you call me?"

"Zsa Zsa. That's my new name for you. Zsa Zsa was a bad bitch. She would never let a man get to her. So, Zsa Zsa, get yourself together, and go put on your clothes. We're going to the mall."

That's why I loved K-Dog. Within minutes, my crying turned into laughter. K-Dog always had the gentle kind of humor that took away my pain.

After he saw that I was feeling better, he ran upstairs to change. Moments later, I ran up behind him.

At the top of the stairs, I observed K-Dog consulting with Zeta about what she should wear. He had a great rapport with her. I think it was because he acted like a kid himself. Not in a negative way, in a free spirited way. He was always the life of the party and he never let anything get him down. I admired him for that.

On our way to the mall, K-Dog got a call from O.B. He said he needed to see him right away. Since we were already in the car, he took us with him. We got to the projects and O.B. was stomping some guy in his head.

K-Dog wasn't sure what was going on, so he told us to stay in the car. It seemed the guy had stolen some money from K-Dog and split town, but his stupid ass made the mistake of coming back. K-Dog ran over to O.B. and told him to calm down, but he wouldn't. The next thing I knew O.B. beat his victim with a beer bottle.

Concerned about Zeta seeing what was going on, I covered her eyes. It was too late. She started crying and that pissed K-Dog off. He couldn't believe O.B.'s behavior. Not only did he assault the man in broad daylight, he did it in front of Zeta. Angry, K-Dog gripped O.B. and pulled him to the side. He whispered something in his ear and came back to the car.

"Zeta Beta, it's okay," he said in a comforting tone. "O.B. was just playing a game with the man." *Yeah, right. What kind of game was that,* I wondered, *human soccer?* After calming Zeta down, we took off to the mall.

K-Dog bought Zeta something from every children's store in the mall. Then it was my turn. We headed to Lady Foot Locker.

"Yeah, I'll take this in an eight," I told the sales clerk.

"What about Zeta?" K-Dog asked.

"What about her? Don't you think she's got enough stuff?"

"Well, that's where you're wrong young lady. She needs to have these and these and these."

"What?" I yelled.

I could tell by the way the clerk sprinted to the stockroom that she was elated. She had a sell for six pairs of shoes and she didn't even have to break a sweat.

I Shoulda Seen It Comin'

As she rung up our purchase, I saw an accepting applications sign on the counter. *Great. I can get a job here.* I waited for the clerk to complete our transaction before I inquired about the positions they had open.

"We have a full-time position open. Are you interested?"

"Yes," I replied.

"OK, I'll get you an application and if you want I'll put in a good word for you."

"You'll do that for me?"

"After the sale you just gave me, you better believe it." She gave me an application and then handed me our bags. "Thank you," she said.

"No, thank you."

I began filling out the application as we sat down in the food court to eat. "Zsaset, why you trying to get a job?" K-Dog asked, as I was filling out the application.

I explained to him that I needed to move out because my relationship with O.B. was over and I needed to get my own place.

"Girl, you know you can stay with us."

"Do you really think O.B. would let me stay in his house?"

"If it was his house...probably not. But since the house in question is mine, I really don't think he has any say-so about the matter."

"What," I said confused. "You mean to tell me that's your house."

"Every nook and cranny." I felt relieved. I laughed so hard I started choking. "Don't you remember what I said to him when you first moved in? I wasn't playing. That is my house and they are freeloaders?" I had forgotten all about that. K-Dog offered Zeta and me to stay. My prayers were answered. The power O.B. had over me was gone.

"K-Dog, I don't know why you are so nice to me and Zeta but I want you to know that I really do appreciate it. If there's anything you need..." K-Dog cut me off.

"Zsaset, it ain't no thing. And I ain't helping you out so you can do something for me. Let's just say you remind me of someone that was special to me that I lost."

"Would I be prying to ask who?" K-Dog was quiet for a minute and he swallowed hard. He started to speak a couple of times and stopped.

Finally he said, "My sister...she was killed a couple of years ago by some niggas that was looking for me."

"I'm sorry, K-Dog." He shook his head.

I tried to lighten the mood a little. "K, I'll be your sister if you'll be my brother. My real brother is a stuffed shirt, know-it-all, so I would prefer you over him any day."

K-Dog smiled and extended his hand. "Deal, sis." We shook on it.

I examined the application one last time before I took it back.

K-Dog sat outside the store with Zeta just in case they wanted to interview me on the spot.

"If they need help that bad they might hire you today," he said.

He was right. The manager interviewed me as soon as I bought my application back in. He asked me a few questions like did I have any experience in sales and what hours I was available to work. He then offered me the position. Of course, I graciously accepted.

I switched from the back and gave the clerk a wink. I figured it was because of her I got the job. I ran over to K-Dog and told him the great news.

"They even want me to start tomorrow," I added. Then it hit me that I didn't have a babysitter. "K-Dog, do you know anyone who baby-sits in the neighborhood?"

"Yeah, the lady next door but she won't be back until tomorrow."

"Oh, God."

I Shoulda Seen It Comin'

"Don't worry. I'll watch Zeta for you." Grateful, I gave him a big hug and kiss. "Don't worry about it," he said.

Chapter Nine

We walked through the door and threw our bags on the couch. O.B. walked out of the kitchen and got in my face. "What the hell you still doing here?" he barked.

"I'll let K-Dog tell you why," I sneered as I ran up the stairs.

I was unpacking my last box when O.B. started ranting and raving. Curious, I went to see what was going on. I was on the last step when I heard K-Dog telling O.B. the good news. It was good news for me anyway.

"Look man, just because you have a problem with her doesn't mean I do. I'm not about to put her and her baby out in the streets, so get over it," K-Dog said.

"This is some bullshit, man," O.B. screamed. "You know there is no way in hell we can stay in the same house."

"Yes, you can. We'll be one big happy family," K-dog said with
    laughter.

O.B. was so vexed he started lashing out at me.

"You think you slick usin' your baby so you can stay here," he said.

"I didn't have to use my baby. K-Dog cares about me and Zeta," I countered.

"Well guess what? I'll let you in on somethin'. I don't care. I never did."

His words shot through me like a bullet. Not only did he accuse me of using my child to get what I wanted, he had the nerve to say he didn't care about us when he was the one who offered me to move to Richmond in the first place. Before I knew it I clawed him like a wild cat. He staggered back into the wall and immediately clutched his face. The anger in his eyes was a sure sign that I was in trouble. As I took off to run, he slapped me across my face sending me tumbling towards the couch. Then he grabbed me by the arms and shook me so hard that spit flew out of my mouth. "What the...!" I screamed. Out the corner of my eye, I saw K-Dog standing behind O.B. He pulled him off me.

"O.B., that was uncalled for, man," K-Dog said, pushing him into the kitchen.

"Fuck that bitch. I should kill her ass for scratching my face," O.B. yelled.

"Go ahead, mothafucka. Do it," I challenged.

"Fuck you," he yelled again.

"Fuck me? No you wish you could fuck me. You can't fuck anyway. You faggot."

I couldn't crush his heart with words so I went for the next best thing— his ego. He lunged at me again but K-Dog stopped him just in time.

I was so mad, I forgot all about my child so I ran upstairs to check on her. She was on the bed with her face buried in a pillow screaming and crying. I tried to calm her down. I rubbed her back and told her that everything was going to be all right. She fell fast asleep. A few minutes later, K-Dog came in the room.

"Ya'll all right?" he said, sitting on the edge of the bed.

"Yeah, but I have to move out. I promised myself that I would never let another man hit me," I said.

"Don't let O.B. run you out of here. Trust me, he'll never put his hands on you again. All you have to do is stay out of his way. Then again I should tell him to stay out your way, Mike Tyson. You sure fucked him up."

Later that night, I plotted my revenge against O.B. Since he and I were the only people home, I felt there was no time like the present. I went down stairs only to find him passed out from slinging back a six-pack of beer. I made sure he was completely out, before I stole his keys. I quickly opened the truck then pulled the brake light out and unscrewed it. When my mission was complete, I bolted back into the house and up to my room.

I awoke the next morning refreshed. As I walked out of my room yawning, I overheard K-Dog on the phone. He soon hung up.
"Your boy got popped last night."
"What do you mean?" I played innocent.
"He's in jail. The police pulled him over for a broken brake light. Then they arrested him for driving with a suspended license again. On top of all that they took my gold and impounded the car. Shit, man. This nigga is getting on my damn nerves," he said, slamming his hand into the wall.
I was so caught up in getting revenge I didn't even think how this would affect K-Dog. The last thing I ever wanted to do was hurt him. He was the only person I could really count on. So I attempted to make myself useful. "You need me to do anything?"
"Naw, I'ma go post his bail later. He should be home sometime tonight. Don't worry. Quan's gonna watch Zeta."
"Alright, well I'll see you when I get home."

I didn't know how Zeta was going to react to me leaving so I tried to sneak out. "Bye, mommy," her little voice yelled.
"Bye, baby. I'll see you later," I said as I closed the door tightly.
Wanting to make a good impression, I arrived 15 minutes early. I walked in and was greeted by the clerk from the day before.
"Hi, so are you excited about your first day?" she said.
"Yeah, but I'm a little nervous."
"There's nothing to be nervous about, you'll be all right. By the way,
my name is Vicki," she said, extending her hand.
"My name is Zsaset."
"I know. Larry told me."

I Shoulda Seen It Comin'

She helped me fill out my paperwork then told me about the company's policies. We talked before the store opened and she gave me the low down on all the employees. I got a crash course on how to work the hustlers that came in and what to do if I had any problems with the girls from the projects. What Vicki didn't know was that I could school her on both topics because I was already a pro.

The first two hours, I trained with Vicki. I watched how she handled the customers. She had skills. She could sell a bald-headed woman barrettes. I was amazed at how she convinced customers to buy shit they didn't even need. That pumped me up to want to jump right into the game.

I noticed Larry watching closely. After the young lady with the pink Reebok sweat-suit left, Larry came over to me smiling. "Good job, Zsaset. I like the fact that you suggested socks with the lady's shoes. If you like, you can go to lunch."

The taste of the special sauce on my Big Mac made me drift back to when my relationship with O.B. was like being in paradise. It was relaxing and romantic. He was a little rough around the edges at times, but I never thought he would hit me. Especially after the way he reacted when Deonte hit me. Before I moved in with him, he promised me he would never do anything to hurt me, but they were just empty promises he couldn't keep. In his mind, I suspect he was dealing with me in the way he thought I was accustomed to being dealt with.

Anxious to find a permanent babysitter, I walked next door to see if our neighbor was back from her trip. The door opened, and a large-framed, white woman greeted me. Her beautiful smile overpowered her weight.

"Hello I'm Zsaset," I said, extending my hand.
"Oh are you Zeta's mom?"

"Yes I am." She welcomed me in and I took a seat on the fluffy couch. Her house was beautifully decorated in a shabby chic décor.

"So what can I do for you?" she asked.

"I was wondering if you could baby-sit my daughter while I work?"

"Sure, I would love to. Your daughter is such a sweetheart."

"Thank you – you met her?"

"She was out on your patio earlier watching my kids play in the pool. I asked if she wanted to join them and she said, 'Yes,' but the gentleman watching her said she should wait until you got home."

I was a little relieved to hear her say that. Zeta was shy. I tried several times to get her to go out and play with some of the other kids but she wouldn't.

"I know it's short notice, but can you start tomorrow?"

"No problem," she said.

It was settled. I finally got a babysitter.

Hearing Zeta screaming, "Mommy, Mommy you're home," made me forget how badly my feet hurt.

"Were you a good girl today?" She nodded her head yes and gave me a big hug and kiss.

"I don't know why mommy even asked you that. You're always a good girl," I said as I took my shoes off.

The smell of fried chicken lured me into the kitchen.

"I hope you're hungry because I'm cooking up a storm," K-Dog said.

He wasn't lying either. He was cooking a Sunday dinner on a Tuesday.

"So how was your first day?"

"It was cool. I learned a lot. I guarantee you in a couple of weeks I'll be runnin' the joint," I said with confidence.

"Where's O.B?" I wanted to know.

"He should be home soon. I posted his bond, but he had to wait for them to do the paperwork. Anyway, enough of that, grab a plate and dig in."

I bit into the fried chicken breast and almost died. He could cook his ass off. I ate so much I was too exhausted to do anything else. So I took a nice long bath and got into bed.

The morning started off calmly considering O.B. was back home. As I dressed Zeta, I explained to her she would be spending the day with Miss Brenda, the lady with the big pool. She was delighted since she was already acquainted with her kids.

Before I could get down the stairs Zeta was screaming "C'mon, Mommy."

"Zeta, slow your roll, little girl." I grabbed my purse and took her next door.

The store was unusually packed for a Wednesday. I clocked in and headed for the sales floor. My day went well. By two o'clock I had done $600 in sales. It was time for lunch.

I felt like some McDonald's that day. I stood at the counter shocked by what I saw. A cute petite white girl took my order. If I were to close my eyes, I'da sworn I was listening to a sista.

"What's up, girl? Whatcha need?" she asked sounding like she was straight out the hood.

I laughed because I couldn't believe she was the manager.

It took me a while to find somewhere to sit. I soon found out the first of the month brought all the bad ass kids and their mommas to the mall. One of those little suckers almost knocked my food out of my hands. I had to find a seat quick. As I looked around, I heard a familiar voice trying to get my attention. I turned and saw it was the manager from McDonald's. Nodding my head, I gave her the okay. "Thank you," I said, sliding my tray on the table. It was awkward at first. We sat there quietly for what seemed like a half hour.

"My name is Cindy," she said, breaking the silence. "What's yours?"

"It's Zsaset."

"So how long have you been working here?" she asked.

"It's only my second day," I replied after taking a sip of my drink.

"I've been here for 2 years. I like it but it doesn't leave me much of a social life."

That didn't surprise me. Big corporations always work you like a dog and pay you scraps. We talked until my break was up. Cindy seemed cool. And I wouldn't mind kicking it with her again.

I returned to the store and the music was blasting. I stared at Vicki for an explanation. She informed me that Larry had left for the rest of the day.

"You know what this means don't you?" Vicki asked.

"No, what?"

"It means we can chill for the rest of the day."

I didn't know about her, but I wasn't here to chill I had bills to pay and a child to feed.

At 4:00 p.m., in came the closing crew. Vicki introduced me to two female employees. Londa, the slim, dark-skinned, medium height one didn't seem very friendly. The other one, Michelle was quiet.

Londa was lazy as hell. She just stood around acting stank while I helped all the customers. No problem…more money for me. A couple of times I caught her cutting her eyes at me. I was going to step to her but I felt kinda sorry for her. Nobody in the store liked her. I don't think she even liked herself. Not only was she rude to us, she was rude to the customers. But stank or no stank, I will slap her.

"Vicki, what's Londa's deal?" I asked.

"Oh, don't pay her any attention. She has issues."

"She's gonna get a fat lip if she don't stop giving me attitude."

I Shoulda Seen It Comin'

We busted out in laughter as we clocked out.

I drove up to the front of the mall where Vicki was standing. "Do you need a ride?"

"No, that's all right I'm waiting on my momma. She'll be here soon." "All right, well I'll see you later," I yelled.

I honked and waved good-bye.

Walking into the house and seeing O.B. made me want to go back to work and pull a double shift. He was his usual cold self. He even called a girl and held a very intimate conversation with her on the phone to get a rise out of me. I tried to ignore his stupidity, but it was impossible not to get upset. That was when I realized that I needed to get the hell out of there. The emotional abuse from him was too much, way too much for me to bear. It was even starting to affect Zeta. She started wetting the bed at night and having temper tantrums.

My daydreaming was interrupted. "What you doing?" K-Dog asked.

"I'm just thinking."

"Thinking about what? Let me guess. O.B. right?"

"Not really. I'm thinking about how nice it would be to have my own place."

"Zsaset, you have to stop letting O.B. get to you like this."

"I know but it's hard. As soon as I get enough money I'm outta here."

"Well, if you need any help just let me know," he said.

"Thanks. I will. Give me a minute and I'll start dinner."

"Take your time," he said, closing the door.

I pulled myself together and went downstairs to cook dinner.

The next couple of weeks proved to be a real test of my strength. Not only did I have to deal with O.B.'s crazy ass I had to deal with Londa. One day she kept staring at me like she was crazy.

"Why are you staring at me?" I asked with an attitude.

"I'm not staring at you," she said.

"Yes, you are. If there's a problem, let's solve it right now so I can get on with my day," I said sharply.

She was so shocked she didn't even respond. As a matter of fact, she was on her best behavior for the rest of the day. She wasn't a bad person. She just needed someone to put her in her place and I was the right one for the job.

Around 5:00 p.m., our assistant manager told us to clock out for dinner. She must've been hungry because it's rare for her to tell us when to go. She can't leave the store until we've eaten.

I snatched my purse off Larry's desk. Before I could get out the door good, Londa yelled for me to wait. Unsure, I hesitated then stopped.

We walked and got to know each other better. Londa explained to me that her attitude was a result of her problems at home. I knew exactly what she was going through.

"Londa, I understand you have problems at home. But problems at home are just that-problems at home. That doesn't mean bring that shit to work with you and make everyone else miserable." She tilted her head and pouted. I wasn't moved.

As we stood in front of McDonald's trying to decide what we wanted, Cindy motioned for me to get in her line. Smiling, she handed me a tray with a Big Mac, fries and a Dr. Pepper drink. *Damn she remembered what I ordered yesterday,* I thought to myself.

While we ate, I found out that Londa and I had some things in common. We were both dealing with lunatics at home. I had O.B. and she had her mother. She told me that her mother was schizo. Her mom thinks she's a FBI agent. Londa said her mother carries five loaded guns on her everyday. She swears someone's after her. She even pulled a gun on Londa one day saying, "I know you tryin' to get me."

I was like, "Damn!" I saw why she was so stressed. It turned out she wasn't as bad I thought. In fact she had some jokes.

I Shoulda Seen It Comin'

What shocked me was she even laughed about her crazy-ass mother. I hadn't cracked up that hard in a long time. Just as we were about to leave, Cindy interrupted us. "So what's up girl?"

"Nothing much," I said pulling out a chair for her. "This is my co-worker, Londa."

They exchanged greetings as Cindy sat down at the table.

"Your assistant manager mentioned you were looking for a place," Cindy said.

"Yeah, why you know somewhere?"

"There are some apartments not far from here that are reasonable," she said as she wrote down the address. "If you need a roommate look me up."

"I'll do that."

I headed to the front of the store when we returned. While I was straightening the shoe wall, a nice looking gentleman with a limp walked in. He was 6'3 with big brown eyes and curly hair. Iced out with diamonds, he wore a colorful Coogi sweater and jeans. *Damn he's fine.* I rushed over to greet him.

"Can I help you find something today?" I said flirting.

"No," he snapped.

What the hell is his problem? He strolled over to the children's section and picked up two styles of Nike sneakers.

"Get me dhese in a 13 1/2, and don't take all day," he said in a nasty tone.

I gripped the shoes, and switched to the stockroom. As I walked back out onto the floor, I noticed his eyes widening.

"Any day," he yelled.

"Excuse me?" I asked bobbing my head.

"You heard me. Hurry up."

"Look, I don't appreciate you talkin' to me like that."

"Do I look like I give a fuck about what you do or don't appreciate? Just ring my shit up," he said, throwing the money at me.

Londa knew I was about to let his ass have it, so she quickly walked up to the register and took over the sale. As she handed him his bags he gave me one last glare and left.

"Zsaset, do you know who that was," Londa said.

"No, and I don't care. Don't nobody talk to me like that."

"Girl, that was Dolo. He's the biggest and most dangerous drug dealer in Richmond. He has murdered people for looking at him wrong."

"Oh well, he'll get over it," I said as if I didn't care.

"I don't know how guys are where you're from, but here they kill girls just as quick as they kill guys. They don't care about nothing or no one. Just watch yourself," she said.

I tossed and turned all that night. The cold look in Dolo's eyes haunted me, so I just stared at the ceiling. *How can a man that fine be such an ass?*

Just before dawn I fell asleep until noon. Casually dressed, I set out to find an apartment. I had to find a place close to K-Dog's house, so I could keep Brenda as my babysitter. Zeta was already comfortable with her. I didn't want her to have get use to someone new.

I drove maybe two miles before I lucked up on some apartments. I walked into the rental office and inquired about a two-bedroom. To my surprise, the complex was running a special.

Still half asleep, I filled out the application and paid the $30 application fee. The rental agent said she would get back to me in three days. Before leaving, I turned towards the lady and asked her how soon I could move in if I got approved.

"You can move in as soon as you want. I already have some apartments ready."

That was all I needed to hear. For the rest of the day, I just kept imagining myself in my own place. Being in the house with O.B. was like serving a life sentence in prison. He made my life miserable. I just wanted to be free and clear of him once and for all.

I Shoulda Seen It Comin'

During the next two days, I was on pins and needles. I couldn't eat or sleep. The first thing I did when I got home was check the answering machine. It was day three and I still hadn't heard from the rental agent. And that worried me. Finally she called that evening. I needed a co-signer since I hadn't been employed for six months yet. I was devastated. *Now what was I going to do?* I had no choice but to find someone. Then it hit me. Cindy was looking for a place too. I called McDonald's and asked to speak with her. She got on the phone and I explained what happened and asked if she would be my roommate. Without hesitation, she agreed. "I'll go fill out the application tomorrow," she said.

I was so nervous I couldn't concentrate. I figured if I prayed hard enough God would get tired of me whining and grant my wish. Sure enough he heard me. I knew it when Cindy came bursting into the store screaming.

"We got it. We can move in next Saturday," she said, jumping up and down.

"Thank God," I said, throwing my hands up in the air.

"Well, I have to get back to work. I'll talk to you later, roomy. Let's go out and celebrate tomorrow, Zsaset. We deserve it."

"What?" Vicki and Londa said in unison. They wondered what all the hype was about.

"Me and Cindy got our apartment. We're gonna go to the club Saturday to celebrate."

"Well count us in," Londa said.

"Of course," I said, prancing around the store.

Everyone sat in the living room when I came home. "Cut off the T.V," I said. "I have something to tell ya'll." O.B. huffed and rolled his eyes. They all looked at me. "It's been real but I'm moving out next Saturday." It was a bittersweet moment. They were happy for me but sad at the same time, with the exception of O.B. He gave me a devilish grin. I was determined to wipe it off his face. Now was not the time, but I made a mental note to get his ass later.

Chapter Ten

I pulled up in front of Vicki's building and blew the horn. I was anxious to celebrate our new apartment and get my party on. Londa and Cindy were going to meet us at the club, a place called Ivory's, that they swore would be rockin'.

Vicki forgot to give me her apartment number. Disturbing neighbors was tacky, especially where Vicki lived. It was a quaint middle class neighborhood mostly occupied by whites. They were peeking out their windows and staring at me like I was crazy. I even saw one woman trying to write down my license plate number. She probably was on the phone with the cops trying to get me arrested for disturbing the peace. Vicki waved at me from her patio after a few seconds. I rolled down my window and asked if she was ready. She shook her head no and motioned for me to come inside.

I was a little ticked, but curiosity got the best of me. I wanted to see if Vicki's mother was as nasty in person as she was on the phone. Every time she called I wanted to hang up on her. I could tell she treated Vicki like shit because she came to work crying all the time.

I entered her apartment only to find it dark and dreary. There was a mausoleum type silence that made my skin crawl. Then she appeared—the witch herself.

"Hi, I'm Zsaset." I couldn't believe it. The bitch didn't even speak back. She gritted on me and kept moving. I laughed out loud as I thought to myself, *some dick could fix you right up*. It was on the tip of my tongue to say, but I held back.

Vicki came into the living room. I scoped her from head to toe. *Oh hell no,* I thought to myself. She is not going out with me like that. Here I was dressed sharp as a knife with my black cat suit and black platform shoes and this bitch had on a sweat suit.

"Vicki, please tell me you're not wearing that to the club," I said as I did a double take.

"Why? Everyone dresses like dis at Ivory's," she replied.

"What?" I said, getting a headache. "And it's not dis, it's this with a th."

"Oh, shut up and let me see what you got on, Zsaset."

I stood up and gave her a few poses like Naomi Campbell on a runaway. "You look like a hooker."

"Well at least I look like a well-paid hooker," I said as I snapped my fingers.

She laughed. "Let's go, crazy."

Londa and Cindy waited in the dimly lit parking lot when we arrived.

"Zsaset, girl what do you have on? That suit is fly," Cindy said, stepping back to get a better look.

"Finally someone with a little class around here," I said eyeing Vicki.

"I didn't say I didn't like it. I just said you look like a hooker in it, that's all," Vicki said.

"Put down the Gatorade and take some notes," I yelled walking towards the door.

I was a bit too much for them because when we got inside, everyone was staring at me like I was a masterpiece at an art museum. I didn't mind because I was there for one reason and one reason only…to get a man.

After a couple of drinks, we were all on the dance floor. I was having the time of my life. It had been a long time since I had been out and I felt the weight lifting off my shoulders. I didn't even allow myself to think about how messed up my life was. I just focused on moving into my new apartment and moving on without O.B.

Four songs later, I was exhausted so I sat down and ordered a drink at the bar. Turning around in the chair to check out the prospects, I spotted a familiar face. I couldn't place where I had seen him until he glanced at me with his chilling eyes. *Oh my God. That's Dolo.* I was so shaken I almost spilled my drink. I quickly left the bar, and went to the dance floor to see if I could find Londa. I searched for her but came up short.

"What's up, girl?" I felt someone grab me by the arm. "You havin' a good time," Londa said.

"I was until a minute ago."

"Why, what's wrong," she asked.

"I think I just saw Dolo."

"You probably did. He comes in here with his crew all the time. Don't worry. He probably won't even remember you. He's not the sharpest knife in the drawer."

"Londa, if that was supposed to make me feel better, it didn't. Most killers aren't very bright or they wouldn't kill people."

I continued to look around to make sure Dolo didn't spot me. "Oh shit, there he is," I said, covering my face.

Seeing him again reminded me of the horror of our first encounter.

"What's your name, shorty?" he said, towering over me.

"Jazzy," I answered.

"Jazzy, I'm Dolo. I'm quite sure your friends at the store told you all about me."

"What store?" I asked.

"Aren't you the chick from Lady Foot Locker that got smart with me?" And Londa said he wouldn't remember me. I think she's the one with the loose screws. I knew I was going to have to talk my way out of this situation.

"I wouldn't say I got smart with you, I was just merely stating that you were being very rude to me and I didn't appreciate it. If I offended you in anyway, I'm very sorry."

"That's okay, I usually don't like it when people talk to me that way, but there are always exceptions, especially when they're as beautiful as you are, Jazzy." He puffed his cigar. "Where are you from?"

"I'm from the Virginia Beach area."

"That explains why you talk like a white girl."

"I don't talk like a white girl. It's called using correct English," I said to him and thought to myself *you ignorant bastard*.

He laughed as if he was saying, whatever, bitch. So without hesitation, I told him to excuse me. I didn't even give him a chance to respond. "Let's go," I said, turning towards Londa.

"Jazzy," Dolo shouted. "How you just gone walk away while we in the middle of a conversation?" I didn't want a scene. I contemplated for a moment and then turned back around and took a few steps back towards Dolo.

"My friends are ready," I said.

"Well can I call you?" Dolo said. At this point, we had a small audience. I knew I shouldn't embarrass him.

"Um, alright." I quickly wrote down a fake number and turned to leave.

"You better not be playing with me, Jazzy. This number better be good." Not only is the number wrong, the name is wrong too, I thought. It probably was not wise for me to do that, but I didn't know what else to do.

The club was starting to let out when I finally found Vicki and Cindy.

"Where the hell have y'all been all night?" I said.

"Talking to dhese guy's from the north side."

"What the hell is dhese? The word is these. Say it with me, *these*."

"Zsaset, you always correcting people like you don't use slang."

"The only time you'll hear me speaking slang is when I'm mad."

They weren't buying it, so I just left it alone.

I Shoulda Seen It Comin'

Walking towards the car, Cindy noticed the payphones. She dug around in the bottom of her purse and pulled out a quarter.
"Who you callin' this time of night," I asked.
"None of your business."
"It must be a booty call," I insisted.
"That's right, it's a booty call. It's my new man. You'll meet him soon. He's gonna help us move in."
I was dying to know if he was white or black, so I asked. When she said he was black it didn't surprise me, considering she acted like she was black herself.

She dialed the number and I took a seat on the stoop next to the phones. I watched as guys driving hot cars pulled over to talk to Vicki and Londa. I couldn't believe all the attention they were getting. They both could've made the worst dressed list not to mention they weren't very attractive. They gave a whole new meaning to the phrase, beauty is in the eye of the beholder. Shit, you had to be blind as hell to find them beautiful. *Damn, I gotta check myself. I'm actually jealous.*

Cindy was on the phone maybe five minutes when I heard a commotion near the club. I saw a crowd of guys fighting in the street. It looked like the L.A. riots. I witnessed a guy bust another guy in the head with a beer bottle. I tried to get my girls' attention, but they were all preoccupied with men.

I bent over to re-tie my ankle strap when I heard a loud car engine. I first looked up and saw a figure coming in my direction. I then turned side- ways and a bright orange Maxima slowly drove by and as it did, shots rang out and the crowd began to scatter. I couldn't believe it, but this guy was actually shooting right next to me. The thugs in the car shot back. I heard girls screaming in fear.

Too afraid to move, I dropped to the ground and shielded my body with my arms. It happened so fast, I didn't have time to concern myself with where my girls were. The shooting seemed like it was never going to end. When the shooting was over, two bloody bodies laid on the ground beside me. I couldn't tell if they were dead, but it appeared if they weren't, they would be soon. I was so out of it, I didn't realize my hairpiece was on the ground when I got up. I stepped around the bodies and took off like a bat out of hell. I headed straight for the car. I heard the sound of sirens growing closer as I fumbled for my keys. I shook like I had Parkinson's disease. The key would not fit in the hole.

Scared and confused, I sat in my car choking down a cigarette. I was relieved when I saw my girls running up to the car.

"Girl, are you alright," they asked.

"I think so," I said, lighting up my second smoke. "I was so scared something happened to y'all. Who was that guy shooting at people?" I asked.

"Girl, that was Dolo," Vicki said trembling.

"What," I said blown away. "Let's get the hell out of here. I'm not used to no shit like this."

On the way to Vicki's house, the events replayed in my head. I was so fucked up in the head, I thought I was gonna need a doctor.

"All I have to say is that was the last time I'm goin' to that club. I'm not losin' my life because a bunch of gun-happy niggas want to declare war on each other," I said.

"Zsaset, I'm with you girl. That was too close for comfort. Are you sure you're okay? Dolo almost shot you."

"Yeah, but I thought I was gonna die. Who is this Dolo fool anyway? Where is he from?" I said.

"New York and he is dangerous as hell. Besides being the biggest drug dealer in Richmond, he's a cold-blooded killer. Just last week, he walked right up to a guy downtown and shot him in the head in broad daylight. The guy shot him back in the leg. That's why he has a limp."

"So why isn't he in jail?" I asked.

"No one will testify against him. He has Richmond locked down."

For the rest of the ride we sat in silence.

I Shoulda Seen It Comin'

I dropped Vicki off just before dawn and headed home. All of the commotion at the club wore me out. I just wanted to get into bed.

I opened the door and found O.B. lying on the couch. The TV wasn't on and there wasn't any music playing. It was almost as if he was waiting up for me. I shut my bedroom door and as I listened quietly on the other side, I heard him get up and come upstairs. "Awww, he still cares," I mouthed. Now it was obvious he was waiting up for me, or so I thought. I guess he was worried. This was the first time I had been out since our break up. I thought to myself - *maybe I had over-reacted about O.B. and the chick in the car.* Then I thought- *don't be stupid, Zsaset, this nigga is luncheon-be over it.*

Chapter Eleven

The sun was shining through my blinds so bright I had no choice but to get up. I picked Zeta up from Brenda's then made myself some breakfast. "I heard that nigga, Dolo, thought he was a cowboy last night shooting up shit. Did you see what happened, Zsaset?" Quan asked.

"Yes, Dolo has issues, but if you don't mind, I don't want to talk about it front of you know who," I said, pointing to Zeta.

"That's right, not in my front of my Zeta Beta," K-Dog said.

The last thing I wanted to do was re-live last night, so I cut the conversation short and went upstairs to get back in bed.

The sound of toys banging awoke me. I rolled over and looked at my clock. Still stretched out on the bed, I asked Zeta if Quan and K-Dog had left.

"Nope," she said, jumping up on the bed.

Seeing all the boxes on the floor made me realize we were actually moving in a week. I pulled out my book and started to jot down notes for my move. I called Cindy to discuss how we would split the bills, but we decided to hammer it out over dinner instead of on the phone.

That evening, I met Cindy at Golden Corral.

"Cindy, this is my daughter, Zeta."

"Oh, she is so cute," she said, giving her a hug.

"Thank you. You guys should get along really well. I've been blessed to have an angel for a daughter," I said proudly.

We put our coats down and headed to the salad bar. Zeta wanted to start with desert but I convinced her to eat some food first. With our plates full of food, we went back to our table. In between stuffing our faces, we worked out a plan.

"I can't wait to move in," Cindy said.

I Shoulda Seen It Comin'

"Yeah I know girl. My ex is driving me crazy."

"So what happened with you guys?"

"To make a long story short, he made me believe there was a future for us. But now that he got the goodies, he's through with me."

"That's a man for you. Don't let him get you down. Trust me, I've had my share of dummies too, but I think I've found true love this time."

Hearing Cindy say that gave me hope. Zeta was falling out of her chair. Her crawling on the floor took the cake. "She's getting restless. I better get her home," I said to Cindy. I told her I would see her tomorrow.

It must have been the food Zeta ate because she was wired. As I pulled out of the parking lot, the new jam by Biggie Smalls blasted on the radio. Zeta began to sing word for word. *"I love it when you call me Big Poppa. The showstopper,"* she sang. I turned to my baby and smiled. I knew my baby girl was too hip for her age. She knew plenty of rap lyrics but no nursery rhymes. She could do all the video dances, but she didn't know the hokey pokey. In the back of my mind, I knew it was because of my lifestyle.

Stuffed, we staggered in the house and there was my favorite lying cheating thug.

"So when are you moving out," O.B. asked.

"None of your business," I said, adjusting myself in my seat.

"I was just trying to be nice to your stupid ass."

"Oh, now you want to be nice to me. It's too late for that." I gritted on him. *How dare he even open his mouth, after the way he's been treating me. His very presence was making me sick to my stomach.*

"Well, is it okay for me to ask when you're leaving," K-Dog inquired.

"It most certainly is K," I said, rolling my eyes at O.B.. "I'll be leaving this weekend. Are you going to miss us?"

"Of course I am. Who am I going to have drippy eggs and a tall glass of milk with?" he said, sitting next to Zeta.

"Me," she said, wrapping her arms around his neck.

"That's right, we can still have breakfast together. I just have to come and pick you up sometime."

I could tell our moving out saddened K-Dog. But it was for the best.

"Do you need help moving in?"

"Well we could use some help with some of the heavy lifting."

"You know I got your back on whatever you need, Sis." I strolled over and gave K-Dog a big hug and cut my eyes at O.B..

"Thank you K," I said.

Chapter Twelve

It was move-in day. Hallelujah! Neither one of us had much except clothes and personal items. Although it only took us two hours to move in, we sweated like slaves. I plopped on one of the boxes and drank an ice-cold beer. I couldn't believe it. I was finally here, in my new apartment.

The split-level, roommate style apartment had its benefits. Our rooms were on opposite ends of the apartment. That was perfect because I didn't want to hear her getting busy. I'm glad we each had our own bathrooms. I'm petty about my bathroom. There was a large kitchen, a small courtyard in the front for Zeta to play in, and a swimming pool was only steps away from our door. *I can finally breathe again.*

My thoughts were interrupted by a knock at the door. I opened it and to my surprise it was the last person in the world I expected to see.

"What the hell are you doing here?" I said taken aback.

"To take care of business. Why the hell are you here?" he said. O.B. paused for a moment and then said, "Wait a minute – this isn't your new place is it?"

"What the hell you think, stupid?" I stood there debating my next move. Just as I was about to close the door Cindy came running down the steps.

O.B. looked over and saw her and then grabbed me and whispered in my ear, "Please play along."

I was squirming and trying to wiggle out of his embrace. "Hey, I assume you two know one another," Cindy said.

"Damn straight, Cindy, this is my sister. You didn't tell me you were rooming with my sister."

Danette Majette

"Your sister? I didn't know you had a sister." *He doesn't,* I thought to myself. "I thought you just had brothers." She stood there confused and a little suspicious. O.B. sensed her distrust and continued with his performance.

"Zsaset, you talked to Ma – what she doing?"

I stumbled over my words. "Ah, ah, yeah, I mean no I haven't talked to her in a long time."

O.B. grinned real big. "Yeah, well you know you better call her – you know how she gets."

Cindy interrupted, "O.B., come on in and chat with your sister. I have to run to the store for some hangers." She plastered a big wet kiss on his lips on her way out.

I couldn't believe it. Cindy was dating O.B. In shock, I stood there motionless.

As soon as the door shut I looked at O.B. "Why did you tell her I was your sister?" I asked shooting him a nasty stare.

"I didn't know what else to say."

"How about the truth, you sack of shit?" I said throwing a roll of paper towels.

"I couldn't," he screamed. "Look, I care about Cindy a lot. Don't mess this up for me."

"You son-of-a-bitch. You didn't have a problem hurting me, but you have a problem hurting her."

"Look, I cared about you, but it just wasn't working."

"Why didn't you just tell me that? I'll tell you why. You're selfish."

He stood there for a few minutes. "So are you going to tell Cindy we used to date?" he asked.

"I don't know what I'm going to do. I can't think right now."

I ran up to my room and closed the door. *What the hell am I going to do? If I tell Cindy I used to date O.B. she'll be crushed. The last thing I need is a fall-out with Cindy because of O.B. It would make our living arrangement unbearable.* I was so mad at O.B. for putting me in this situation. At the same time, I was hurt that he loved her and not me. I poured my heart and soul into our relationship and he just threw it away.

I contemplated what to do then went downstairs and told O.B. that I wouldn't say anything. I could tell he was relieved because he hugged me.   "So, I'm your sister, uh," I asked.

"I guess so."

Not only did he tell her I was his sister he told her K-Dog and Quan were his brothers. I went from being an only child to having three brothers in one day.

"What am I supposed to do when she starts asking me questions," I said.

"Just make up somethin'. You act like you don't know how to lie."

"I don't lie, thank you."

"Yeah, whatever you say. Tell Cindy I had to make a run and I'll call her later," he said walking out the door. He sped out the parking lot and I went to my room.

Tired of unpacking boxes, I went downstairs to see if Cindy was back from the store.

"You finish unpacking already?" she said from the kitchen.

"Not yet. I just wanted to take a break before Deonte got here."

The doorbell rang. It was K-dog.

"I just dropped by to see the new crib," he said snooping around.

"Boy, I'm glad to see you. Let's talk out here." I pulled him by the hand and led him to the courtyard.

"What's wrong?"

"K-Dog, I can't get rid of this mothafucka to save my life. Guess who my roommate's boyfriend is?"

"Naw," he said, dropping his jaw. "Please don't tell me."

"Yep, my biggest nightmare," I screamed.

I explained the whole twisted story to K-Dog to get his opinion. Shrugging his shoulders, he just rubbed his head as if he didn't have an answer to my question.

"This situation calls for a Newport," he said. "That nigga, O.B., is crazy as hell."

"No, if anyone's crazy it's me. I can't believe I agreed to go along with this shit. I moved to get away from him and now I have to see his ass everyday. And with another woman at that. Ain't that a bitch?"

We were laughing when Deonte drove up in the moving truck. K-Dog and I said our good-byes.

I met Deonte at the truck. When he stepped out he asked if I was all right.

"Yeah, I'm just having a bad day," I said, leading him inside.

I just stood there for a moment admiring Deonte's compassion. I couldn't believe he was still concerned about me. After all we've been through, I was sure he hated my guts.

"So did you bring everything?"

"Yeah, everything except the TV, I didn't have room for it."

"That's fine. I'll just buy another one. I'll go get Cindy so she can help us," I said.

"Okay, I'll start pulling the furniture out."

Because Cindy and I are petite women, it took both of us to move in the heavier boxes. Deonte was pressed for time, so he enlisted our neighbor to help him with the furniture. Once we were finished, I kicked up my feet on the couch, and drank another beer. I was exhausted. I could tell Cindy was too.

"I'm going upstairs to take a shower. I'm quite sure you and your husband could use some privacy," she smirked.

"I don't think so."

"You never know, Zsaset. You never know."

I watched Deonte and Zeta play in the courtyard. They were happy to see each other. I hated to break up the fun, but Deonte and I had business to talk over. I tapped on the window to motion him to come in.

"Now let's be serious, I'm quite sure you didn't volunteer to bring my stuff up here out of the goodness of your heart," I said, wiping the sweat from my head.

"Look, you may not always be my wife, but you're always going to be the mother of my daughter. So what affects you affects me."

"Wait, stop the press. Where is all this going?"

"From my heart to yours," he said with sincerity.

"Bullshit, Deonte. Just spill it!"

He went on to feed me some crap about how us not living together, but still being married, bothered him. Deonte beat around the bush about wanting to divorce my tail. "Well, we've both moved on with our lives...blah, blah, blah," he dragged out. I was pissed off.

He had no idea I was seconds away from knocking out his two front teeth. "If it's a divorce you want, you can have it. But on one condition—I want $550 a month and full custody."

"Fine. All you have to do is sign these papers. You don't even have to show up for court. My lawyer will take care of everything."

"Oh, I just bet he will." I snatched the pen from his hand and signed the papers. "You got what you came for...now leave." He watched my back as I switched upstairs. Halfway up, I yelled, "Zeta, come say bye to Daddy." She came hopping downstairs with her ponytails swinging.

"Bye, Daddy," she said, holding tightly to his waist.

"Bye, baby, I'll be back soon." He gave me a sorry glance and strolled out the door.

Cindy walked in the den with a towel wrapped around her head. "So, did ya'll get reacquainted?"

"No, we're getting divorced."

"Oh, Zsaset. I'm so sorry."

"I'm not. Our marriage was over before it started. It was only a matter of time before we made it official. Now we can both move on."

The rest of the day, our apartment was like Grand Central Station. K-Dog and his friends were in the kitchen talking shit when Vicki and Londa arrived. I led them to the kitchen.
"Vicki and Londa, these are my brothers K-Dog and Quan and their friends."
Londa even brought her pretty friend, Clova, along for the visit. She wore jeans that she obviously cut up herself and a shredded t-shirt. Once I sized her up, I gave her the privilege of meeting everyone.

"I thought you only had one brother that you said was a stuck up stuff shirt. Neither of these could be him," Londa whispered fixated on K-Dog and Quan.
"That is what she told me also," Vicki said.
"Oh naw, ya'll got the story twisted," I said
"Girl, they are fine," Londa said.
They chilled with them in the kitchen and left me to do all the unpacking. Minutes turned into hours and I was ticked off. Everyone was so busy cracking jokes and having fun, they completely forgot about me. But I quickly changed that. I slammed down the centerpiece on the couch and stormed into the kitchen.
"If ya'll not gonna help me unpack, ya'll can roll up outta here! Don't think ya'll gonna be comin' over here loungin' and shit. Now find somethin' to do."
All eyes were on me as I switched out of the kitchen like somebody's momma. Next thing I knew I heard dishes hitting the cabinet and hammers banging against the wall. I leaned against the doorway of the kitchen, put my hands on my hips, smiled and said, "Now that's what I'm talking about—teamwork."

I Shoulda Seen It Comin'

They all laughed, but I had the last laugh because I still sent them bammas home anyway. I was tired as hell.

Chapter Thirteen

Things were finally going my way. I spent my days at work and my nights at home with Zeta. Cindy and O.B. were really hitting it off. Surprisingly, I was all right with it. Of course, he practically moved in with us. Suspecting that I was annoyed with him being there all the time, she sat me down. "Zsaset, does it bother you that I'm dating your brother?"

"No, why?"

"You just seem like you're always in a bad mood when he's around."

"Girl, he just rubs me the wrong way. I told you before, we don't get along too well. What can I say?"

I didn't have the heart to tell her the truth, so I just left it at that. I knew it was wrong, but I didn't want to rock the boat and be right back at square one. As much as I despised him, I relied on his hush money to pay my rent. I wanted to keep the lifestyle I was accustomed to. I hated deceiving her, but I wasn't dating her. It wasn't my place to tell her.

Our apartment was the favorite hangout spot. There was always loud music, food, and lots of alcohol. Things really got out of hand when K-Dog and his friends came over. They would make so much noise when they were gambling that my neighbors would call the police.

One night my girls and I all stayed up half the night drinking and talking about our love lives. Everyone was having men problems. They seemed to all tell the same stories about men cheating on them and treating them like shit.

"Why don't ya'll just dump them? Then you don't have to sit here boring me with these stories," I said.

Clova laughed. "I'm with you, Miss Thang. Why ya'll putting up with their shit anyway? Just get what you can get from their ass and roll out."

She was known around the city for being a freak, but she had a good heart and I liked her personality. Girls hated her, but she didn't let that stop her from getting her money. Guys actually paid her to sleep with them. They paid all her bills and bought her whatever she wanted. They gave her everything but love. That was fine with her though, she didn't care about love. I think that's what I liked about her. She too had been in relationships with men who dogged her. So she flipped the script on them. She started dogging them.

After our third round of beers, Vicki told us that she had met a really nice guy. We all gave each other a look like here she goes again.

"Who is it this week?" I asked.

"Seriously, I think this one is Mr. Right," she said in a serious tone.

"You said that last week," Londa said, hitting her in the back of the head.

We laughed our heads off.

"I know, but it's for real this time. And guess what, Zsaset? He has a brother who wants to meet you."

I looked at her ass like she had two heads. "Oh, no. I am not interested," I said, waving my hand in the air.

"Zsaset, I'm telling you if his brother looks anything like him you are in for a treat."

"Vicki, the last time I thought I was getting a treat it turned out to be a trick. So just leave me alone."

Was she crazy? The last thing I needed was a man complicating my life again.

Clova interjected saying, "Girl, it's just a date. You gotta eat. Just look at it as a free meal. I don't know about you, but I don't get free offers like that too often. I always pay some price whether it's with my body or my mind." We all got quiet. A large part of me felt sorry for her.

I didn't want to go, but Vicki was damn near on her knees begging me. Against my better judgment I finally agreed. That didn't mean I had to fall in love or anything. I'll just go out and have fun without any strings attached. At least that's what I thought.

The next day at work Vicki asked what time I was going to be ready.

"Ready for what," I asked.

"We're supposed to go out tonight."

Upset I shook my head. I thought she was talking about next week sometime. But no, they wanted to go out that night.

"I don't know about that, I don't have a babysitter."

"Ask Cindy," she said.

I didn't want to ask Cindy because she was always laid up with O.B., but Vicki insisted because she had already told them we would go out with them.

"Well just tell them we can't."

"Fine," she said, grabbing the phone.

"Wait. Let me see what I can do when I get home."

After putting my purse down, I heard laughter coming from the den, so I made my way there.

"Do you two have any plans tonight?" I asked plopping down in the chair.

"No, we're just gonna watch a movie. Why?" Cindy said.

I asked her to baby-sit and she was more than happy to. She said I was overdue for a date. *That was easy enough,* I thought as I walked up the stairs. But as usual I had spoken too soon.

"Who are you going on a blind date with," O.B. yelled from the bottom of the stairs.

"Well, if I knew that, it wouldn't be a blind date now would it," I said as I rolled my eyes and continued up the stairs.

I Shoulda Seen It Comin'

I was so nervous I completely demolished my closet. It was like I was going on my first date. I didn't know what to wear because I wasn't sure where we were going. So, I played it safe and decided on my chocolate halter Donna Karen dress and matching stilettos.

I stood in front of the mirror admiring how nice the dress made my ass look. Then I went downstairs.

Cindy complimented me on how pretty I looked, but pretty wasn't the look I was going for. She turned to O.B. to ask him how I looked. It was written all over his face, he was fuming. I could feel his eyes burning holes right through my dress. Poor Cindy was so naïve. She figured he was jealous because of the thought of another man touching his sister, and not his ex-girlfriend.

"She looks all right," he answered with tight lips.

It felt so good seeing him jealous, I let him have that one.

"I'll see you guys later," I said as I pranced to the door. I kissed Zeta on the way out and checked my makeup one last time before leaving to go outside to meet Vicki and the guys.

Halfway down the sidewalk, I noticed Vicki walking towards me like she'd seen a ghost.

"What's wrong?" I asked.

"Umm, I have some bad news," she said as she threw her arm around me.

Just as she started to speak, a guy walked up. "You must be Zsaset," he said, showing his pearly whites.

My attention went immediately towards him. "Yes, I am. You must be Tee."

"You got it, shorty."

Both his accent and his gear screamed New York. He wore a tweed sports coat, Versace jeans, and cowboy boots. The brother looked like he had just stepped out of a GQ magazine.

Their ride was still several cars away and I peered over to it attempting to get a glimpse of my date. In light of how Tee looked, I figured my date couldn't look too bad. I neared the car

Danette Majette

and a guy emerged to greet me. He sported a Coogi sweater, taupe colored pants, and the biggest diamond-stud earring I ever saw in my life. I thought to myself that he looked vaguely familiar. I took about two more steps and stopped dead in my tracks, but my date was already moving towards me. I spun around on my heels and peered at Vicki with heat coming from my ears. She looked at me with eyes that said *I'm sorry*. Out of all the men in Richmond, she set me up with Dolo.

"So, Jazzy, we meet again," he said with a smile.

I was so shocked to see Dolo standing there in front of me. I just stood there for a minute in complete silence.

"So you're my date," I asked wanting to fight Vicki.

"I guess so. Is that a problem?" I hesitated so he continued. "If it makes you feel any better, I'm just as surprised as you," he said. *For some reason, I didn't think so. I felt like he set this whole thing up.*

He proceeded to the opposite side of the car and opened the door for me. I no longer wanted to look sexy. I adjusted my dress after I sat down not wanting to reveal any private parts. I didn't want to give this fool the impression that he was getting anywhere with me. It was out to dinner then home.

"Ay, Tee, I want to go to that new restaurant down at the Bottoms," Dolo said.

No this mothafucka didn't just say where he wants to go. What about where we want to go? I thought to myself.

I turned in my seat. "What do you think, Vicki?" I asked with a fake smile.

"Um, yeah that sounds good."

Vicki was still shook. You could tell from the sound of her voice. She had fucked up big time and she knew it. She set me up with the man that almost killed me.

The drive to the restaurant was quiet. Tee tried to loosen things up with cheap talk, but it didn't work. I was too paranoid to talk. I was sitting next to a wanted killer. There were people who wanted this man dead and I was in the car with him. What the hell was I thinking going out with him? I had to get out of this and fast.

By the time I came up with a good excuse, we were at the restaurant. The maitre'd seated us then our waiter came over. "Can I get you something from the bar?" he asked.

"Definitely. I'll take a double shot of Hennessey," I said. I needed something to calm my nerves.

I quickly downed my drink after the waiter sat it on the table. I looked around the restaurant for any suspicious characters.

"Zsaset, is somethin' wrong?" Dolo asked.

"No. Why?"

"I don't know. You're actin' like your hidin' from someone."

"I'm kinda nervous because it's my first time out since I broke up with my last boyfriend." I almost felt bad lying to him. I should have just told him how I felt. But when he said I was in good hands and promised to show me the time of my life, I got scared. The time of my life sounded like the end of my life.

I was so busy caught up in my fears that I didn't notice how attentive Tee was to Vicki. He was gentle and seemed to dwell on everything she said. She would tell corny ass jokes that only he got and they called each other little pet names. I couldn't believe he and Dolo were brothers. They were total opposites. Just as I was about to ask Dolo a question the waiter came with our food. I took a couple of bites and then decided to go for it.

"So do you have a girlfriend?" I asked.

"Not right now, but I got my eye on someone."

"Oh that's good," I said taking a bite of my T-Bone steak. *What the hell was I saying? Anyone crazy enough to get involved with him needed to be committed.*

"So I guess you're not seeing anyone since this is your first date since your last man."

"No, I'm not going down that road again."

"Yeah, that's what they all say."

"What do you mean by that?"

"It just means you don't strike me as the type of woman who's gonna let one man stop her from loving again. Just wait and see. You'll have a man in your life again real soon."

I know he ain't even thinking about being my man. Now I know I had too much to drink, but what was his excuse. He had to be crazy if he thought I was going to let him in. Little did he know, our first date was our last. Dolo had three strikes from the door. One, he was one of Richmond's most hated men. Two, he was a notorious drug kingpin. And to top it off, he was a cold-blooded killer who almost killed me during one of his shootin' rampages.

He broke my train of thought when he rubbed my leg under the table.

"Umm, Zsaset to Earth," he said. I jerked and almost knocked over my drink. I knew it was time to go. I gave Vicki the time to roll signal. She kissed Tee once more and grabbed her purse.

"Tee, we'll be at the front after we freshen up in the bathroom." I followed her out and left them to pay the bill.

Vicki and Tee decided they wanted to take a drive. I hated to cut Vicki and Tee short but I was ready to go straight home. So Tee asked Dolo if he would take him to pick up his car. When we got to Tee's car he asked if it was okay if he and Vicki took off.

"My brotha'll get you home safe."

"Naw, let's just drop her off first," Vicki said. I could tell I was cock blocking, so I told Vicki to go and have fun.

"Dolo can take me home," I said to Vicki.

"Are you sure?" she asked.

"Yeah, I'm sure." Vicki kissed my cheek and waved goodbye as she ran to the car.

The ride home was long and uncomfortable. I only lived ten minutes away, but the short drive seemed like eternity. *Home at last,* I thought to myself. I stepped out the car and walked around to the driver's side door.

"Thank you for dinner. I had a good time."

"No, you didn't," he said, knowing I was lying. He was right. I was a nervous wreck. "So what's the deal? Why are you so uneasy around me?"

"Well, I guess it started when you came in the store and got nasty with me. And then I saw you at the club and I don't know if you know it or not, but you almost shot me."

"I almost shot you. How did I almost shoot you?" he said in amazement.

"Well, I just happened to be standing right next to you when you shot at those guys that night at club Ivory's."

"First of all, those niggas started shooting at me."

"Well, when you started shooting back I was standing right next to you."

"No wonder you were acting so strange at dinner. Well since you gave me a fake name and number at the club, can't we just call it even?" He flashed a wide grin and we both laughed.

We stared at each other for a few seconds and then he broke the awkwardness by asking, "So people talk real highly of me, uh?"

"I wouldn't say that."

"Oh really," he said with sarcasm.

"So are they lying?"

"They're not lying, they're just not telling the whole truth—if that makes any kind of sense to you."

"No, it doesn't. You're gonna have to explain that one to me," I said.

"I'll explain it to you the next time we go out. That's if you go out with me again."

"We'll see," I said with a smirk. *What was I saying,* I thought.

I turned away. "I'm tired and I have to work tomorrow so I better go."

"Alright well, I'll talk to you later," Dolo said as he touched my hand.

As I walked to my door I took one last look at him. I forgot all about the bad boy lifestyle. Instead, my thoughts went straight physical. He looked so good with his broad shoulders and muscular arms. "Zsaset, snap out of it girl," I whispered.

I was up half the night thinking about my evening with Dolo. I enjoyed talking to him, even though I definitely shouldn't have been in his company. Scary as it was, I knew I would see him again.

At work the next morning, I waited by the door for Vicki. I was exhausted, but not too tired to curse her out for hooking me up with Dolo.

"Hi, Zsaset. How was your night? I hope it was as good as mine," she said, looking spaced out.

"Somehow I doubt it," I said angrily.

"Did you forget who I was with last night?"

"No. And I bet you're not going to let me forget it either. C'mon, Zsaset, everything went okay. You got home safe, didn't you?"

"Yes I did. That's not the point. You set me up with a drug dealer slash killer."

"You know I didn't know, Zsaset – but honestly, Dolo didn't seem that bad."

"No, he's probably worse," I said.

"So you're telling me, his bad boy image didn't turn you on at all?"

"Not even a little bit." Still frustrated I went on, "Why do I even talk to you."

"Uh-huh. I knew it. You wanted him, didn't you?"

"Vicki, I'm gonna act like I didn't hear you say that."

"Okay. I'll let that be our little secret," she said in a playful tone.

Vicki was on cloud nine the rest of the day, and I was jealous. It had been four months since I was intimate with

I Shoulda Seen It Comin'

someone, and I think it was starting to get to me. I was beginning to rethink this independent woman philosophy about how I didn't need a man. I did need a man. Normally Dolo would not be my pick of the litter, but when you're batting zero, the bottom of the barrel looks good.

Chapter Fourteen

I hadn't heard from Dolo since our first date. In a round about way I tried to get some info on him from Vicki, but she never gave me a straight answer. Her attention was strictly on Tee. All I heard was Tee this and Tee that. She was falling for him hard. She had even stopped coming over to my apartment.

It was raining so hard one night everyone decided to stay home. It was the first time the apartment had been that quiet since we moved in. I played a few games with Zeta until she fell asleep. Feeling depressed, I took off my clothes and went downstairs. Prepared for an evening of television and popcorn I curled up on the couch. With my Heineken in one hand and remote in the other, I flipped the channels only to find nothing on.

I was so bored, I found myself hypnotized by the hard falling rain. As I let go of the curtain, I saw a pearly white Lexus pull up. "Who in the world could that be?" I said to myself. It was a male figure, but it couldn't be for me. So I closed the blinds and grabbed an Ebony magazine from the coffee table. I thumbed through the pages until I came to an article about Whitney Houston and Bobby Brown. *Whitney you're not alone, girlfriend. I'm attracted to a bad boy too.*

I heard a knock at the door. I stared at it for a few seconds before I moved. "Who is it?" I asked. There was no response. So I put my eye against the peephole and someone's finger blocked my view. I got nervous and ran to the window but I couldn't see a thing. "Who is it?" I asked again getting pissed. Still there was no answer. "Alright, let's see if you say something when I put one in your ass." I headed to the closet.

"Girl, it's me, Dolo," I heard him say as I wrapped my hand around my piece.

I Shoulda Seen It Comin'

Oh my God. What is he doing here?

"Umm. One minute," I said as I pulled the scarf off of my head.

I opened the door and there he was, standing in front of me with a black, velour Adidas sweat suit.

"Hi, what brings you by?"

"I was in the neighborhood and decided to drop in. I hope that's okay," he said with a smile that made me want to melt.

"I guess. Come on in."

Dolo was drenched from the rain. I took his jacket and hung it behind the door. He sat on the couch like he owned the place. Dolo scoped out the living room until he came across a picture of my children.

"Whose kids?" he asked.

"Mine." Dolo gave me a look as if to say cut the bull. "Oh, I didn't tell you I have two kids."

"No you didn't. But it's cool I have a daughter myself." He smiled.

I offered Dolo something to drink for what turned out to be a really long night. We talked for hours about our personal lives. I guess he was starting to feel comfortable around me because he dropped the bomb that he and Tee had been abandoned by their junkie mother when they were 3 and 5 years old and grew up in an orphanage. I don't know why but people always wanted to tell me their darkest secrets.

By the time we finished our conversation, I understood why he was fucked up in the head. We really didn't have too much in common. I guess that's what drew us together. They say opposites attract.

It was three o' clock in the morning when the credits rolled to the movie we were watching. We both fought back sleep. I eased a few inches away from Dolo. "Well, I'm about to turn in," I said yawning.

"Yeah, I better get going. It's raining kind of hard and I live across town."

Danette Majette

"You wanna stay here tonight? It's only a couple of hours before morning anyway." *What the hell was I thinking? I can't believe I invited him to stay.*

"You sure?" he asked.

"Yeah. C'mon, we can go up to my room. I'll make you a bed on the floor."

When we got upstairs to my room, he noticed Zeta on the bed.

"Is that your daughter?"

"Yes," I said, pulling the blanket over her.

"She's a cutie like her mother."

"You think so?" I said with a seductive look in my eye.

"I know so." He pulled his T-shirt over his head.

I layered the floor with blankets and quilts. He slipped under the blankets like he was sleeping on a Serta. By the time I returned from the bathroom, he was snoring like a fat man. Dolo was knocked out cold. I moved Zeta to the other side of the bed so that I could keep my eye on him. Leaning over the edge, I was surprised at what I saw. For just that moment, Dolo had a sort of angelic innocence about him. Instead of a bad boy, he actually resembled a baby boy.

Dolo and Zeta were already up by the time I awoke.

"Good morning, Mommy," Zeta said.

"Good morning, baby. Whatcha watchin'?"

"I'm watchin' cartoons wit the man," she said.

"I see," I said, staring at Dolo.

"Well, I hate to break up your little party but I have to get to work. And Miss Zeta Beta you have to go to Brenda's."

"I don't wanna go, Mommy."

"I know but Mommy has to go make some money."

Feeling sorry for Zeta, Dolo said, "Why don't you just take the day off?"

"Everybody can't live like you...Mr. Don Corleone. I could tell his ego was pumped by the way he smiled. It tripped me out how Italian mafia criminals were always super heroes to the boys in the hood.

He reached in his pants pocket and pulled out a handful of money. He then proceeded to peel off five, one hundred dollar bills and handed them to me.

"What is this for?" I asked.

"You said you wished you could take the day off, but you have to pay bills, right? Now you can take the day off and still pay your bills."

I wasn't sure if I should keep the money, but I was tired and a day off from work was what I needed. I thanked him and walked him downstairs to the door.

"Can I see you later?" he asked.

"I don't see why not. But can you keep this between me and you?" I asked. Dolo's smirk was filled with many questions. "I have my reasons and one of them is that I don't like people all up in my business."

"I see. Well, will you explain your other reasons to me?"

"Maybe later."

He kissed me on the lips and left. "Thanks," he said as he walked away.

"Thanks for what," I inquired. He stopped and turned around.

"For not judgin' me like everyone else. I'm really not all that bad."

"Yeah, well that still remains to be seen." I smiled seductively and closed the door.

After spending the whole day with Zeta, I needed some time to myself. I dropped her off at Brenda's for the night. I stopped at the convenience store in the strip mall of our complex to get a beer and some snacks. Throwing my car in park, I looked up and noticed a homeless man standing in front of the store harassing people. As soon as he saw me coming, he started to scream.

"You think you too good for me, don't you? Well, bitch, we'll just see about that," he yelled.

I tried to avoid him, but he followed me into the store. I quickly grabbed my sandwiches and drinks and headed to the checkout counter. As I stood there waiting, he kept making crazy siren noises and staring at me. I tried to keep my cool, but before I knew it I exploded.

"Why don't you find a fuckin' job or something and leave people alone with your dirty-ass self," I yelled.

"Fuck you, bitch."

"Fuck you, smelling like you pissed on yourself," I screeched before I left the store.

He watched me leave the parking space with this sick look in his eyes. I got to the corner and had to pull over. I felt nausea. For some reason, I knew I was going to regret what I said to him. People who feel like they have nothing to live for will kill you without a second thought. They have to be dealt with carefully. I was not trying to be a statistic. Richmond's crime rate was already at an all time high. It was so bad, the state police had to step in to aid the local officers.

I returned home to find Cindy and O.B all over each other on the living room floor.

"Ya'll need to take that shit up to your room," I said.

Cindy laughed and asked if I wanted to watch a movie.

"No, that's alright I don't want to be a third wheel."

"Girl, please we're just watching a movie. Besides you never do anything with us. I'm starting to think you don't want to spend time with us."

I glanced at O.B. He had a smirk on his face.

"Come on, Sis," O.B. said with a wide grin. Since he was so sure I wouldn't, I decided to fuck with him. I accepted her invitation and

I Shoulda Seen It Comin'

chilled with them. After all, I had moved on from O.B. wanted to show him I was long over him.

About thirty minutes into the movie, there was a knock at the door. I could hear Cindy telling the visitor I was in the living room. I peeked around the corner and it was Dolo.

"Hey, I thought you were gonna be tied down...I mean tied up all night," I said jokingly. He laughed.

"Real funny. I'm actually free for the rest of the night so I decided to stop by. I hope that's okay."

"Sure, sit down. We're just watching a movie. By the way, this is my brother, O.B. and my roommate, Cindy." There was a hint of jealousy on O.B.'s face, but of course he tried to play it off as he gave Dolo some dap.

He spoke and then sat next to me on the love seat. I could tell Cindy was uncomfortable so I asked her to help me get some beers from the fridge.

"Girl, you didn't tell me you're messing with Dolo," Cindy said shocked.

"I didn't tell anyone because I'm not messing with him, we're just chillin'."

"Uh-hum. I bet," she said, twisting her lips. "Zsaset, did you see the ice on his watch."

"Yeah, I did. It's not about the money. It's about the man behind the money."

"Oh okay. I gotchu. He's fine as hell though."

"I know. That's what's keeping my interest," I teased.

"You be careful, girl. He's a baller." She got serious.

"Oh don't worry, a sista can take care of herself."

After our conversation, Cindy seemed more relaxed. The movie ended and I invited Dolo up to my room. This time I had no plans to make him a bed on the floor. He was going to sleep with me that night. It had been a long time since a man held me. And no matter how much I tried to deny it, I wanted that feeling again.

Danette Majette

I knew that our relationship could never amount to much, but I was going to enjoy it for as long as it lasted.

"So what side do you want?" I asked.

"The side you're on," he said in a sexy tone.

I winked and sashayed towards the bathroom.

"Get comfortable, I'll be back shortly," I said.

I twisted the knob in the shower. The water steamed just the way I liked it. Tonight would be special. So I lathered my body with a mixture of Jasmine Vanilla and Cotton Blossom body wash, compliments of Bath & Bodyworks. I gave my legs a close shave for a smooth touch. When I got out of the shower, I slipped on my Fredrick's of Hollywood sexy black one piece. I appeared from behind the door and Dolo's yo-yo expression was priceless. He laid on the bed speechless and dumbfounded.

"What's wrong," I asked pretending not to know.

He didn't reply at first because he was too busy drooling at my breasts. After letting out a heavy sigh he replied, "Nothing."

"I take it you like what you see."

"I like what I see. I like it a lot."

He tried hard not to stare, but it was too impossible. The sight was enough to make a blind man see. The lady at Fredrick's told me I would get this type of reaction and she was right. I slid in the bed and pulled just enough covers over me to tease him.

Afraid to make the first move, I waited for him. Ten minutes passed and I was still waiting. Dolo just laid there under the sheets.

"You know, when I told you not to try anything," I said, breaking the silence, "Well... um ...I was just playing."

"I know. I just don't want you to think that this is all I want from you," he said. "I can get sex from any girl I want. Unfortunately, I can't get friends as easily. That's what I want with you. I haven't been this comfortable with someone in a long time. Believe it or not, I value our friendship."

"Don't worry, we'll always be friends. Now come over here and let's be lovers. If you know what I mean."

I Shoulda Seen It Comin'

"Whatever you say," he laughed.

I wasn't prepared for what was about to happen. Dolo caught me totally off guard. He crawled like a P.O.W. to the edge of the bed. *What is he doing,* I thought. When my ass was at the bottom of my mattress, then I knew. Dolo had yanked me by the ankles. With one hard pull, my one piece flew off like it was attached with Velcro. I thought he was losing his mind. *This nightie cost too much money for him to be destroying it.* He was so rough it scared me.

I attempted to kiss Dolo, but he pushed back my forehead with his hands. What he did next went overboard. He stroked his fingers in and out of my mouth as if he was finger-fucking my face. *I don't know where the hell his fingers been.* I was so turned off. "Baby, slow down," I gagged as he slowly pulled them out one at a time.

"Look, this is my show. You gotta play by my rules," he groaned.

I decided to be a pawn in his game. *Didn't he know sex was a two way street?* Dolo flipped me on my stomach and instantly began licking the soles of my feet. That made me wet as hell. His hands slid up my inner thigh. They felt like a hundred fingers gripping my flesh from all angles. When air hit the middle of my cheeks, I held on for dear life. He swirled his tongue around the inner wall of my ass. At the same time, he rammed his fingers inside my booty. One finger, two fingers, three…I screamed at the top of my lungs. Clawing at the headboard, I tried to get away, but he snatched me back down.

Slamming me onto my back and gripping my titties roughly, he wasted no time plunging his dick in me. The friction from his thickness scraped my sugarwalls and my booty felt like it was on fire. I wrapped my legs around his back, trying to get into his rhythm, moving fast--up and down, again and again.

Dolo pulled out and forcefully grabbed my shoulders and pushed me down to my knees. Sick as it may sound, his forcefulness was such a turn on. He pushed my head forward and the hard edge of the bedpost caught me under the chin. I sucked enthusiastically on his jimmy like a hungry baby on a bottle of Kool-aid. *Damn, I felt like porno hoe.* Fire burned between my legs. He pressed my head deeper and deeper until he was all in. Massaging his balls, I made him soar into another level. He yelled like a girl. I did it. I finally had him at my mercy.

I had a sense of satisfaction. I felt like this man was going to be my destruction. Part of him was gentle, kind and handsome on the outside, but I knew there was a devil in disguise on the inside.

Chapter Fifteen

Our first customer at the store the next day was a strange one. He kept eyeing me suspiciously and he was starting to make me nervous. At first I thought he may have something to with Dolo. Aside from his pot belly and medium frame, I could tell he was no young cat from his salt and pepper hair. My mind was put at ease, once he asked a couple of questions. He seemed less interested in purchasing and more interested in how I felt about my job and the company. *Is he working for the competition,* I thought. "Why so many questions?" I asked.

He looked at me. "Baby girl, I'm gonna be straight up with you. My name is Dre and I'm the manager of the Foot Locker downtown. I'm looking for a new sales associate and you would be perfect."

"What makes you so sure?"

"First of all, you know your shit." I jerked back my head in curiosity. "Oh yeah, this isn't my first time in here. I've been watching you for some time. You're a double threat. You got the brains and the beauty."

I asked him what my looks had to do with it.

"Have you ever been to our store?" he asked.

"No, I haven't."

"Well, why don't you come down and check us out, then you'll see what your looks have to do it. I guarantee you'll be callin' me." I don't know what made him so sure of himself, but it sounded like it was worth checking out. I took his card and stuck it in my back pocket.

My curiosity got the best of me. So on my next day off, I drove downtown to check out Dre's store. I parked, paid the attendant and strolled up the street into the mall. The store was half the size of the one I worked in. But it was packed with wall to wall niggas. I pushed my way to the counter and asked the salesman if Dre was available.

"Yeah, let me get him for you," said the young Alonzo Mourning look-a-like.

"That will be $361.97," the sales associate said as I patiently waited.

I couldn't believe his bill was so high. But it didn't look like it was hurting his pockets too much. He pulled out a knot of money and threw it on the counter.

"Baby girl, what's up? Nice of you to drop by. What do you think about our store?" Dre said, coming from the stockroom.

I peeped around. "It's a little small, but I see you rollin' in the dough down here," I said.

He asked me what he had to do to get me to work for him. I told him I needed more money and more time to spend with my baby.

"You got it," he said pressed.

I was loving the job and hadn't even started. Dre topped fat-ass Larry's salary by two dollars more an hour. Plus I wouldn't have to close at night because their work day ended at six. Now I could be home early with Zeta.

"Deal," I said shaking his hand. "I just need to give Larry two weeks notice." He told me to call him when I handled my business. Dre said my schedule would be ready by then.

As I drove home I had a lot on my mind. *What was I going to tell Larry? I felt bad about leaving since he gave me a chance. But it was already a done deal. So I was just going to tell Larry the truth and hope he understood. If he didn't, the hell with him. After all, I had to look out for me and my child.*

Cindy was sitting in the dining room doing her schedule for work when I walked in the house.

"Girl, guess what? This man from another Foot Locker offered me a job."

"Where?" she asked.

"Downtown."

"Whoa," she said in a shocked tone.

"What?"

"Isn't it dangerous down there?"

"Not really. I went down there this afternoon."

"You would make a lot more money. All the hustlers shop down there," Cindy added.

"I know. You should have seen the traffic they pulled in."

"I guess so. They don't like to come out to the country because they get harassed when they're in our suburban mall. They can't walk in groups of more than three and they say the Feds take pictures of them."

"What?"

"Yeah, girl. The Feds are all over the place—watchin'. They're just waiting and biding time. One day, I bet they're gonna lock all of their butts up. All I can say is, be careful, girl," Cindy warned.

"I will."

That next morning at work I was so nervous, I couldn't even sell a pair of shoes. I walked around torn and confused until I couldn't take it anymore.

I took a deep breath and headed back to Larry's office.

"Zsaset, how can I help you?"

"Larry, I need to talk to you about something," I said taking a seat in the beat-up leather chair.

"Go ahead, shoot."

"I have another job offer." He raised his bushy eyebrows. "If you can match their offer, I'll stay. But they are also adjusting my schedule so I will have more time with my daughter."

"I can't do it," he said with a smirk on his face. He told me no so fast, it was as if I was of no value at all to him as an employee. He didn't even give it a second thought. Larry's attitude irritated me so much that I decided to only give him a week's notice and take a week off to myself.

Chapter Sixteen

My relationship with Dolo was moving fast. We spent most of our nights at the movies and dining at the finest restaurants. On the weekends, we would shop in the Big Apple. My favorite store was Century 21, next to the World Trade Center. It sold the hottest designer clothing at half the cost. Being with him was magical. But all good things come to an end.

One night, Dolo and I had just finished making love and the last thing I would ever expect to happen, did. I had just lit a cigarette when all of a sudden I heard a thump in the bathroom. At first, I thought maybe Dolo dropped something in there. But then I heard strange rubbing sounds on the floor. Curious, I went into the bathroom to see what was going on.

"Oh shit," I said rubbing my head. I ran to call 911 but decided that may not be the best thing to do for Dolo, so instead I started yelling for Cindy and O.B. Immediately, Cindy and O.B. ran into the bathroom.

"What happened!" Cindy screamed.

"I don't know. I heard a noise so I got up."

Shaking his head and looking at me like I had horns, O.B. asked if he was dying.

"I don't think so and stop looking at me like that. I didn't do anything," I yelled. Dolo's muscular naked body lay on the floor with his arms and legs flailing.

"It looks like he's having a seizure. Help me turn him over so he doesn't swallow his tongue," Cindy commanded. The bathroom was so small we couldn't get him on his side without pulling him out first.

"Oh my God," I kept repeating as I paced the hall floor. Dolo's body continued to jerk out of control. I could only see the whites of his eyes because they rolled in the back of his head. I thought I was watching a horror show when foam dripped out the side of his mouth. He looked like the possessed dog foaming at the mouth in the *Cujo* movie. That brought my pace to a halt and I couldn't move.

    Cindy yelled at me to get myself together. She needed me to get some towels. I grabbed them and covered his naked body. I couldn't take it anymore. I couldn't let this man die in my house. I decided to call 911. If he was wanted by the law, he would have to suffer the consequences. As soon as the operator answered and said, "Emergency, how may I help you?" Dolo came out of it. Cindy sat him up. I told the operator that I misdialed and hung up the phone.

    "I need some orange juice," he said barely breathing.

    O.B. ran downstairs for the juice. After taking a few sips, Dolo's seizure seemed to be under control.

    "Thanks, man. I'm alright now," he said wheezing.

    "Are you sure," Cindy asked.

    "Yeah," he said.

    O.B. and Cindy went back to her room.

    "I think you need to go to hospital," I said.

    "No. This happens sometimes."

    Dolo composed himself then got in the bed. I just stared at him as he curled up like a baby. I was so scared and confused I couldn't even think straight. Worried that it might happen again, I tried to convince him to go to the hospital.

    "Look, I'm all right I just need to lay down for a minute," he said frustrated.

    "Well what's wrong with you? I mean, did we over do it or something?"

    He giggled. "No. I have diabetes. When I took my shot today, I was supposed to eat somethin'. But I was doing so much runnin' around I forgot."

    "Oh my God. You never told me you had diabetes."

    "I know. I just didn't want to freak you out."

I Shoulda Seen It Comin'

"Well, what do you think passing out on my bathroom floor did? At least, if I had known about your condition, I would've known what to expect. What if Cindy wasn't home? You could have died because I didn't know what to do. You really are crazy."

"I'm crazy because I didn't tell you I'm a diabetic."

" Look, I think you need to just go home. Do you need me to call someone to pick you up?"

"Yeah, call my brother."

I called Tee and told him what happened. He was there within minutes to pick Dolo up. As I walked back to my apartment, Tee stopped me. "I'm glad my brother didn't die in your house. Because if he did, I probably would have killed you," he said, looking at me suspiciously. I couldn't believe he was threatening to kill me.

He came closer. "Look, Zsaset, my brother keeps a lot of cash on him when he comes over here and I probably would've thought you killed him for it. I'm just lookin' out for him."

"Look, let me tell yo ass something. Your brother gives me whatever I want. All I have to do is ask. Now if you want to look out for him, then take him home and get out of my face."

I stormed inside my apartment and dropped to my knees. I couldn't believe he would say something like that to me. I knew Tee was a little obsessive over Dolo, but I had no idea it was that serious.

I drank two beers and smoked almost a whole pack of Newports before I went to bed. But I couldn't sleep. I just kept hearing Tee's voice in my head and wondered if he would really kill me. I had feelings for Dolo, but what if it happened again? I couldn't take that chance, so I decided it would be best if I didn't see him anymore.

I waited about an hour before I picked up the phone. I asked if he was okay then dropped the bomb—straight, no chaser. "Dolo, after what happened tonight I don't want to see you anymore."

Danette Majette

I didn't even give him a chance to respond. I just said what I had to say and hung up.

Anyway, it must have been contagious because the same week I broke up with Dolo, Cindy and O.B. called it quits and so did Vicki and Tee. We spent our nights, once again, sitting around my living room drinking and dogging men. It was back to our NM days—No Men.

Chapter Seventeen

It was July 10, 1993, my birthday. As a gift to myself, I bought a 1992 black Acura Integra. The first place I hit was Vicki's house. She wasn't home. I drove around the corner to Clova's to see what she was up to, but she wasn't home either. *Where the hell is everyone? No one even called me to say Happy Birthday.*

Disappointed, I went home to celebrate by myself. That evening Londa showed up with two huge beautifully wrapped boxes from Nordstrom's.

"What's this?" I asked.

"Open it and see."

What lay in the box made me cry. It was a crème sheer dress with matching shoes.

"It's from all of us," she said, kissing me on my cheek.

"Oh my God. It's gorgeous. I thought you guys forgot about me."

"Girl, please. No one forgot your birthday. Clova and Vicki had to run some errands but they're going to meet us at the club. Get dressed and I'll be back to pick you up at nine."

Dressed and ready to party, I called K-Dog to see if they wanted to go out with us, but he said they couldn't because they were out of town. I was so mad at him. I had talked with him at least two times the day before and he never mentioned anything about having to go to New York. Deciding not to make a federal case out it, I told him I loved him anyway and I would see them when they got back.

Moments later, Londa arrived to pick me up.

"So where are we going again?"

"Would you just sit back and relax. We'll be there soon." We pulled into the parking lot of a club not far from my house.

"What are we doing here, I thought this was a private club," I said.

"It is, but it's opened to the public tonight."

When the attendant saw Londa, he quickly ran to the car and took her keys.

"Where is he going with your car?"

"He's going to park it. It's called valet parking, girlfriend."

"Bitch, I know what it's called," I said with anger. "I ain't dumb."

"Well excuse me, Miss Zsaset. But can you do me a favor?" she said.

"What?"

"Stop asking so many got damn questions."

The doors to the club were opened by two guys who had strange looks on their faces. It was like we were walking into a trap. Well, *we* didn't walk into a trap. I did. I walked right into a room full of people yelling, "SURPRISE!"

My heart skipped a beat and then I let out a heavy sigh as I covered my face. It was a surprise birthday party for me. Everyone was there. They even arranged for my girls, Sheba and Brina to come up to Richmond and celebrate with me. I ran over and gave K-Dog a big hug. I was so happy and it was all because of him. I could tell by the look of the place it cost a pretty penny. And the only one with that kind of money was K-Dog. He might have paid for it, but he sure wasn't on the decorating committee.

The club was so beautiful. There were floating candles on each table. Chilled bottles of Moet lined the bar. And the buffet was packed with buffalo wings, potato salad, chilled shrimp, and deviled eggs—all of my favorite foods. Anyone who knew me, knew that eating was my favorite pastime.

I Shoulda Seen It Comin'

Then there was my birthday present, the human beat box and great entertainer, Doug E. Fresh. He performed his hit "Lottie Dottie" then posed in a picture with me. I was in heaven. This was sure to be a birthday I would never forget. Literally.

I was dancing when I saw a familiar face in the dark corner of the club. *What the hell is he doing here?* I turned to Londa.

"Look over there in the corner," I said. Our eyes met briefly. "Did you invite him?"

"No. I wouldn't invite him to your birthday party. I know you guys don't talk anymore."

He strolled over to me. "Happy Birthday," he said, handing me a gift.

"Thanks, but I can't take this," I said handing it back to him.

"Why not? Because you broke up with me?" he said eyeing me up and down.

I wanted to pull him close and kiss his lips, but I couldn't allow myself to get caught up again. Not with his lunching-ass brother, anyway.

"I think it's fucked up how you just broke up with me because I got sick at your place." He gave me a disappointed look. "I thought we were better than that."

"The problem wasn't you. It was what your brother, Tee, said to me that night." He frowned his face. I knew what he was asking for, so I told him the whole story.

"Zsaset, why didn't you just say somethin'? I would've straightened him out," he said.

"I didn't want to cause any problems between you and Tee."

"Our brotherhood is stronger than some broad." Dolo came close and whispered, "That was no reason for you to break up with me." My attention was distracted by K-Dog. Following my eyes, Dolo turned around.

"What, that nigga keeping tabs or somethin'?"

"That's my brother. He's just lookin' out."

"Yeah, anyway back to my brotha," he said.

"Look, Dolo, I'm not trippin' off your brother. But he shouldn't have said that punk-ass shit to me."

"Why Tee gotta be a punk?" Seeing his nose flare made me question why I even said that. Just when I thought our conversation was going well, it took a turn for the worst. "Bitch, you must be fuckin' mad talkin' about my brotha."

"Who the fuck you callin' a bitch?" My finger pointed in his face. Out the corner of my eye, I could see K-Dog coming. I knew Dolo was outnumbered, so I showed my ass. I started yelling words about how he wasn't invited in the first place. As I continued to break bad, I stepped back once I saw his hand rest on his gun. K-Dog stepped in front of me in the knick of time.

"Yo, son, what you tryin' to do?" K-Dog said, gripping his own piece.

I knew it was about to be on and poppin'. So I pulled K-Dog to the side. "Look this is my day. I'm not gonna let some stupid shit ruin it." They both stared at each other like pit bulls about to attack.

"Dolo, just get out," I screamed. Thank goodness we were outside in the hallway away from the party or else there would've been major chaos.

Dolo backed out the door. "I'll see yo ass in the streets, nigga," K-Dog said to Dolo before the door shut.

The two of us went back to the party as if nothing happened. The rest of the night was off the hook. After the Dolo incident, I drank one drink after another. I was out of control. I danced on top of the table like a stripper at Magic City. It didn't matter to me how much of a fool I made of myself. After all, it was my birthday.

Everyone headed to my house for the after party. Since Cindy was there, O.B. decided to go hang out with Quan and some of their other boys. We did what we knew best, and fell off to sleep. Sheba, K-dog, and I slept in my bed and everyone else slept wherever they could. I stepped on a few of them because there was nowhere to walk. They were so drunk, they didn't even feel me.

The next morning, I overheard K-Dog talking to O.B. on the phone. "What's wrong," I asked?

"O.B. and them got into a shootout last night."

"What. Are they alright?"

"Yeah, but my car is fucked up. I knew I should have made them leave it."

A while later, O.B. walked in the house with his tail between his legs.

"Where's the car," I asked.

"It's outside. What's left of it anyway."

Afraid to ask what he meant, I went outside. All of the windows were completely shot out of K-Dog's Delta 88. And the doors were filled with bullet holes like something out of an action movie scene. I walked in and went back upstairs. I had to lie down, and collect my thoughts.

Shit was definitely about to hit the fan.

K-Dog could tell by the look on my face that it was bad. So he went outside to check for himself. I could tell by the expression on his face he was mad as hell, but as usual he just let it roll off his shoulders. He told O.B. not to worry about it.

"It can be fixed," K-Dog smirked. Then he looked at me. "Can't it?"

"I guess it can. If it can't, O.B. will just have to buy you another one," I said.

"Now ya talkin'," K-Dog said.

Since O.B. was already in hot water, he just sat there shaking his head in agreement.

Chapter Eighteen

My son Ryan, came to visit me two weekends before school started. I hadn't seen him since I left so I was excited. Brenda agreed to watch him for me while I worked. I was so glad he and Zeta were finally getting to spend some time together. I could tell by the way they played that they really missed each other. And I loved having both of them together. I thought about having him stay, but I knew that would upset my mother. She considered him her son, even though I had given birth to him. Ryan was good company for her because she was always sick.

Aside from Ryan coming to visit, everything had been normal. Weeks went by since I'd heard a word from Dolo. One night he called out of the blue.

"Hello," I said.

"Yeah, it's me, Dolo. You up?" he asked.

"No, I'm sleep."

"Well, get up. I gotta talk to you about somethin'."

"Can't this wait until tomorrow?"

"No, it can't. Get up." I could tell from the tone in his voice that something was wrong. "Some of my peeps told me that it was your brother, K-Dog, blazing at me about two weeks ago."

"Dolo, what are you talkin' about?" I said, sitting up in my bed.

I told him his sources were wrong. But he didn't believe me. Instead he told me to tell K-Dog he was going to kill him.

"You're such a bad boy, you tell him?"

"I will, bitch."

At this point, I was fuming. "Bitch. Now, I'm a bitch."

"That's right. You were just a trophy to add to my collection."

I Shoulda Seen It Comin'

"Well, did your other trophies fuck you like I did? Did they make your weak ass fall out in their bathrooms?" He was quiet for a moment. "I didn't think so," I said.

"Oh, okay, since you want to be a smart ass, I'm gonna go down to where K-Dog be at and I'm gonna kill his ass then I'm gonna wet your ass up and everyone in your house."

I was finally seeing the real Dolo. Scared, I quickly dressed the kids and ran next door. My next door neighbor was a police officer, so I thought I would be safe there. I knocked on the door and waited for someone to answer. When Shawn came to the door I told him what happened. I couldn't believe it, he told me to go to the police station.

"I would love to help you, but I have a family, so I can't get involved." Then he rudely closed the door in my face and locked it. I was finally seeing what Vicki was talking about. No one went against Dolo. Not even the police.

Panicked, I grabbed my sleeping children and hurried to my car. I drove to a remote area near my apartment and parked. I forgot my purse, so I couldn't call anyone. I prayed K-Dog would be alright. Then I just sat there hypnotized by fear. I must have dozed off, because the next thing I knew the sun was shining.

I went over to Lina's house looking for K-Dog and O.B. Before I could turn the engine off, she was opening my car door.

"What's going on, Zsaset?"

"Are K-dog and O.B. alright?" I said, cutting her off.

"I don't know. Why? What happened?"

"I'll tell you as soon as we get in the house. Help me with the kids."

I told Lina about my fight with Dolo. All about drama, Lina grabbed her phone and dialed K-Dog's number.

"Girl, he's on his way," she said slamming the phone on the kitchen counter.

I could tell that things were about to get out of control and there wasn't a damn thing I could do about it.

"Zsaset, it's about to be on. They don't play that shit. Nobody, I mean nobody threatens them. And on top of that, he said he was going to kill you and the kids? His ass done fucked up now. You hear me?"

With his tires screeching, K-dog came flying around the corner. He and O.B. jumped out of the car like two mad men.

"What the fuck is goin' on?" K-Dog said all worked up.

"It turns out the guy O.B. got into the shootout with was Dolo. He thinks it was you. It's probably because you two had words at my party," I said.

Lina stood up waiting for more details.

"And last night he told me he was going to kill you and then kill me and the kids," I said.

Lina, frustrated that we ignored her, spoke with an attitude. "Wait a minute, wait one minute, what words? What ya'll talkin' 'bout?"

"Lina, it was nothin'," K-Dog said. He turned to me and laughed. "Zsaset, he's just talking shit. Real niggas don't talk about what they're gonna do. They just do it. Like Nike. But he didn't. You know why?"

"Why?" I asked.

"Because he's a bitch, that's why. He knows not to fuck with me for real, for real."

Feeling secure that K-Dog would handle the situation, I took my kids and left. We went to the pool so I could get their minds off everything that had happened. Ryan was older and full of questions, but taking them to the pool worked. Without a care in the world, they played for hours. I hoped they would never mention it to anyone. Of course, Ryan did. The day he went back to Norfolk, I received a call from my mother. She questioned me about the confusing story Ryan told her and wanted me to clear up the details. I told her he must have had a bad dream because I had no idea as to what he was talking about.

I Shoulda Seen It Comin'

I thought I was dreaming when the phone rang at two in the morning. My first thought was that it was Dolo calling to harass me again. My heart raced as I hit the talk button.

"Hello," I answered as my hands shook uncontrollably.

"Hey, I'm just makin' sure you're all right," K-Dog said.

It was such a relief to hear his voice. "Yeah, I'm cool."

"You cool now. But from the way you answered the phone I would say yo ass was scared to death," he said teasing me.

"I ain't gonna lie, I thought you were Dolo."

"You don't have to worry about him anymore," he said.

Dolo had somehow got in touch with K-Dog minutes before he called me. He told him he wanted to squash the beef between them. But I didn't believe that for a second. He was up to something, I just couldn't figure out what. I knew it wasn't over, not by a long shot.

I tried to forget about all the chaos, by working day in and day out. But it had somehow gotten back to Dre.

"Baby girl, I ain't tryin' to get in your business, but I heard what happened the other night. You alright?"

"Yeah. I'm fine," I answered trying to avoid eye contact.

"Well, you don't look fine. Your eyes are red. You're jumpy and I ain't never seen you smoke this much."

I quickly cut the conversation short. I just wanted to put it out of my mind. I hugged him and thanked him for his concern. Then I asked him not to mention the situation to my co-workers. My business was my own and that's the way it was going to stay.

I think K-Dog was feeling guilty. He hadn't been over in a while so he decided to stop by and play cards with me. I was out of beers so we drove up to the store. When we got out of the car, I noticed the homeless man I had gotten into an argument with standing in front of the store. He looked straight at me and started smiling.

"What the hell are you smiling at?" I asked.

"I'm smilin' at you, pretty lady," the homeless man said with a sinful grin.

K-Dog walked over to him and shook his hand. "What's up, man?"

"Don't tell me you know this old fool," I said disgusted.

"Yeah, this is my man, Ra, from New York."

I was through when K-Dog told me that. If he knew like I knew he wouldn't spread that shit around. Not being able to stomach his pissy smell, I went into the store. K-Dog followed. By the time he walked in, I was already at the counter ready to pay for my beer.

"Damn! What ya'll went up?" K-Dog yelled, scaring the Asian owner.

"You good customer. I take off two dollar," the man said.

"Yeah, that's more like it," K-Dog said as he paid the man.

Before we pulled out of the parking lot, K-Dog yelled out the window, "Yo, Ra, I'll see you later, man. Oh yeah, be nice to my sister from now on."

"Okay, Dog. You got it, man," he said with this sneaky look in his eyes.

Cracking open a beer, I sat down at the table and started shuffling the cards.

"You ready to get your butt beat again?"

"Yeah whatever," K-dog yelled as he slammed his stack of money on the table.

We played cards until about two that morning. I didn't have enough energy to walk upstairs, so I slept on the couch.

Still drunk, I awoke to the phone ringing.

"Hello," I answered.

"Hello, may I speak to Cindy?"

"Yes, hold on for a second."

I yelled up the stairs for Cindy, but she didn't answer. I looked out the window to see if her car was there.

I Shoulda Seen It Comin'

"Sorry, she's isn't here."
"Could you tell her to call her mother?"
"Okay," I said, hanging up the phone.
Cindy had never talked about her mother. From what I understood, they didn't get along too well. She and Cindy had a fall out about her dating O.B.. Cindy said it was because he was black. I couldn't believe there were still people in this world who were prejudiced. You would think after all of the race mixing, they wouldn't see color anymore.
An hour later, the phone rang again.
"Hello," I said in an angry tone.
"Is Cindy home yet?"
"No, she isn't."
"Are you sure she's not there?"
I didn't want to disrespect her mother, so I tried to remain calm. "Like I said before, ma'am she's not here, but I'll tell her you called."
Upset with my answer she called me a nigger under her breathe.
"Did you call me a nigger," I yelled.
"Yes, I did. That's what you are. You and your brother."
That bitch must've been drinking. And if she wasn't drinking then she needed to have one to rest her nerves.
I was still asleep when Cindy came home. The phone rang again and this time she answered it. I was half asleep, but I heard her arguing. It was her mother again. I didn't hear everything Cindy was saying, but I did hear her saying, "It's my life. I can live with whoever I want." Then she slammed down the phone.
K-Dog and O.B. came in just as Cindy laid the phone down on the couch. She apologized for her mother's behavior.
I tried hard to change the subject, when K-Dog asked me what was going on. But he could tell I was upset and insisted on knowing why.
"My mother called Zsaset and O.B. niggas," she said, holding her head down.

I slowly arose from off the couch and began up the stairs.

"Wait a minute. Where are you going?"

"K-Dog, I'm going upstairs. I have a feeling it's about to get ugly. Personally, I don't want to be around when it does."

I could see smoke coming from K-Dog's ears. He quickly turned to Cindy. "Your mother should really watch what she says. I mean someone could hurt her for saying some shit like that."

O.B. added his two cents. "I should go over there and fuck her up."

"That's not necessary. Just because she's ignorant doesn't mean we have to be. Now if ya'll don't mind I'm going back to sleep," I said.

The tension in the house was thick. So K-Dog and O.B. didn't stay long at all before they left.

Hearing all the noise from Cindy's room made me get up. I peeked in and saw her packing.

"Where are you going?" I asked.

"I think it would be best if I leave. I'm scared they might try to hurt my mother."

"Girl, please. Ain't nobody gonna hurt your momma."

"You don't know that. I know what kind of people your brothers are," Cindy said with tears.

"What the fuck are you trying to say? It didn't seem to matter to you when you were dating one of them and spending his dough."

"Look, I cared about O.B. but he hid his true self from me for a long time. I didn't know about his violent side until it was too late," she said.

"Bitch, please. You ain't green. Tell that to someone who's buying it, 'cause I ain't. You knew O.B. ain't have no job, but had plenty of money. You ain't have a problem with that, did you?"

"Look, I don't want to argue with you." Cindy quickly ran out of the room. "I'll pick up the rest of my stuff later."

"No, you won't. Take your shit now. And if you think you're gonna stick me with the rent, you better think again," I yelled.

Ignoring me she called her mother.

"Did you just tell your mother to come over here after she called me a nigga? Bitch, you better call her back. Then again, let her come over here so I can whip her ass." She had me so heated I started throwing her shit down the stairs. "Get out. Get out. 'Cause you and your mother are about to be a blast from the past fuckin' with me."

"Zsaset, I'm going as soon as my mother gets here with her pick-up."

"No you're not. You're going right now. Wait for her dumb ass outside."

She grabbed as many of her things as she could and waited outside in her car.

Her mother arrived with the police. The fine black officer veered toward Cindy.

"What's the problem here?" the officer asked pulling out his notebook.

We each told him our version of what happened.

"Technically, both of you have the right to stay here, but it might be a good idea for one of you to voluntarily leave so no one gets hurt," the officer said.

"Officer, I was trying to leave when she got all crazy. Can you stay here until I get everything? She might try to do something to me and my mother."

"Oh my God. Give me a fucking break. Ain't nobody gonna do nothing to you. Get over yourself," I uttered in disgust.

The officer waited in his squad car until she got the rest of her stuff. I couldn't believe this shit was happening. I never saw it coming. My concentration was shot to hell for the rest of the night. I had just bought a new car, so I couldn't afford to pay all the household bills by myself. I needed another roommate and I needed one bad.

Danette Majette

The following morning, I went to the rental office. I needed to know what recourse I could take against Cindy for moving out before the lease expired. She informed me I could take her to court. The only problem was that the courts were backed up. She said it would take at least a month or two before my case would even be heard. Frustrated, I came to the conclusion it wouldn't be worth it. *I'll just do what I have to do,* I thought to myself.

Chapter Nineteen

I hated to admit it but I missed Cindy. It was actually kind of boring around the apartment without her presence. However, I was still angry with her for leaving me in a bind. Before I knew it, it was the first of the month. It took every dime I had to pay the rent and the rest of my bills. My car was almost on 'E' and my refrigerator was empty. My finances were spinning out of control and I didn't know what to do. The situation left me with only one solution—borrow some money from K-Dog. It was the last thing I wanted to do, but I had no choice. It was either starve to death or ask for help. I preferred the latter.

One evening on my way home, I stopped in the projects to see K-Dog. Embarrassed, I asked him if I could borrow some money.

"This should hold you over for a while," he said, peeling off two g's from his bankroll.

"Thanks," I said, wrapping my arms around his neck. I gave him a big juicy kiss on his forehead. He was embarrassed.

The first place I stopped after I left the projects was the convenience store. Me and my baby needed some food.

Not again, I thought as I opened my car door. I looked Ra up and down and wondered how anyone could allow themselves to look like that. His clothes looked like he just rolled around in a pig's pen and his teeth looked like they hadn't been brushed in years.

"How you doin', Miss Lady? You lookin' fine as ever."

"And you're looking dirty as ever. Now get out my face," I said as I slammed my car door and headed towards the store. Figuring I'd only be a minute and that I could still see my car from the inside of the store, I had left Zeta sleeping on the back seat. I

scooped up two sandwiches, a beer and some chips and waited in line while the man in front of me decided if he wanted lambskin or ribbed condoms. *Just get the lubricated, and get the fuck out the line so I can go,* I thought as I noticed the bum stagger through the door.
"One of these days," he snarled.
"One of these days, what? What? I'm so sick of you and your little slick comments, I don't know what to do."
"Like I said, one of these days, I'm gonna make you respect me."
"Yeah, right. Wait on it. Then again maybe if you get a job and get cleaned up, I might let you...umm let me see...take me out...Not!" I said as the clerk bagged my food.
I let out a hearty laugh and walked back to my car. I slammed on the gas pedal and drove home in an uproar. *Why do I let him get to me? He is just a bum. A bum that is unworthy of even an ounce of my energy.*

I warmed up the sandwiches and sat at the table with Zeta. We hadn't even said our grace yet when the phone starting ringing.
"What?" I yelled into the receiver irritated.
"Zsaset, I need a favor," K-Dog said.
I put down my sandwich. "Whatcha need?"
"My boy is here from New York and he needs a place to stay. He's good peeps so you don't have to worry about him bringin' any drama to your crib. And he's willin' to pay all of the rent."
Thank God, my prayers were finally answered.
"When does he want to move in?"
"Tomorrow, if that's okay."
"Sure, bring him by so I can meet him."
"Cool, we'll be there shortly."
It took them ten minutes to get to my place. When he walked in, I inspected him thoroughly. He was a dark-skinned, short cutie with a slim build. His sexy light brown eyes gave him

I Shoulda Seen It Comin'

that extra umph. I couldn't keep my eyes off the ice that dripped from his neck.

"Bisal, this is Zsaset. Everyone thinks she's our sister," K-Dog said.

Bisal shook his head and laughed. "I know. Just go along with the story if anyone asks." K-Dog gave him a pound.

"Welcome to the family, Bisal. Mi casa es su casa. O.K. that's the extent of my Spanish, now come over here and give me a hug." I hugged him. We chilled for a while. It was more of a two way than a three way conversation. Bisal spoke all of five words the entire time, which was a good thing because the last thing I needed was someone beating their gums.

"Zsaset, I'm gonna run to the store. Do you need anything?" K-Dog said as he got up grabbing his jacket from the back of the chair.

"No, I just left there. I got everything I need."

"Cool. I'll be right back."

I figured while K-Dog was gone, I would try to get to know Bisal a little better. I kept asking him questions hoping he would open up a little, but I was seriously wasting my time. So I decided to give him a tour of the apartment. Just as we were finishing up, there was a horn blowing outside. It was K-Dog summoning Bisal to come outside and get his bags. I followed to help, but ended up talking and laughing for about a half an hour with them.

"Alright crazy, I'm going in the house. I have to go to work tomorrow," I said.

"Word, I got to go too. Bisal man, I'll pick you up tomorrow."

"Alright, Dog. What time we doin' that thang?"

"As soon as my man calls."

"What thing," I asked out of curiosity.

"None ya," K-Dog said.

"Ha Ha," I smirked. Bisal and I turned and went in the house.

Danette Majette

By the time I got upstairs, Zeta was asleep in Cindy's old room. As loud as she snored, she must've been playing hard that day. I felt bad that Zeta had taken over Bisal's spot so I tried to wake her, but he insisted I let her sleep.

"I'll sleep on the couch," he said. I handed him some blankets and thanked him for taking the couch.

I was incredibly tired and anxious to get in bed. I turned down my bed sheets, took off my clothes and went into the bathroom to take a shower. After finishing, I came back into the room and was surprised to find that it was dark, because I was sure I had left the light on. I hesitated for just a moment and then figured Zeta must have come in, turned out the lights and got in the bed. Actually, I could hear her breathing in the bed. Plus, I knew Basil was downstairs or I would probably have been slightly alarmed.

I groped my way over to the bed and sat down to lotion up. I wasn't sure if Zeta was actually asleep or not so I whispered to her.

"Good night, Zeta Beta." She didn't respond.

As I slid one leg between the sheets, I heard a familiar voice say, "Bitch, I told you, you gonna respect me." My heart pounded.

"What the hell are you doing in my house? Get out," I screamed as I jumped out of bed, ran, and tripped over my shoe. I knew who it was. It was Ra, the lunatic from the convenience store. Without hesitation, I started yelling at the top of my lungs. Bisal came running upstairs to my defense. But neither one of us were prepared to defend ourselves against a gun. Ra grabbed me around my neck.

"Look, son, don't hurt her. What you want…money…huh? I have plenty of money downstairs. Just let her go and we can go and get it."

Ra, offended by Bisal's offer, tightened his grip on my neck and sneered.

I Shoulda Seen It Comin'

"This ain't 'bout no money, nigga. It's about this bitch treatin' me like I ain't nothin'. Every time she see me, she spit on me like I ain't shit."

In a rage, he dragged me back into my room and yanked the phone cord out of the wall. With the gun pointed to my head, he shoved us both down the stairs.

The situation was so surreal. I was helpless. Here we were sitting in my dining room with a gun pointed at us. This man was completely out of control. His eyes were blood shot and he was shaking like a tree in the middle of a storm. I couldn't grasp what was happening. But reality set back in when he started preaching. "At last, you're gonna feel the wrath of my madness. I told you, didn't I? I told you that you were gonna respect me. But you didn't believe me. Well, I bet you believe me now, bitch," Ra said while laughing insanely.

Bisal and I were forced to sit down on the sofa as Ra tore through the house like a deranged animal. I didn't have proof, but I was sure he was on drugs. Out of breath, he sat at the table drinking Gin straight from the bottle. *No this nigga ain't drinking up all my shit. That was a brand new bottle.* Mixing the drugs and the gin made him even crazier. We were fucked.

Scared for our lives, Bisal and I sat motionless for an hour listening to him read scriptures from the Bible. *Ain't this a bitch? He's trying to school us on the Lord.* Fed up with his psycho game, I jumped up. "What the hell do you want?" I screamed.

Agitated by my question, he pulled out his gun and held it to my throat. "I'm gonna tell you what I want. I want you to sit your ass down and shut the fuck up."

My knees weakened when I heard the tone in his voice. I was a lot of things, but a fool wasn't one of them. I sat my ass down and quick. Bisal patted me gently on my leg. "Keep cool, Zsaset." He didn't have to tell me twice. I didn't say another word.

Ra broke everything. He pulled the stove and refrigerator out of the wall and pushed them over. He even broke the television with his bare hands. He was so out of it, he didn't even notice that his hand was bleeding profusely. "They're going to find your daughter hanging in the bathroom with her heart cut out. Then after I finish with her, I'm gonna kill you, your mother, and your mother's mother," he said barking. All I could think was, *what the fuck is this mothafucker smoking?*

My biggest concern now was Zeta. What if she startled him and he shot her? Or, what if he lost control and shot us? What would he do to her? I was fed up with the whole situation. I had been held hostage in my own home for over an hour. And whether Bisal was with me or not I was going to do something.

While Ra was distracted in the kitchen, I snuck up the stairs to grab Zeta, although Bisal tried to keep me from making a move. I was just in time, because she was walking out of Cindy's old room crying when I got to the top of the stairs. I carried her quickly into my room and locked the door. I looked under my bed and pulled out my nightstick. I was sure Ra had followed me, but he hadn't.

At this point, my only concern was to get Zeta out of the house safely. But how? My first thought was I could drop her from my bedroom window. That wouldn't work because she might get hurt. So I decided I would jump out with her, that way I could be her cushion.

It was then that a little voice in my head said calm down and look in the closet. When I did, I saw a small trim line phone. I immediately grabbed it and plugged it into the wall, which was a miracle in itself considering how badly my hands were shaking. Confused and scared half out of my mind, I dialed K-Dog's number and told him what was happening. "Don't worry, I'm right around the corner. Stay in your room."

Although it seemed like hours had passed, within minutes, I heard some loud thumps. My heart sank with fear so I hid in the closet with my daughter. We were both sobbing. Then I heard footsteps coming up the stairs toward my door. "Zsaset, open the door. Open up the door."

I Shoulda Seen It Comin'

It was K-Dog and O.B. I had never been so happy to see them than I was at that moment. It was truly a miracle that they were on their way home when I called. K-Dog clutched Zeta and started kissing her. "You're safe now. Uncle K-Dog is here."
"Is he still here?" I asked still trembling.
"Yeah," K-Dog said in an angry tone.
"Well, let's call the police."
"No. He'll be right back out on the streets tomorrow," K-Dog insisted.
"So we're just gonna let him go?"
"Hell no. We'll take care of him. O.B., take them back to my crib."
"Alright," O.B. said, ushering me out the room.
It was the first time in months that O.B.'s arms held me. He guided me down the steps behind K-Dog.
I could tell there was something wrong because they tried to shield me from looking in the dining room. As we walked to the car, I could hear K- Dog yelling at the top of his lungs, but I couldn't make out what he was saying. All I know is it wasn't nice.

I needed a drink by the time I got to K-Dog's house. I couldn't believe this was happening to me. My daughter and I could have been killed. My fear quickly turned into anger. I didn't know exactly what
K-Dog meant when he said they would take care of it. But I hoped it meant they would make him pay for what he put me through. Threatening my life was a mistake. But threatening my child's life was an even bigger mistake.

The next morning, I overheard O.B. telling K-Dog he would try. "Try to what," I demanded to know. "What's going on?"
"Nothin'," O.B. said.
"Don't tell me nothin', take me home, please. That bastard made a mess and I need to clean it up."

Danette Majette

I asked O.B. to take me home several times. Each time, he refused. I knew then that something terrible must have happened in there. Anxious to get home and see what was wrong, I called Clova. "Girl, I'll be there in a few," she assured me.

I walked next door and asked Brenda if she could watch Zeta. Without wavering she said, "Of course."

Within thirty minutes, I was on my way home. I knew I was going to need help cleaning up, so I called Vicki and Londa and told them to meet us at my apartment. As we pulled up, I had this eerie feeling at the pit of my stomach that got worse once I got inside. If I didn't know better, I would've thought someone had tied my intestines in knots.

"Oh my God," Clova screamed. I couldn't believe this was the same apartment. We had to have been in the wrong place.

"Somebody please pinch me. And tell me I'm having a nightmare," I said holding both sides of my head. Blood was spattered all over the walls. A big hole near the hallway closet was in the shape of someone's head. Everything was broken. I mean everything.

When Vicki and Londa arrived, I was sitting outside dazed. I just couldn't put my mind around what had happened. My apartment looked like the Valentine's Day massacre.

They all huddled around me and tried to assure me everything would be all right. But I wasn't convinced. With so many unanswered questions, I called K-Dog. He was reluctant to talk to me on the phone. So, I demanded he come over and talk to me.

He arrived about ten minutes later, with a look of guilt on his face. "What happened after I left?" I asked. K-Dog pulled me away so that we could speak alone.

"Zsaset, he was so fucked up he tore through the place."

"Why didn't you stop him?"

"Look, Bisal said he did it while you were upstairs. Just look at it this way, material things can be replaced. You and Zeta can't."

I Shoulda Seen It Comin'

I understood where he was coming from. I just didn't want to hear it. With all the blood, I didn't want to catch a murder wrap. After all it was my apartment.

"Look, we're family and family looks out for one another. So, I did what I had to do to make sure he never bothers you again. Believe that. Now, don't ever mention this again. Forget about last night. It's over," he said with a serious look in his eyes.

Everyone pitched in, but it was useless. I didn't care how clean we got it. I knew I would never be able to sleep in that apartment again.

"What's wrong?" Clova asked noticing the distressed look on my face.

"I just don't think I could live here anymore. There're just too many memories about last night," I said as I started to cry.

"Zsaset, did he do somethin' to you?" Clova asked.

"No. He didn't touch me or anything. He just scared me. I think I'm just upset about the images of having that gun pointed to my head. And the things he said he was going to do to Zeta."

"What do you think K-Dog did to him? It looks like they shoved his head into the wall. Do you think they killed him?" she asked.

From what K-Dog said to me, I was pretty sure that they killed Ra, but Clova didn't need to know all that. "Naw," I said. "You need to stop watching so many mafia movies."

"Well, how do you explain all that blood?"

"I don't know. Stop asking me so many questions," I yelled.

Overwhelmed, I ran up to my room to see if anything was damaged. Thank God. The last thing I needed was to have that psychopath destroy the upstairs too. I sat on the edge of my bed and tried to replay where I went wrong. I had so many unanswered questions. *How did he get in the house? Better yet, how did he know where I lived?* Then it hit me. When I was standing outside with K-Dog and Bisal last night, I left the door opened. He must have slipped in while we were talking. Oh my God, I left Zeta in the house. What was I thinking? He could have hurt her.

Danette Majette

I ran down the stairs and out the door. Vicki came running behind me yelling, "Zsaset, what's wrong?"

"I can't stay here. I can't."

"Let's think," Vicki said, trying to comfort me.

We sat on the curb for about ten minutes and then with a loud outburst she said, "I got it."

"You got what?"

"Call your landlord and tell them someone broke into your apartment."

"What are you talking about?"

"Look, there have been a lot of break-in's around here lately. And I heard they've been moving the victims into new apartments. I guess so they won't be sued. I bet any amount of money if you tell her that you and your child were almost killed last night, she'll move you. If she doesn't we'll just tell her you're gonna go to the news. The last thing they need is bad publicity. They're already losing tenants."

"I don't know. What if it doesn't work?"

"Well, you won't know until you try. I'll go get K-Dog's phone so you can call her."

I sat there for a few minutes trying to get my lies straight. I knew her first question would be why didn't I call the police. I'll just tell her there was no reason to. The person didn't take anything. They just trashed the place. Maybe that would fly. If it didn't, I would have to go back and live with K-Dog and O.B. Oh hell no. I was not having that. It had to work.

Dialing the numbers to the rental office proved to be a task for me. My hands were shaking so bad, Vicki had to take the phone. "Do you want me to do it?" she asked.

"No, I can do it."

I took a deep breath then continued to dial the number. When the property manager answered the phone, I explained my situation.

I Shoulda Seen It Comin'

"I would love to move you into another apartment. The only problem is that I only have a one bedroom apartment vacant," she said in a sympathetic tone.

"That's fine. My roommate moved out, so it's just me and my daughter."

"Alright, but it's gonna take me a day or two to get it ready."

I informed her that I would be staying with friends, so she could call me at work.

Zeta and I stayed with Clova. The next morning, K-Dog took me to work because I was still too shaken to drive myself. I had only been at work about two hours when Dre called me back to his office. I was sure he couldn't possibly know about what had happened at my apartment. Dre often surprised me with the information and gossip he had, so I braced myself. But to my dismay he said, "Baby girl, business has been slow since them indictments were just handed down. I'm sorry but I have to cut back."

"Does this mean I'm fired?" I asked.

"No, I just have to give you an extra day off."

"Oh. I thought you were firing me."

"No, I wouldn't do that. I'd fire one of their lazy butts before I let you go," he said, pointing to my co-workers.

I didn't have a place to live and on top of that my hours had been cut back. That was the last thing I needed. But at least I still had a job.

I finished my conversation with Dre, then grabbed my bag and clocked out. I stood in front of the store and waited for K-Dog to pick me up. An hour passed and there was no sign of him. With his system pumping and new car shining so bright it almost blinded me, Dolo pulled up. "Need a ride?"

Was this fool crazy? I was not about to get in the car with his psycho ass, especially after he threatened to kill me and my kids. Forget it.

"No thank you, I'm waitin' for someone."

"How long you been waitin'?"

"About an hour. He must be stuck in traffic."

"Umm, there's no traffic at this time of day, shorty. Look, I know you don't trust me, but I was wrong. It wasn't your brotha who shot at me, it was someone else. So get in the car and let me take you home. Anyway, it seems whoever was supposed to come and pick you up forgot all about you."

I hated to admit it, but he was right. K-Dog had forgotten about me. As much as I detested Dolo, I needed to get home to Zeta. So I let him take me to Clova's. On our way, I noticed that his mood was very somber.

"What's wrong with you," I asked.

"You didn't hear about my brother? Someone killed him at a club on the Southside. Sorry bastards popped him while he was pissing."

"Damn, Dolo, I'm sorry about that. Tee was a good guy and I know you guys were more than close. I'm so sorry." I thought to myself *Damn, what a way to go*. I lied about Tee being a good guy, but I had to say something to comfort Dolo. Even though I wasn't feeling Dolo anymore, I felt sorry for him.

It had been a long time since we talked to one another. And it was like old times, but it was over and it was going to stay that way. We said our good-byes and shared one last kiss before I went into Clova's apartment. *If only he wasn't such an asshole*, I thought.

My new apartment was ready the next day. It was smaller, but free from all the evidence of a murder. I didn't have much to move in, since Ra had broken everything. Starting over was a big transition. K-Dog promised he would replace all of my possessions. *But, who was going to replace my sanity?*

I managed to get my life back on track a few weeks later. Work picked up and I was learning to love myself instead of looking for someone else to do it for me. I started to find solace in the word. I quickly learned that the problems I was having were from an underlying issue—my need for male attention. I never knew my father, but I often wondered if my life would have been different had he been around. My mother raised me the best way she knew how. It was impossible for her to play both mother and father, but damn if she didn't try. But her working two jobs only left me to raise myself. The streets became my parents. And guess what my new parents gave me…a big belly at fifteen.

My mother never really spoke ill of my father, but she was never short on stories about him. One story that always stood out in my mind was the story she told me about how she had to sneak money from him just to get pampers and milk. Although the story was comical, it often angered me. What kind of man fathers a child and then refuses to take care of it?

Being a father is more than just sending a check to your baby momma. It's giving that child love and teaching them to have confidence and high self-esteem. All the things I lacked. I subconsciously looked for the love and nurturing I didn't get from my father in my intimate relationships. No wonder none of my relationships worked. My standards were set too low. Who can blame me? I didn't have anyone around to show me how a real man loves and cares for a woman.

A few days later, a friend of Dolo's called the store to get my new number. He had been picked up by the Feds earlier in the week and needed to talk to me about something. I had no idea what it was, but nevertheless I was curious so I gave it to him.

When he called, we chatted for a few minutes about old times then he gave me a heartfelt apology. His apology seemed sincere, although I wondered why he decided to tell me after he had gotten locked down. *Why didn't he tell me this sooner?* Was he lonely and in need of a friend? Everyone knows once a hustler gets locked down, friends are far, few, and in between. They lose their male friends because they're paranoid. Then they lose all of their groupies because they don't have the money, power, and respect they had on the streets. Hell, chicks would just move on to the next hustler. Like they say, money talks and bullshits walks.

Before I knew it, we were talking on the phone everyday. He even had one of his friends bring me money to keep me afloat.

One day, one of Dolo's friends told me that it was going be the last time he would bring me money. I didn't understand why until a few days later. It seemed the word had gotten out about indictments being served on all of Dolo's friends. Then one by one, anyone who was associated with him was put away. Rumors were all over Richmond about who the snitch was. When the trial started, everyone was amazed to find out the snitch was Dolo himself. I was shocked. People even started questioning me. *Like I knew he was going to roll over like a bitch.*

Chapter Twenty

A year after a year after the Ra incident that I hit rock bottom. K-Dog and O.B. were out of town most of time, so I usually sat in the house alone. As far as I was concerned, my life was over. I started smoking and drinking heavily to forget all the crazy things I had been through. And before I knew it, I had shut my friends out and started missing work on a regular. With no one to console me, I sank into a deep depression. I would go days without a shower and there was food and dishes all over the living room. My hair was fucked up and my nails needed a fill-in so bad they looked like someone gnawed on them. It seemed the more I tried to get my life in order, the worse it got. One day I decided to just end it all.

I sat for an hour with a razor to my wrist ready to take my own life, when a voice said to me. *"You're better than that. Just hold on. It will get better, but you have to want to make it better. What about your daughter? She needs you more than ever now."* The voice was right. I was better than that and my daughter did need me. She was a strong little girl, but how much can one child take?

The air coming through my window was refreshing. I opened my eyes to another day, and a whole new outlook on life. It was the breaking point of my depression. I started my morning off by having breakfast, then I went and got my hair and nails done. You would be amazed at how your appearance can make you feel better about yourself. I was among the living again. I started hanging out with my friends and I even started going out to the club. It was all about self-love with me.

Danette Majette

One particular morning, I arrived at work an hour early. As I passed the jewelry boutique, I noticed a very attractive girl waiting by the store. By the texture of her hair, I could tell she was mixed. Dressed in some cute acid-washed jeans and a tightly fitted tee, I wondered who she was.

"Excuse me, do you know what time Foot Locker opens?" she asked in a soft tone.

"We don't open until ten. Are you comin' to see someone?" I asked, sizing her up.

"No, I'm interested in a job."

"Our manager, Dre, will be here in about thirty minutes. What's your name?"

"Rachel."

"Oh, I'm Zsaset. I'm one of the sales associates."

"Is your manager, Dre is his name, right, hiring?"

"Yes. His name is Dre. I don't know but I can ask."

"If you could that would be great. I really need a job bad."

"Here he comes now," I said.

I left Rachel outside until it was time for the store to open up. She was the first person to walk in. Dre gave her an on-the-spot interview, probably because it was close to the holiday season and business was about to pick up. She seemed so desperate for work I felt sorry for her. I told her to wait while I went to talk to Dre. Because he had a soft spot for me, I knew he would hire her.

"Baby girl, we don't even know her."

"You took a chance on me and look, our sales have increased." I batted my eyes.

"Yeah, I guess you're right."

"And besides, she was here before me and I was an hour early. That should tell you something."

He agreed with me and gave her a chance. The only catch was that I was responsible for her. I went back to the front of the store and told Rachel the good news.

"Since you're gonna be workin' here, don't you think we should get you a uniform and a schedule?" Dre said eyeing me.

I Shoulda Seen It Comin'

"Yes, sir," Rachel yelled.

Needless to say, Rachel started a couple of days after her interview. Although she was a natural and worked hard like the rest of us, Rachel had skeletons in her closet.

Dre was Richmond's gossip columnist. Well respected by everyone, especially the hustlers, he knew all the dirt. Some guy from Woodcroft told Dre that Rachel was an ex-con who was brought up on child neglect charges.

I wanted to know the scoop, so I invited her to my apartment to hang out with me and my girls. We finished our shift and headed to my apartment to meet Clova, Vicki and Londa. By the time we arrived, they were already there.

"It's about time ya'll got here," Clova said.

"Whatever. Shit, some people do work for a living," I hissed.

After guzzling down four rounds of E&J, the craziest thing happened. Out of nowhere, Rachel started to spaz out. She quickly came out of her high.

"Oh shit," she screamed.

"What's wrong, Rachel?" I asked.

"I missed my curfew."

"Curfew? You have a curfew?" Vicki chuckled.

"Yeah, it's a long story. Zsaset, can I use your phone, I have to call my grandmother."

"Sure."

We got dizzy watching her dial the numbers so fast. "Damn, bitch, is that smoke I see comin' from the keypad?" Londa said. We fell out laughing. Rachel was so shook up she didn't hear a word Londa said. She concentrated on the yelling coming from the other end of the receiver. Her grandmother must have been scolding her like she was a child. The tears fell from her face like a rainstorm and she hung up the phone.

"What did she say?" I asked.

"She said, 'don't come home'," Rachel said sobbing.

"What? What does she mean don't come home? What dah hell kinda shit is that? Where does she expect you to go?"

"I don't know. But do you think I could stay with you for the night?"

I sat there in a daze. She blew my flow. For a few minutes, I sat there saying nothing. *Snap out of it Zsaset. She needs shelter, not a kidney.*

"Sure, your grandmother probably just needs to calm down and come to her senses. She'll let you come home tomorrow."

Boy, was I wrong. She was even worst the next day. I took Rachel home and her clothes were thrown outside scattered all over the ground. As we approached the door, her grandmother started cussing and yelling at Rachel to get her stuff and go. The old bitty even threatened to call the police. I didn't want any part of that scene so I quickly helped her and we rolled out.

Being the kind-hearted person I was, I let her move in with me. She slept on a pullout bed in the living room. I told her that I understood that she was going through a tough time, but so was I. Another person in the house meant a higher electricity and food bill. In other words, she had to help out with the bills. I just couldn't afford it.

Rachel and I got along great. It was like we had known each other all our lives. Wherever I was, she was. Of course, my girls weren't feeling her. But that was only because they were jealous of the time I was spending with her. But, I still took heed to their warnings. As my mother would say, don't always judge a book by its cover.

Chapter Twenty-1

My day at work was going fine until this annoying guy came in. He was 5'5", medium build, with a low fade haircut. Wearing baggy jeans, a Miami Hurricane jersey and baseball cap, he walked over to me and licked his lips.
"Yo, what's up, cutie?"
"Are you talking to me?" I asked rolling my eyes.
"Yeah, I'm talkin' to you," he said like he was the mack.
I don't know who told him he was fine, but they lied. As a matter of fact, they played a cruel joke on his ass.
Not impressed, I looked him up and down. "I don't think so, sweetie," I replied as I walked to the back.

Sitting at Dre's desk, I began to get the closing paperwork together. It had been a long day and I was ready to get out of there. Suddenly, Rachel came running to the back. "Girl, that guy spent three hundred dollars," she said impressed.
"And?" I said still working.
"Well, he told me he wanted to get with you."
"That'll be the day. My dating days are over," I said.
She was trying her damnedest to get me to go out with him. She didn't seem to get the message that her pleas were falling on deaf ears.

The whole crew started in on me when we walked back onto the floor. For some reason, everyone felt they had to put their two cents in. *Who was he anyway?* The last thing I needed was another psycho in my life. And with my track record, I needed to ban men for life. But that was easier said then done considering he started coming in our store everyday.

I was standing at the cash register when I saw that same fool pimpin' in again. He made a beeline straight over to me.

"What's your name, baby?" he said.

This nigga is relentless. "It's Zsaset," I said irritated as hell.

"Hi, Zsaset. I'm Pit."

As in pit bull, I thought to myself. *Come to think of it you do look like a damn dog.*

"Zsaset, do you think I could take you out some time?"

"I don't think so," I said in a rude manner.

He wouldn't take no for an answer. "I guarantee you, after one date with me, you'll change your mind," he said.

"Whatever," I said walking away.

I blew him off for weeks before I gave in. That nigga finally convinced me to have one dinner with him. He promised to take me home if he zigged when he should've zagged. I figured it was a win-win situation for me. So I asked Rachel to watch Zeta that Friday night. I was hoping she would say she couldn't so I wouldn't have to go. But that didn't pan out. *What was the big fuss? After all, it was just a meal. And it was gonna be a cheap meal. That way he couldn't expect anything afterwards. It was not that kind of party.*

I told him to meet me at the store in my complex because I didn't want him to know where I lived. He might try to camp out at my home like he does at my job.

Pit rode up in a brand new, champagne colored Infiniti Q45. It was beautiful. It had a banging system, television, phone and rims. *If only he looked like his car.*

In between the times the waiter at Darryl's came to the table, Pit had me rolling so hard my stomach was hurting. He wasn't so bad after all, but he was still a little stuck on himself. He didn't mind spending money either. That was a plus. Our bill came to $80.00. My chunky tail ordered one of everything off the menu. I

I Shoulda Seen It Comin'

felt kind of bad spending his money like that because he sure wasn't gettin' none.

After dinner, we met my friends at Ivory's. They found him to be very polite. If he could just get over himself, he would be an okay guy. Well maybe I'm lying. He still could use a little plastic surgery. Just enough to make him look like a man and not man's best friend.

There were a dozen red roses and breakfast waiting for me the next day at work. Compliments of guess who...yep, Pit. He was no fool. He knew the only way he would have a chance with me, was to court me. I called him and thanked him for the flowers. Before I knew it, I had agreed to another date. Since he was a perfect gentleman the first time, I figured I would order lobster this time. But I needed to lay down a few ground rules. I told him that I wasn't ready to be serious with anyone. And sex was definitely out of the question. He seemed to be cool with it.

We dated for about a month before the honeymoon was over. My friends dropped a mega bomb on me. Not only was this nigga a drug dealer, which I could handle, but he was shackin' up with his baby momma. Now that shit I wasn't puttin' up with.

"Londa, are y'all sure," I asked.

"Yeah, girl. Her name is Kim and she is trouble with a capital T. Forget that heffer, he wants you," Londa said.

"Why does it matter what he does for a living," Clova asked.

"Because it does. I don't need no man bringing me down. I've worked too hard to pull myself up."

I was so mad at them for telling me, that I snapped. I knew it wasn't their fault, but I had to take it out on somebody. They were my girls and they were just looking out for me. When I calmed down, I apologized and thanked them for having my back. After all, he was the one who lied to me and he was going to pay.

That night, I told Pit to come over because I was horny. He was there before I could hang up the phone. *Desperate bastard.*

Danette Majette

As soon as he walked through the door, I started by gently rubbing his back. My little strip tease in my new panty set was the icing on the cake. He was so aroused, he sweated and trembled like a crack head going through withdrawal symptoms. Then I made my move.

"Get the fuck out," I yelled.

"Whatcha talkin' 'bout, girl? I thought we were about to do somethin' here." He looked so dumb, I felt like knocking his ass out.

"That's what your dumb ass gets for thinking."

I got dressed and walked downstairs. "Let's go, Rover. Your ticks and fleas got to go."

He kept pleading with me to tell him what he'd done, so I told him.

"You lied to me, that's what."

"Lied to you about what?"

"I don't know, let me see…maybe about your occupation. Oh, don't forget about the baby momma you live with."

"Will you please calm down and let me explain?" He tried to explain for an hour, but I kept ignoring him. His words sounded hollow. Finally, he grabbed me by the arm and threw me down on the floor. He straddled me so I couldn't move.

"Let my damn hands go," I said trying to break free.

"Listen to me. I'm sorry, I didn't tell you. But I'm workin' on legalizing my money so I can get out of the business. I ain't tryin' to retire off this shit. As far as Kim is concerned, we live together but we're not together. I sleep in one room and she sleeps in another. I'm only there because I want to be close to my daughter."

"You expect me to believe some bullshit like that," I said blowing air out of the side of my mouth.

"If I was serious about her, do you think I would be takin' you out and showin' you off in public? No. I would be tryin' to keep you on the down low. You met my momma, didn't you? Come on, man, that's gotta count for somethin'."

I Shoulda Seen It Comin'

"Well sorry, your account here is now closed. Get off of me and just leave."

This nigga rested on me like I was a chair, trying to figure out what language I was speaking. *English, nigga, now get up.* After five minutes of silence, he finally decided to get up. He walked out the door without another word.

Pit called me at work the next day. "What do you want? Don't call me no more," I screamed. Dre looked at me as if to ask if I was alright. I shook my head to let him know I was fine.

"I want you to tell me how I can make this up to you," Pit said begging.

"You can't. So get over it."

"You're not gonna tell me I don't mean anything to you," he said. He was right, but I wasn't going to give him the satisfaction of knowing it. "Zsaset, can we just please talk about this?"

"Pit, there's nothin' to talk about."

I tried hard to convince him and myself that it was over, but I couldn't. I allowed him to come over that night. Faced with an ultimatum to move out of his baby momma's house and stop selling drugs, Pit stared at me in confusion. I knew I was basically asking him to give up his life, but hell this was his chance to redeem himself. And if he wanted me bad enough he would do it. To my surprise, he agreed.

Chapter Twenty-2

Things between Pit and me were going well. He packed his things and moved into a hotel. He was in the process of handing over his drug connections to his cousin, Romeo, fulltime. I began to feel more secure about our relationship. Pit was definitely making moves in the right direction.

Something inside warned me not to get too happy, because all good things come to an end. We tried to keep things quiet as long as we could, but after a week of dating him exclusively, it was all over Richmond. It got back to Kim that he left her for me. I even heard the lynch mob was out to get me. Kim and her girls were on my trail. My friends warned me that she may try to do something to me, but I wasn't worried. She was going to be in for a rude awakening when she came my way.

On the day before Christmas Eve, we went to D.C. to do a little shopping. That city was like one big candy store. Our first stop was Houston's in Georgetown. Then we headed up Wisconsin Avenue to the upscale fashion stores, Neiman Marcus and Saks. We were having a good time, but I could tell he was upset about something.

"What's wrong?" I asked.

"I'm tired of Kim's shit. She's trying to keep me from seeing my daughter."

I told him to take her to court. As a father, he had rights too. Me telling him that didn't change his mood, he was still distant.

Trying to lighten his mood, I invited him to ride with me to pick up my mother in Williamsburg the next day. Without hesitation, he said he wouldn't miss it for the world. It would be a chance for him to clear his mind.

I Shoulda Seen It Comin'

We got back to Richmond around eight that night. Pit dropped me off at home then made another attempt to see his daughter. I prayed Kim would come to her senses and let him see her, but she didn't. Instead things got ugly.
I thought when Pit came over he was going to burst. He said she showed her ass. She cut up the rest of his clothes and set his car on fire right in front of the house just days earlier. What pissed him off even more was when she cussed him out saying he wasn't shit as a father, with his daughter, Shanique, glued to her hip. He said her last words were, "I'll rot in hell before I let you see your daughter again." Pit's hardcore exterior quickly turned into mush. I never had a rough neck cry on my shoulder before. Seeing him so upset made me mad. I couldn't wait to get my hands around that bitch's neck.
"She's nuts and I'm telling you right now if she comes this way. I'm gonna tap that ass good."
"You crazy, girl." He broke a smile. "Look, I don't want you to worry about her. I'll take care of everything," he said, pulling me close. Still not convinced, he looked me in the eye and told me he loved me. That was all I needed to hear.

I was excited about my mother's and son's visit. I threw on my Bongo jeans and leather jacket and we drove to the Williamsburg outlet to meet them. My mother looked great. She had her hair fixed in a bun and wore a beautiful crème velour sweat suit. My son had grown so much, I almost didn't recognize him. I could tell my mom was feeding him plenty of her famous pork chops and gravy because he picked up a lot of weight. I appreciated my mother taking care of him. It was hard for me to let him go, but it was for the best.
After the introductions, the shopping was on. The first stop...K-Bee toy store. I wanted to see what they were interested in. Seeing so many things they wanted sent my kids into a frenzy. I told them that there was no need to get excited, Santa Claus was coming later that night.

Danette Majette

"Mommy, can we please buy one thing now," they sang in unison.

"No. We have to go," I said.

With their mouths poked out and attitudes flaring, they just stood there pouting. Finally I gave in. Pit made matters even worse, by telling them to get whatever they wanted. By the time they were finished shopping, my son walked out with the new Nintendo game system and every game his little hands could hold. And my daughter had a new Barbie doll collection.

"Baby, you haven't told me what you want for Christmas," Pit said.

"What are you getting your baby momma?" I said in a sassy tone.

"I don't know. But I have to get her somethin' or she'll really never let me see my daughter again."

"Well, I want the same things you get her. Whatever she's worth, I'm worth."

He had no idea where I was coming from. But I heard from several people that he spent dough on her. So I was going to make sure he did the same for me.

It was Christmas Day and my mom and I were in the kitchen cooking when K-Dog arrived. As usual, he spoiled me and Zeta rotten with expensive gifts. He even bought Rachel and my mom both gift certificates to Hecht's. Everyone seemed to be enjoying themselves. I checked the clock and it was 5:00 p.m. Pit still hadn't come or called. I was beginning to wonder if he'd gotten lost. Soon my wondering came to an end. He walked in with six beautifully wrapped boxes and they were all for me.

"What's all this?" I asked taking the packages from him.

"You told me everything she got, you wanted, so here you go."

I tore through the boxes like a kid. A rush of anger ran through me when I got to the last box. It was a ring. "You bought her a ring?" I said with my eyebrows raised.

"Yeah, but it was a cheap one. As you can see, yours isn't cheap."

Pouting, I walked into the kitchen. Pit followed me. No matter how blasé he tried to be about the ring, he knew he had fucked up.

"Zsaset, it's Christmas. Can we please just enjoy our time together without thinking about her?" he said kissing my neck.

"I guess, but she doesn't deserve a ring and you know it."

"Well, it's her last one. Let her enjoy it," he said in sneaky tone.

"Yeah, it just better be," I said as I walked back to the living room.

Sitting on the sofa, Pit leaned over and whispered in my ear. "Guess what?" Pit asked. "You can have one more gift. So, what's it gonna be?"

"Did Kim get this privilege too?"

"Hell naw. She ain't gettin' another dime out of me."

"Good, glad to hear that. Now let me see."

I thought long and hard. I knew exactly what I wanted, but I was sure it was a long shot. He sat on the couch with a curious look on his face. "Damn, it cost that much," he said laughing.

"Yeah, kinda," I said.

"What is it?"

"I want my own store."

"Is that all? Wait right here," he said winking his eye. He returned from his car with a large brown duffel bag. "Merry Christmas," he said as he emptied the bag onto the coffee table.

"What is this?" I asked stunned.

"Twenty G's. You said you wanted your own store. Now you can have it."

I just sat there speechless. I couldn't stop the tears.

"What's wrong? It's not enough?" he said, picking up a stack of money.

"It's not that. I can't believe you would do this for me."

"I told you I wanted to do the right thing. Now I know it's gonna be your baby, but can I at least be your partner?"

"Hell yeah. You can be whatever you want to be."

I was on cloud nine. I was finally going to be my own boss and I had a man who cared about me. All of the excitement got me in the mood. So after everyone left, I put the kids to sleep. My mother was still wide awake so I asked her if she would watch them while Pit and I took a ride. Little did she know it was a ride to the Marriott.

I had rejected the idea of making love to Pit for weeks. But I felt it was finally time to take things to the next level. Of course, I told him that we were just going there to get away from everyone. I wanted it to be a surprise. As soon as we got into the room, I immediately went to the shower. I returned wrapped in a towel. I stood in front of him, dropped my towel and pushed him back onto the bed. Unable to bear it, he put his hands over his eyes and shook his head.

"Zsaset, why are you playin' with me like this? This shit ain't even funny."

"Who says I'm playin'? Now shut up and get out those drawers." I didn't have to tell his ass that twice.

As he nibbled on my earlobe, Pit whispered sultry words into my ear and caressed all the right places of my body. Sliding his tongue up and down my neck and in and out of my ear made my juices flow. Getting harder and harder by the second, he slowly slid into me. With my arms stretched and positioned over my head, Pit took my fingers and intertwined them with his. His kisses were so warm and sensual, they made me feel loved. That was it. *Pitt was making sweet love to me.* I appreciated the way he cared enough to make me feel special. And I was glad to know that when I was in that kind of mood, he would be a generous and passionate lover. But it had been a while, and right now, I knew exactly what I wanted to do. I wanted to fuck. I was too shy to ask until he hit that spot.

"Harder," I said boldly.

I Shoulda Seen It Comin'

"Like this?" he asked while spreading my ass cheeks apart and pounding deep inside me.

"Yeah, baby, just… like… that! Fuck me, fuck me," I screamed loudly. "It's all yours, do what ya want!"

Just then, he slipped his thumb in my ass and started sucking my fingers like tootsie pops, now digging deeper and harder than before. I had to fight hard to control my urge to pee. Damn, it felt so good, it brought tears to my eyes. Moving fast and hard, I rocked my hips until I felt my body start to twitch, bringing me to my first orgasm. The second and third ones soon followed and by then, I was sure that Pit was *the* man for me.

It was New Years Eve and there was a knock at my door. I opened it and to my surprise it was Pit and a bunch of his friends.

"What's goin' on?" I asked.

"I'm moving in and I'm out of the business for good."

I was flabbergasted. I guess he really did want to be with me.

As Pit and his friends moved his stuff in, I noticed three large safes. He sat them in my room. "What's in those?" I asked?

"Nothing much, just my jewelry and some important papers," he said, blowing me off.

Damn, he sure has a lot of jewelry.

Chapter Twenty-3

During the week were living in bliss. During the week we would go see a movie and then go have dinner and drinks at cozy little restaurants. On the weekends, we would cuddle up at home and watch television. He enjoyed that sense of family and I did too. More importantly, it was the way he bonded with Zeta. Even though she wasn't his, he always treated her like she was. He would give her horseback rides and read her books until she fell asleep. Everything seemed normal and I couldn't have been happier. I was in love and I didn't think anything or anyone could spoil the happiness I felt.

It had been a long day and proved to be an even longer night. Somehow Kim got her hands on my phone number. She called me up threatening me and screaming every name in the book that she could think of.

"You know what? You can call me all the hoes, sluts, and bitches you want. I still got your man," I said teasing her.

I threw the phone at Pit and told him to handle it. To make sure he did, I went into the living room and picked up the receiver.

"Hoe, I know you on the phone," she said.

"Damn right, bitch. You called my house. So if you want privacy, you better call him on his cell."

"Fuck you," Kim shouted.

"No, fuck you. You may have these other chicks around here runnin' scared. But you don't put no fear in my heart." Kim and I went back and forth until Pit finally intervened.

"Look, Kim it's over. Don't call here no more."

"Fine. I'll call the Feds instead."

This bitch is dumb as hell. "What the hell do the Feds have to do with me fuckin' yo man? I asked with curiosity.

I Shoulda Seen It Comin'

Pit tried to over talk her, but it was too late. She let the cat out of the bag. "You know those safes in your house? They're full of dope and money."

Heated, I dropped the phone and ran into the kitchen. He stood without any movement for a few minutes and then just dropped his head. He had been caught in a lie and had no recourse. "Tell me she's lying. Tell me you don't have no dope up in my house."

He hung up the phone and quickly ran over to the safes and opened them. "Does this look like dope to you?" He was right, there was just money and jewelry.

He immediately called Kim back. I could only hear from the receiving end, but from the reaction on his face, I assumed she hit a nerve. She probably told him he couldn't see his daughter again. Girls like Kim always use their kids when they can't get their way. That's that baby momma drama for your ass.

Pit was cold as ice in bed that night. Every time I tried to touch him, he would tense up. I don't know what Kim said to him, but it had his ass all shook up. "How the fuck did she get my number?"

"Does it really matter?"

"I guess not."

Tired of trying to figure him out, I fell asleep.

I opened the registers and waited for the first customer. It was hard not to let what Kim said get to me. I knew if I didn't keep my eyes and ears opened, she and her crew might try something. So as a precaution, I kept a blade in my pocket.

I was busy with a customer when an old friend walked in and greeted me. Ironically, her name was Kim too. I met her in the projects where
K-Dog and them hung out. She had just gotten out of jail and was looking for work. She was from New York and was not to be

fucked with. She was known for slicing and dicing a bitch. I told her to fill out an application because I knew I could convince Dre to give her a chance. Sure enough he did.

"Girl, I heard you got beef with Kim from the North side."

"No, she got beef with me because I mess with her baby's daddy. She can't stand that shit."

"Well watch your back. That bitch is wicked. Not too wicked for me to whip that ass though."

That's what I liked about Kim. If she was your friend, there's nothing she wouldn't do for you. She was a soldier. She even did a bid for K-Dog and he respected the hell out of her for it.

I invited Kim to come over and have some drinks one night. My mouth dropped when I walked in and saw Pit had moved out without even a word. I immediately called him on his cell phone to ask him what was up.

"I had to leave."

"What do you mean you had to leave?"

"Kim threatened that if I didn't come back, she was gonna call the Feds. Zsaset, she knows everything. Baby, I just couldn't take that chance."

When I asked him where we stood he paused. "We can still be together, but we have to keep it quiet." He was definitely using his own product. I wasn't about to be his chick on the side. He could forget about that.

I was so distraught, I asked Kim to stay. It was Mary J. Blige time. With the *My Life* CD playing and cigarette in hand, I just cried like a baby.

"Look, it's gonna be alright. Fuck that nigga. You're a beautiful, intelligent woman with a shape to die for. Hell, any man would be lucky to have you," Kim said, trying to comfort me.

It was easy for her to say, but I couldn't do this shit again. Just when I thought I was going to live happily ever after, I was back to square one.

I Shoulda Seen It Comin'

Days went by and there was no sign of Pit. I didn't know what to do about the store so I called Romeo and told him to come and pick up the money Pit gave me. Immediately, Pit called and asked me what I was doing.

"What? I know your ass don't expect me to still go into business with you."

"Why not? I told you we were still gonna see each other."

"So, now I'm gonna be your secret lover? I don't think so."

He sat on the phone quiet for a minute and then he said in a firm voice, "This was your dream and I'm not gonna let no one take it from you."

"You're a fuckin' joke, you know that," I said, slamming the phone in his ear.

All I wanted was to be happy, but Kim destroyed that. Was I going let her get away with it? Hell no.

Kim, the convict, was so pissed, she wanted to go over and fuck Kim up. But I had a plan of my own. She had fucked with the right person. She wanted a fight so I was going to give her one. I knew Pit had strong feelings for me, so I was going use that to my advantage. "Kim and Rachel, take notes, 'cause my mind is too advanced for these dump chicks. I'm about to beat her at her own game. And she don't even know it yet."

It took every ounce of strength in me not to kick Pit out when he came over. Unfortunately, the only way my plan would work was to get him to trust me. So I had to be calm, cool, and collected. In a childlike manner, I sat down next to him and told him that I understood what a tough situation he was in and that the only problem I had was the way he handled things.

"I know. But I knew if I told you what was going down, you would try and talk me out of it," he said.

"So how are we gonna work this store thing?" I said, scooting closer to him. "You know we'll have to spend a lot of time together. How is Kim gonna feel about that."

"I already told her about the store, so I don't think she's gonna be a problem." *That bitch is already a problem,* I thought to myself.

Pit and I worked side by side on the store's opening. We made several trips to New York, but never alone. He would always bring someone. It didn't matter though. We always ended up in bed together. Never underestimate the power of the P.

It was February and we were having the grand opening of my new store, *Top of the Line.* I was so excited. I was able to get Steady B to sign autographs. I was surprised to see we sold over $3000 in merchandise that day. We did the closing paperwork, locked the doors then went to the Redman and Method Man show. It was off the hook. I wore my leather shorts and bustier just to get a rise out of Pit and it worked. He couldn't keep his eyes off me the whole night. Neither could Kim.

The whole crew went out to breakfast after the show. Sure enough, Pit and his boys were there. After several botched attempts to get my attention, he sent Romeo over to the table where me and my girls were sitting to give me a message. "Hey, Zsaset, Pit said he'll be over your house after we finish eatin'."

He didn't have to tell me that. I already knew he would. He was beginning to be so predictable. Nevertheless, I wanted him.

Convict Kim and Rachel fell asleep as soon as we hit the door. I jumped in the shower and then decided to lay down to wait for Pit. Just as I was about to fall asleep, there was a knock at the door. It was him. Too tired to deal with him now, I turned on my side and went back to sleep. Not knowing I wanted to be alone, Convict Kim let him in. He was so drunk, he fell asleep on the floor. I pulled him up on the bed, kissed his forehead and went to sleep.

"Who the hell is blowin' up his pager," I mumbled as I reached for it on the nightstand. His baby's momma was on a rampage too early in the damn morning. Since Pit was asleep, I decided to handle it. I grabbed the cordless phone and tiptoed to the bathroom. As I dialed her number, I figured this was my time to get back at her. I pretended I didn't know who she was.

"Who is diss?"

I wanted to tell her ignorant ass the word was this, but I thought I would fuck with her instead. "Diss is Zsaset. Who is diss?"

"Put Pit on the phone."

"I'm sorry, I can't do that. He's sleep right now."

"Whatever, bitch, he ain't over there."

"See that's where you're wrong. He is here. He's always here. If you like, I could wake him up for you. Pit...Pit, wake up, baby...someone's on the phone for you."

He was so out of it. He grabbed the phone and said hello. That was all she wrote. She went slam off. And I didn't waste no time laughing either. "Zsaset, why you do that, man," he said, tightening his jaw.

"Fuck her. As a matter of fact, fuck you too."

He rang me out for what I did as he got dressed. Of course, I ignored him. So he left. Determined not to let his abrupt departure mess the rest of my day up, I hung out with my girls. We took Zeta out to eat and then sat in the house for the rest of the day. I sat staring at the walls, trying to figure out my next move. I knew Kim wasn't going to let me get away with humiliating her again. So I had to be ready for her wrath.

Chapter Twenty-4

My day started off as usual. Rachel went to Foot Locker and I went to my store. Vicki showed up just as I was about to leave. She wanted to take Zeta to have her pictures taken. Her offer was a gift from God because I had a lot of work to do.

I felt a little strange as I walked in the store. I tried not to dwell on it, but as time went by it got worse. The store was a mess from the grand opening so I decided to reorganize the clothes and put up a few displays. I had just finished putting up my final display when the unthinkable happened.

"What the hell are you doin'?" I yelled.

"What does it look like, bitch? We're shoppin'."

"Not in here you ain't. Go shop somewhere else," I said, pointing to the door.

"Who's gonna stop us? Not you."

"Look, get out before I call security," I screamed.

"Call security, bitch." I ran over to the phone and dialed the number to the security office. "You can call security all you want. My man gave you the money to open this funky ass store. So if I want somethin', I can get it." If Kim only knew how stupid she sounded, she wouldn't have said that.

"That's right, your man gave me the money. Just like he gives me that dick when I want it too," I spurted off.

"You ain't gettin' shit from him. Do you really think he cares about you?" Kim said, still grabbing clothes. I could tell that my words were fucking her up for real, so I decided to go in for the kill.

"Do you think he cares about *you*? You're running around here all fired up about a man who doesn't even want to be with you. If he did, he wouldn't be sniffing around me. And I'll let you

I Shoulda Seen It Comin'

in on something else. Everything you got for Christmas, I got. As a matter of fact, he wasn't even with you on Christmas. He spent the whole day with me and my family."

By this time, we were all in each other's space. She wasn't backing down and neither was I. I had to let that bitch know I wasn't scared of her ass. So I hit her with a two-piece. We scrapped like Muhammad Ali and George Forman. *Damn, this bitch is strong*, I thought to myself. But it wasn't just her. One of her friends had jumped in on the action, realizing Kim couldn't handle me. Kim grabbed a platform boot off my display and hit me over the head with it. Infuriated, I slammed her into a wall. She fell to the ground kicking and screaming for her friend to help. The next thing I knew her friend jumped me from the back. I don't know what the hell she thought she was doing. I was in the Marines for four years. I was trained for situations like this. So, I threw her ass forward and started stomping her in the face when I noticed the other friend coming from out of the corner of my eye. The whole scene played out in slow motion. I felt myself pause for a moment. When I did, I noticed Vicki had the other friend in a choke hold. Thank God she came when she did.

Kim and I were holding each other by the hair when the police arrived on the scene. "Ladies, break it up," one of the officers demanded.

"Tell this bitch to let my hair go," Kim yelled.

"Tell her to let my hair go," I yelled back.

Stubborn, we both stood there refusing to let go. Finally, the police officer told us that if we didn't break it up, he was going to take us both downtown. I didn't want Zeta, who'd seen enough already, to see me getting cuffed, so I let her go.

"Someone wanna tell me what's going on here," the other officer asked chewing on a toothpick.

"These dummies were trying to steal some clothes from me," I said, pointing to Kim and her friends.

"Is that true?"

"No," Kim said with a stupid look on her face.

The officer glanced around the store. "Are there any witnesses?"

Although a small crowd was now gathered in my store, no one said a word. Not even the guy who worked for me. I wasn't surprised considering he was Pit's friend. "I saw everything, officer," the man who rented the space next to me said. "They were trying to steal from this young lady. She asked them to leave, but they wouldn't."

That was all she wrote. The officers cuffed Kim and her friends and took them away. I ran over to my daughter immediately. I can only imagine how upset she was. It's not an easy thing to see your mother fighting like some street thug.

"Mommy, Mommy! You got a boo-boo on your face."

"I know, but it's okay. Mommy just hit her nose. I'll be just fine."

"You want me to kiss your boo-boo?" Zeta asked trying to comfort me.

"Oh baby, that's not necessary. It doesn't hurt," I said laughing.

I fired Pit's friend, closed up shop and went home. With every bone in my body aching and a major headache, I walked into the bathroom to check out the damage. Two scratches. *That's all they did.* I was on my couch relaxing when my girls arrived. "Zsaset, what happened, girl?" Londa asked

"Kim and two of her girls *tried* to jump me."

"You fought all of them at the same time?" Londa said looking me over.

"What kinda dumb-ass question is that? Isn't that what jumped usually means?" I yelled.

"Are you okay?" Convict Kim asked.

"Yeah, I wasn't in the Marines for nothing. Hell, I retained what I learned. I would've stabbed that bitch if Zeta wasn't there."

I Shoulda Seen It Comin'

My girls were mad as hell, especially Convict Kim. "Yo, Zsaset, those bitches gotta get it, man. I don't play that shit," she said, her New York accent stronger than normal.

"Kim, don't even worry about it. Look at me. They ain't do shit. Meanwhile, I have all their jewelry and I'm gonna go pawn it tomorrow."

Kim chuckled, but I knew she wasn't going to let it go. A little while later they left.

News of the fight was all over Richmond. Of course, Kim and her girls put their own twist on things. They told people they broke my nose, gave me two black eyes, and cut my face. Pit called as soon as he heard what happened. He tried to act like he was concerned, but I knew that was all an act. "I heard they messed up your face," he said.

"Yeah, I'm all fucked up."

"So you still gonna go to the Craig Mack show?"

"Naw, I better stay in the house."

I cut the conversation short, so I could call my girls to put my plan in order. Kim, Pit, and everyone else in Richmond were in for the shock of their lives.

Around 10 p.m., we were headed to the club. We found a parking spot, then Clova worked her magic to get us in through the back way. I didn't want anyone to see me until I got in. I wanted to make a grand entrance.

I walked through the crowd with sheer elegance. And then I made my way over to Pit and his crew. I wanted him to be the first person to see me up front and personal. "I thought you said they messed your face up," he said, inspecting my face.

"No, that's what you said. Let that be a lesson to you. Don't believe everything you hear."

We made our rounds and then copped a table in the back of the club. K-Dog and O.B. were nearby for backup. Kim and her crew showed up just before last call. They all walked pass me in amazement.

"Yeah, that's right. Your girl lied. The only person that got they ass whooped was you three," Convict Kim said as she pointed to Kim and her girls.

I don't know who moved first, but Convict Kim, already hyper, grabbed one of Kim's friends and slammed her into the wall. She slid down the wall like Jell-O. It was unbelievable. I knew Convict Kim was strong, but I didn't know she had that kind of strength.

Then all hell broke loose. There was complete mayhem in the club. Security was all over the place, but they wouldn't find us. If they wanted us, they were going to have hit I-95.

Chapter Twenty-5

Things were finally getting back to normal. Vicki and I spent our days in the store. And we all spent our nights at my house drinking beer and smoking.

"I guess Kim learned her lesson about messing with us," Vicki said as she folded some tee shirts. I wasn't convinced. I knew without a doubt she wasn't going to let me get away with humiliating her again. I would bet my life Kim was up to something. Girls like her thrive on keeping shit stirred up. She was going to make a move when I least expected it. So I kept my guards up.

I needed a break and some fresh air so I decided to go out and get my lunch. "Vicki, I'll be back. I'm gonna walk down to McDonald's. Do you want me to bring you somethin' back?"

"Naw, that's okay."

I was walking down the street when something caught my eye. It was an old beat up car with dark tinted windows. It followed me for a block before it pulled up beside me. Scared, I picked up speed. When I looked over to see if the car was still following me, a shiny object appeared as the window was being rolled down. I saw Kim's face. She was smiling. Before I could react, I heard a click. *This crazy bitch is tryin' to kill me for real.* She pulled the trigger several times, but nothing came out. It was jammed. I took off down the street like a bat out of hell. I ran to safety in a church and called the police. Then I called Vicki and told her to close the shop and meet me at the police station. The police took my statement and told me they were going to bring her in for questioning. Since there were no witnesses, it wasn't too much they could do. But they assured me they would investigate the matter.

That wasn't good enough for me. I was going to have to take matters into my own hands. I didn't waste any time either. I went home and called my mother and told her I was coming home, then I called K-Dog.

"Well, I think that's best. No tellin' what that crazy broad might try to do to you or Zeta," he said. "Of course I could always take care of it for you."

"Naw, today was just a sign that it's time for me to go."

It only took me a week to find an apartment. There were only two left so Vicki and I drove down to Virginia Beach to fill out the application. We got back late that evening. I wanted to keep my leaving a secret so I told Vicki not to say a word to anyone about where I was moving. "Can I go with you," she asked.

"Go with me where?" I said with my eyebrows raised.

"To Virginia Beach. I'm tired of Richmond and my momma."

I knew where Vicki was coming from. Her mom was a nut case. She was a foster mother of four and would get children just for money. To make matters worse, she never took care of them. She always made Vicki watch them, even though she had two other children older than Vicki. I never understood why she never made them watch the kids until Vicki told me that her mother didn't like her. After Vicki's mother got pregnant with her, her father skipped town, leaving her to fend for herself. He never wanted children and told her that if she kept the baby he would leave her. By this time, it was too late for her to get an abortion so she kept Vicki. After she was born, he left town and she resented Vicki for it.

I couldn't wait to get the hell out of Richmond. This place was my worst nightmare. I had seen more heartache in my few

I Shoulda Seen It Comin'

years there than in my whole life. It was time for me to start healing again. All I needed was for things to work out with the apartment. Once that was a done deal everything else would fall into place.

I was sitting on my couch enjoying a cold beer when the phone rang. It was the property manager calling to tell me I had been approved.

"When do you want to move in?"
"When will you have it ready?"
"I can have it ready by the end of the week."

I knew I had to get my stuff packed. So I called Pit's friend and told him he could come back to work for a week because I was sick. His stupid ass fell for it and agreed. Then I called my girls and told them I was leaving. I ran my plan by them and asked them to keep quiet. For the rest of the week, I packed.

On my last day in Richmond, I rented a truck and parked it at the end of the street. I jumped into my car and went to the bank. I cleaned out the account and then closed it. Three thousand dollars wasn't much to live off, but it was a start.

At nightfall, Vicki and I started packing up the truck. I paid two teenagers to help. When the last box was loaded, I went to the store and threw every stitch of clothing in the back of the truck.

With Vicki following me in my car, I headed to the Jackson Ward Projects where Kim lived. I wasn't there to socialize. This was strictly business. I was there to take care of that bitch once and for all. After we got near her apartment, I parked the truck and then ran back to my car.

"Bingo," I said with excitement.
"What, Zsaset?"
"His car is here," I said, looking over the hood of my car.
"I thought you wanted to get back at Kim."
"I do. Stay here while I go to the payphone."
"Alright, but I think we should get out of here before someone sees us."

"Don't worry, I won't be long."

When I got to the pay phone, I dialed 911. "Yes, I just saw a young lady put a gun in her trunk. I'm worried she's gonna do something bad," I said in a granny voice.

"Did you happen to see the license plates?"

"I think I got it. It was XXL-000. Does that help?"

"Yes, ma'am. We'll have a unit there in a few minutes."

I slammed down the receiver and ran back to my car.

"Zsaset, I don't understand."

"Well, Vicki, that doesn't surprise me. You are pretty slow."

"Zsaset, this is no time for jokes."

"I know but I couldn't help it. Anyway, this is the deal." Just as I was about to explain what I had done to Vicki, Kim walked out of the apartment. "Damn," I yelled hitting my fist on the car.

"What's wrong?" Vicki asked.

"She's leaving. Oh never mind. She ain't going nowhere, at least not on her own."

As soon as Kim started up her car, the police were all over her. It was my lucky day too. Not only did they find the gun Pit always kept in the car, they also found a Kilo of dope. That was the final nail in her coffin.

Pitt always worried about what Kim knew. It never occurred to him that I was watching his every move and doing a little investigating myself. While we were still seeing each other, I went through his glove ompartment. I had a feeling his car was in someone else's name. Never in a million years did I think that someone was Kim. After all, he supposedly hated her. As mad as I was about it, I didn't say anything. I always knew the information would come in handy one day.

I watched with great pleasure as they cuffed Kim. Feeling a sense of victory, Vicki and I drove to pick up Zeta, then headed for the highway.

I Shoulda Seen It Comin'

We got to Sheba's house in Virginia Beach around 8:00 p.m. I had arranged to stay with her until I moved in the next day. We sat up for hours talking. I didn't know that while I was away, she was going through it herself. She'd lost a baby in what seemed to be a questionable mishap at a hospital where she was being treated. From what I could see, not only did she lose her baby, but she lost part of her sanity too. After listening to her, I told her about all the bullshit I had been through. Not to mention, the extreme measures I had to take to get home. All she could say is "Girl, you crazy. What if he finds you?"

"He won't. He thinks I'm from New York. Besides he'll be too busy making sure Kim doesn't roll over on him."

    The next morning, we drove the truck over to my new apartment. My mother was there as usual lending a helpful hand. She never questioned me about my abrupt departure. But I knew it was on her mind.
    After we unpacked the truck, I sat on the floor, gazing up at the ceiling. I asked myself how I had gotten to this point. It was because I left one bad situation for another, only to do the same damn thing again. *Wise up, Zsaset, wise up.*

Chapter Twenty-6

I never realized how much I missed being around my family and friends. Most of all, I realized how much of my son's life I had missed out on. I thought that now that I was home, things would fall in place and I could start living a simple life again, but that didn't happen. Instead things got worse.

Vicki and I decided to do a budget to see how long I had before I would have to find a job. It was depressing, considering I only had a thousand dollars left after all of my moving expenses. But I knew what I had to do, so I did it.

First, I made an agreement with Vicki to watch Zeta until she started school in the fall. It made more sense for her to stay at home with Zeta because daycare was too expensive.

I started my day off job hunting. Hours of driving around, I finally found a job at a hotel. It was a dump, but at least it would pay the bills. Then I headed to a parking lot near Norfolk State and sold the clothes I took from the store. *This G should hold me over,* I thought to myself.

After my first day at the hotel, I wanted to quit. The shit they did in those hotel rooms was enough to make you never want to sleep in a hotel bed again.

It only took me a couple of days to get the hang of the job, thanks to this lady named Ann. She knew all the ins and outs of making money at the hotel.

"First, sweetie, remember we get paid by how many rooms we clean, not how well we clean them. So only change the linen if it's dirty. Trust me they won't even know the difference. Half of them are only here for a booty call anyway."

"Are you sure they can't tell?"

"Hell, I'm positive. I been doin' this for 10 years."

I Shoulda Seen It Comin'

We both began laughing so loud it made the other workers look at us suspiciously. I guess they thought it was about them.

"Now here's the next thing. We get paid for the sleepovers too. So go to their rooms first because nine times out of ten, they don't want to be bothered that early in the morning. They'll just tell you to give them some towels. Last but not least, if you get assigned to room 112 or if someone wants to give that room up, take it."

"Why?" I asked.

She got closer. "I'll tell you why. There's this nasty old man in there who tips real well. Sure, you'll want to throw your breakfast up, but trust me, it's worth it. Just hold your breath and go for it."

I did just that too. A couple of days after Ann schooled me, I was assigned to clean room 112. I knocked on the door and tried to prepare myself for the worst. But there was no preparation for what my eyes witnessed. There were dirty clothes thrown all over the bed and a trashcan overflowing with Wendy's bags. And the smell. Thank God I didn't eat breakfast.

I quickly went in and poured Pine Sol all over the bathroom. It helped a little, but not enough. As I cleaned the bathtub, I noticed the old man staring at me. *What a jerk*, I thought to myself. I noticed his eyes piercing through my clothes. I decided to leave the tub as is and move on to the trash so I could keep my eye on him. I cleaned the rest of the room then I walked over to make the bed.

"No thanks, sweetheart. You don't have to make the bed," the man said in a bass tone.

"Are you sure?" I asked.

"Yes, I'm sure."

"Okay, you have a nice day," I said as I walked towards the door.

"You too. By the way, what's your name?"

"My name is Zsaset."

"A pretty name for a pretty girl."

"Oh and before I forget, here's a little somethin' for you." He handed me the balled up bill from his sweaty sock that he had tucked under his mattress.

"Thank you."

I walked out of the room and took the deepest breath ever. I unfolded my hand to see how much he gave me. It was a fifty-dollar bill. Ann was right. I took my cleaning cart back to the laundry room then grabbed Ann to tell her about the man in room 112.

"Did Miss Ann put you down or what," she said like she was twenty years old.

"Yeah, but that's your connect."

"So if I get his room tomorrow, I'll give it to you."

"Honey, you got to do what you got to do. Now that old geezer done got a look at you, Miss Ann don't stand a chance."

Miss Ann and I sat near the hotel at a picnic bench and ate our lunch. It was refreshing to talk to someone from the old school. I valued her words of wisdom. I knew I had a friend for life in Miss Ann. That was until she told me she was moving back to North Carolina on Friday. "Can't make it here in this big city no more, babe."

"Big city? Norfolk is a joke."

"It may be a joke to you, but it ain't no joke to me. You know I also get a Social Security check and a retirement check and I still can't make ends meet. So I'ma move on back home and stay with my sister and her husband. They ain't even gonna charge me no rent. Can't beat that."

"No you can't. Well I guess I'll see you tomorrow, Miss Ann," I said in a somber tone.

"If Lord willin' you sure will," she said.

I left the hotel feeling like I had just lost my best friend.

On the way home, it hit me that I hadn't been to the old restaurant I used to work at. To my amazement, my old manager was still there. Her name was Harriet. She was smart as hell and just as beautiful.

"Oh my God, Zsaset is that you? Where have you been? And more importantly where is that cute baby of yours?

"I moved to Richmond for a while. And that Ryan ain't no baby no more. I got two kids now, my youngest, Zeta, is almost five."

"How did you like it?"

"It was okay." I knew she could tell I was lying, but she didn't press me for any more information. When I told her that I was working at the Travel Lodge, she shook her head.

"That dump. Girl, you better come on back here and work for me. You know I'll look out for you. Not to mention, we'll have fun like old times."

I couldn't believe the whole crew still worked there. They practically begged me to come back. I finally agreed. Since Miss Ann was leaving the hotel, there was really no reason for me to stay.

"So, Miss Lady, when can you start? Please say by the end of the week because my cook is getting transferred and I really don't feel like working twenty-four seven up in this camp, if you know what I mean."

"Yeah, I hear you. I can start Monday."

"Thank you, baby, and welcome back home. I'll see you Monday, okay. I have to get back to work. You want something to eat?"

"You know I do."

"I'll tell my girl to hook you up, alright?"

I ate my food and went home.

Bored, I asked Vicki if she wanted to ride with me over to Sheba's. I didn't have anyone else's address, so I thought I'd go over and kick it with her for a while.

Hanging out with Sheba bought back memories of old times. With a cold Heineken in one hand and blunt lit in the other, Sheba sat on the couch getting bent. After copping a beer, we sat down beside her.

"Alright, give me all the dirt that's been going on since I've been gone."

"Bitch, I hope you got all night 'cause that's how long it would take me to tell you everythin'."

"It's like that?"

"Is it? Girl, Norfolk is off the hook now. I got all these niggas 'round here payin' my bills, gettin' my hair and nails did, and I'm drivin' their whips."

"Well, you gone wit ya bad self."

"Don't worry, I'ma find a baller for you."

"No thanks, I had enough of that shit in Richmond."

"Well you ain't in Richmond no more and them bills gots to get paid. "You think about it." I didn't have to think about it. It was a wrap for me and hustlers and I meant it.

"Girl, what is up with Brina and them?" She hesitated and then went on to give me the low down. It seems things had really changed while I was gone.

Brina married a guy she had met right after I left and moved to Atlanta. Janet, Brina's cousin, was living it up in Chesapeake with her boyfriend who was down with the Wu Tang Clan. From what Sheba told me, she wasn't allowed to associate with anyone or go out to clubs anymore. Trey, who used to live next door to Nicole, was somewhere around and it was rumored that she had the HIV virus, which had everyone in an uproar since she had been through the whole city. Even the girls were worried. Norfolk was so small that most of the girls fucked guys in the same circle. So if she had it, that meant they had it. As for Nicole, she was still just being Nicole—crazy as ever. She had a baby by a Jamaican drug lord who was just as crazy as she was if not worst.

It seems money was plentiful. Norfolk was popping just like Richmond. If you had a nice car and your own place, you were good to go. Conversation was short unless it was, I need my hair

I Shoulda Seen It Comin'

did, or I need some new clothes, or I need my nails fixed. The D.C., New York, and Miami niggas were the ones really getting it though. They were all tied up with the same people because money was floating around from everywhere. The athletes, stars, musicians, and the hustlers were all intertwined together. And just think, all this transpired while I was in Richmond.

Chapter Twenty-7

It was my last day at the hotel and the last day I would see Miss Ann. We cleaned our rooms, shared a tearful goodbye, then went our separate ways.

I arrived home and was greeted by Zeta. She ran to my car with a bag filled with candy in tow.

"Who gave you that?"

"Grandma."

"That figures. She don't have to deal with you tonight."

I was so upset about Miss Ann that I didn't even notice my mother's car in the parking lot.

"What you up to?" I asked hugging her.

"Nothin' much. Just came by to see how you were getting along."

"I'm fine."

"Well what ya'll up to tonight?" she asked

"Nothing I guess. It ain't like I have anywhere to go. Well, I probably could find somewhere to go if I had a babysitter."

"I knew that was comin'. I'll take her tonight. Ryan would love to spend some time with her."

"Speaking of Ryan, I can take him now if you want."

I think the question caught her off guard because she started babbling something about needing him to stay because she was sick. I knew it was an excuse. She just wanted to keep him. She had him so long it was like he was her son. I understood. Besides I couldn't afford to keep him if I wanted. And that made me feel like shit. But I was determined to get my life in order. My kids needed to be together and the only way that was going to happen was for me to get my shit together.

I Shoulda Seen It Comin'

That night, I called Sheba and asked her where the party was. I knew she would know. She lived to party. But although those days were over, I wasn't pressed about going out. My mind was on money and how to make it.

She gave me the directions to Picassos where she was going to be. I was to look for her in a jean mini skirt and Moschino halter top.

We arrived at the club around 11:00 p.m. The parking lot was packed.

"I don't remember there being a club here," I said, looking at the building.

"Maybe they just opened it," Vicki said, throwing a cigarette butt out the window.

She was right. The club used to be a sports store. Some Nigerian bought it and made it a club.

The club resembled the club we used to go to in Richmond. We walked around and I saw a few people from back in the day, but not many. We bought a drink then found a nice spot to stand in to get a good view of everyone. I think every guy in the club wanted to be a mini Biggie Smalls. I saw niggas in fake me out Versace shirts and short sleeved Coogi sweaters. And don't get me started on the Fagazy Gators. They were wack to death. But let them tell it, they were the shit.

Then out of nowhere, I felt someone grab me. It was Nicole's crazy ass.

"Girl, where the hell you been?" Nicole said, hitting me on the shoulder.

"I moved to Richmond for a while."

"So what you just visitin'?"

"Naw, I'm home for good. I got tired of livin' in that country ass city."

"So have you seen Sheba yet? You know she lost her baby."

"Yeah, she told me."

"What else did she tell you?"

"Nothin'. Why?" I asked looking at her with curiosity. I thought she was talking about something else, but she was actually talking about the fact that she too had a baby. "Oh, yeah. So what do you have, a boy or a girl?"

"I got a little boy. Girl, he be gettin' on my nerves and his dumb ass daddy be actin' stupid and shit." I assumed she was talking about the Jamaican Sheba told me about. She then went on to tell me how much more of a freak Sheba was now. "Zsaset, that bitch be trickin' hard now. She done fucked the whole Norfolk, Virginia Beach, Portsmouth, and surroundin' areas. She better not think about fuckin' my baby daddy though. 'Cause me and my girls will not hesitate to fuck her ass up."

Trying not to get in the middle of whatever they had going on, I changed the subject. "So who are your girls?"

"Hey, girls. Come here, this is my girl, Zsaset."

As we were exchanging greetings, Sheba walked up. You could have cut the tension with a knife.

"Hey, Zsaset. I see you found the club. Well when you finish talkin' come over to our table. I got this guy to buy us some Moet."

"Okay," I said confused. "I'll be over in a minute."

After Sheba left, I asked Nicole what was going on between them. "Nothin' really, I just don't like that bitch no more."

In other words, what Nicole was telling me was that she was jealous of Sheba. Come to think of it, she always was. Sheba was a very descent looking girl. Of course that wasn't the reason guys were crazy about her. It was more about her big ass and double D titties. She was the girl every guy wanted to get with. So what was so special about that now? Then it hit me. Nicole's baby daddy must have been trying to hit it.

There wasn't too much Nicole could do about it. If he wanted it and his money was long, Sheba was going to give it to him. Not even an ass whipping was going to stop her flow.

I grabbed a napkin from the bar and wrote Nicole's number down. Sheba and her were no longer friends, but they were both

I Shoulda Seen It Comin'

still my girls and I was determined to get them back on track. We had been friends too long for them to let some shit like Sheba fucking whoever to come between them.

I went over to Sheba's table and lit a cigarette. As I sipped on my Heineken, I noticed Nicole's friends staring at me. One of them even whispered something to her. I started to go over and ask her if she had something she wanted to say to me. *I don't got time for that shit,* I thought to myself. *Nicole will give them the 411. And that's not to fuck with me.*

Hanging out with Sheba brought back a lot of memories. The only thing that was different was everyone had his or her own little crew now. Sheba's crew was all about money. They had to game niggas with their looks and their moves in cheap hotel rooms to get money, clothes and jewelry. They wore Coogi dresses, Fendi, Prada, and Versace and they were all iced out. I bet they thought they were real smart, but just how smart do you have to be to ride someone's dick. You're smart when you can use your head and not your body to get what you want. That was me. I refused to be anyone's hoe. Know what I mean?

Around 1:00 a.m., it was so tight in the club, I thought I was going to pass out. It didn't help that they kept playing Total's song *Can't You See.* I mean damn, all the music on the radio and they had to play that song every five minutes. Norfolk was definitely not like Richmond when it came to music. Where the hell was the Go-Go music? Richmond was considered little D.C.. We would pop to go-go all night in the club.

Just when I was about to give up on the D.J., he started playing Biggie's *One More Chance.* Now that was my shit. Puffy was doing his thang with the music. I danced to my song then Sheba and I decided to cruise around the club. As we were walking, I noticed a large group of guys, who from the looks of their clothes, were definitely not locals.

"Sheba, who are those guys. I recognize some of them."

"Girl, they're called the Reservoir Dogs."

"Reservoir Dogs?"

"Where they from?"

"They're from D.C., New York, Philly, and Connecticut. But they hang over in Brambleton at the weed spot."

Now these were some fly ass niggas. They wore FUBU, Phat Farm, Enyce, and Ecko. And they all were iced out. It was sick. We played our positions next to them. Then out of nowhere, the ugliest guy I had ever seen in my life walked right up to me and asked me my name. This dude was way off base if he thought he could get with me.

"Hey, ma. Whatcha name again?"

"I don't remember telling you the first time."

"I know yo brotha, he told me."

"What?"

"You K-Dog's sister, right?"

I looked him up and down and then turned my head. I didn't know this dude and I wasn't saying shit. If I learned anything in Richmond, I learned not to claim anybody until you knew why. For all I know, he could be trying to kill K-Dog or something.

"I saw you in the projects with K-Dog one time when I was up there re-uppin'."

"I don't remember. And why would you say somethin' like that to me. I could be the Feds for all you know."

"'Cause I know you not. But you right. You right. Sorry."

"Well, next time you see yo brotha, ask him 'bout me."

"You didn't have to tell me that, I was gonna do it anyway." He started to laugh. "Well I'll check you later, ma."

Disgusted with his ugly face, I told Sheba I was about to go.

"Hey, wait a minute. You know Don Juan?"

"Naw, but he claims he knows me from K-Dog."

"Oh, well I'll call you tomorrow."

"Alright, see you."

By the time I got home, I could barely keep my eyes opened. Just when I was in the best part of my sleep the phone rang.

I Shoulda Seen It Comin'

Cursing who ever was on the other end, I reached over and picked it up.
"Hello."
"What's up, sis?"
"K-Dog, I'm gonna kill your ass. I just got to sleep."
"Well wake up, tootsie. I haven't talked to you in a while. What, you forgot about yo big brotha already?"
"No. I've just been working."
"Well you're off work now so let's talk." K-Dog could never take no for an answer. He just kept on talking. He wanted to know everything from how Zeta was doing to who I was dating.
"By the way, some ugly ass guy told me to ask you about him. I think Sheba told me his name was Don Juan or some shit like that."
"Yeah, that's my man from Ni Y."
"I guess that means New York."
"Yeah. That nigga ugly, but he's paid out the ass. That's why I'm callin' you. He owes me money, but he can't drive it up here to me. And I need it like yesterday."
"So what the hell that got to do with me?"
"I was wonderin' if you could bring it to me. I'll tell you right now he'll give you five hundred bones to do it. He might even give you more than that if you play yo cards right. What do you say?"
"I don't know."
"Please. Haven't I been there for you? Won't I always be here for you?"
"Oh shut up. I'll bring it. Besides I do need the money. My car note is due. Call me tomorrow after you talk to Don Juan."
"Will do. Talk to you tomorrow."

It was Saturday morning and if I had my way I would have slept all day. Unfortunately, K-Dog wasn't going to let that happen. He called all morning. Not answering the phone was not working so I decided to get up. After sitting on the edge of my bed for five minutes trying to get my thoughts together, I washed up, made me some breakfast and then sat in the living room with Vicki.

"Who dat keep callin'?" Vicki asked irritating the hell out of me.

"What the fuck is dat? I told you about makin' up words, girl."

"Okay, who was that telephoning all morning, Miss Zsaset?"

"Dat would be K-Dog," I said, walking to the kitchen.

"Listen at you."

"I'm just playing. He needs me to drive some money to Richmond."

"You ain't got no money."

"Bitch, you don't know what I got."

"You right. But I do know that you ain't got no money."

I hated to admit it but she was right. My savings were dwindling. Once I paid my car note, I would be broke. So I decided I better get with the program and call K-Dog back before they found someone else.

I got the instructions from K-Dog then called Don Juan and told him where to meet me. I told him to meet me at the 7-Eleven near my home because I didn't want him trying to pop up later, like he was all familiar with me and shit. It was not going down like that.

Around 2:00 p.m., Vicki and I headed to the store where I was going to meet Don Juan. All the way there we cracked on the fact that his nickname was Don Juan, especially since he was tore up from the floor up. When we pulled into the parking lot, Don Juan was there with this guy I remembered seeing with him in the club. He wasn't anywhere near Don Juan's status. I could tell this from his shoes alone, but he wasn't bad looking. He was medium height with a dark complexion, thick beautiful eyebrows and long eyelashes that give him a magazine-man look.

"What's up, ma? I told you yo brotha knows me."

I Shoulda Seen It Comin'

"That's my brother, and I don't know you so stop calling me ma. My name is Zsaset."

"That's just an expression. I don't mean no disrespect."

"Good, now let's get down to business."

His man looked at me like he wanted to smack me, but it didn't faze me. If he knew K-Dog, then he knew what would happen if he did. So I cut him a slick smile and then turned my attention back to Don Juan.

He dropped a bundle in my lap and then peeled off seven one hundred dollar bills.

"That's for you. Just to show you how I get down just in case I need you again."

There was no doubt that if he needed me again I would be there. Seven hundred dollars to drive an hour and a half round trip was well worth it.

He got out of the car and pimped into the store. As soon as he got out of sight, I picked up the bundle and inspected it.

"How much money do you think that is?" Vicki asked.

"I'm not sure, but it's a lot. I wonder why he just didn't drive it himself. He would've saved himself a lot of dough," I said with a smirk.

It only took us about 40 minutes to get to Richmond and when we crossed the city line, I felt my heart started to pump fast. I hadn't talked to anyone since I had left so I wasn't sure what was going on with Pit and Kim. Last I heard, they both got arrested, but made bail. The last thing I needed was to run into either one of them. After all, I had cleaned out the store, ran off with Pit's money and gotten them both hemmed up. Just thinking about what he would do if he caught up with me made me smoke three cigarettes back to back. It was too late to be thinking about what ifs. So I just said, "Fuck it."

The drive through the projects brought back memories. Norfolk had projects, but they weren't anywhere near the projects in Richmond. People were getting killed left and right. It had gotten so bad, one time they had to call in the National Guards.

That didn't stop them. They even ran them out of the projects. I guess the Guards said fuck that. Let these fools kill themselves, we're out of here.

When we pulled in front of K-Dog's spot, he ran out and grabbed me up in the air.

"What's up, Zsa Zsa? I missed you, girl."

"I missed you too, crazy."

"Okay enough of that shit. Where's my gold?"

"Now that's triflin'."

"I know, but you know me." We stayed while K-Dog counted his money. All of the money was in order so K-Dog gave me five more bones and walked us to the car. "I'll see you next month around the same time."

"What?" I asked.

"I know he paid you well, so I trust when he calls you again, you'll be more than willing to oblige."

"I don't think so. I don't have time to be running up and down the highways. Besides what if I get caught?"

"You still got yo business license, right?"

"Yeah, and?"

"Well there you go. Just tell them that you're on your way to New York to buy some clothes for your business."

"You know, sometimes you're just too damn smart for your own good."

"Well you know, what can I say? I'm just smart like that."

Vicki and I left a little while later.

As we were driving, my mind drifted back to all the shit I had been through in Richmond. I thought going home would get me focused. But just when I thought I was out of the game, I got sucked right back in it. *Damn.*

Chapter Twenty-8

I woke up Monday morning ready to start my new job. I used to love working at Captain D's. We used to have so much fun like when we would laugh at fat customers that came in and ordered damn near everything on the menu.

I was a prep cook and although I didn't eat seafood, I sure could cook it. Then again, there wasn't too much I couldn't cook well. My mother was a great cook and it just filtered down. I didn't realize how much I missed cooking, since I had just about stopped while I was living in Richmond.

I walked into the restaurant with my combat boots on to some familiar and some not so familiar faces. Harriet had a whole new crew of misfits. She introduced me to these two knuckle heads who found me to be funny. See, what they didn't know was that I used to be the prep cook a few years ago, so I knew what I was getting into. Washing big pans, pulling fish out of a fryer two times my size, and breading and divining 30 pounds of shrimp was nothing to me. And believe me, I let it be known. I put them to shame. Just think. It took two of them to do what I did by myself back in the day.

They sweated my skills so much they gave me a high five.

"You worked it today, shorty. By the way, what's up with the combat boots?"

"I used to be in the Marines. When I put in work, I dress the part."

"Oh. Is that why you so strong?" one of them asked.

"I guess you can say that. Just let today be a lesson to you."

"Let what be a lesson to us?"

"Well, when I first walked in, you thought I was a rookie. Remember, never judge a book by its cover. See you tomorrow."

I walked out.

Vicki had this silly grin on her face when I walked in the house.

"What's up with you? What's so funny?"

"Guess who called you?" I didn't know, but I could tell she couldn't wait to tell me.

"I don't feel like guessing, Vicki."

"It was Lucky."

"Who is Lucky?" I asked.

"Remember the guy that was with Don Juan the other day when we met up with him? You know the one who gave you the evil eye?"

"Yeah," I said hesitantly. "What did he want?" I asked pouring myself some juice.

"I don't know. He wants you to call him."

"I don't think so."

"What if it's about us going back to Richmond?"

"Too bad, I'm not in the mood for a road trip tonight. Plus he looked kind of sinister." I paused. "Something seemed kinda strange about him."

"Aw, you being paranoid," Vicki laughed.

Going back and forth with Vicki made me even more tired than I already was. She loved to keep shit going. I loved her to death, but sometimes she could make me want to kill her with all the nagging.

Smelling like I just got off a fish boat, I ripped off my clothes and jumped in the shower. I walked out with my towel wrapped snugly around me and headed to my room. Minutes later, Vicki was standing in the doorway with the phone in her hand.

"Who is it?" I asked annoyed.

"I think its Lucky."

"You think or you know."

"I know," she said, handing me the phone.

"Didn't I tell you I wasn't interested in talking to him?"

I Shoulda Seen It Comin'

"Well I already told him you were home."

I grabbed the phone and plopped on my bed. "Hello."

"What's up, shorty."

"My rent," I said sarcastically. Lucky chuckled.

"So why aren't you interested in talkin' to me? You don't even know what I want." *Her dumb ass ain't even have enough sense to put the phone on mute.*

"So what do you want? I was just about to get into bed."

"Have you eaten yet?"

"No, I'm not hungry."

"Oh, I just thought maybe we could go to the Fisherman's Wharf or something."

Is he kidding me? I just left a smelly fish restaurant and I was not about to go to another one. "No thanks, maybe some other time. I just got off work and I'm kinda tired."

"I hope this isn't because we didn't hit it off the other day."

"How could we? We didn't say two words to each other."

"I know. That's what I mean. I was havin' a bad day. Not to mention, you were rollin' off with over $30,000 of our money."

"So you didn't trust me, uh."

"I don't trust anyone."

"That's nice to know."

"I didn't mean it like that. It's just that I didn't know you and we were supposed to just trust you because you were my man's sister."

"That's alright, I understand. You didn't trust me."

"I guess you ain't gonna cut a nigga no slack, uh?"

"No. Cut a Nigga Some Slack Day is tomorrow."

I could see his smile through the phone and before I knew it we were laughing until three in the morning. He was funny and I enjoyed our conversation, but I just wasn't interested in getting involved with anyone. That didn't stop him from trying though. He called me everyday after that.

Danette Majette

Working at Captain D's was going well. I learned the new menu in a matter of days, but going home everyday smelling like fish bugged the hell out of me. I stuck it out though because I knew it wasn't going to be for long. I had bigger plans for my life and it didn't include working in someone else's kitchen. I wanted to be a clothes buyer, but I needed to get my degree first. Having a high school diploma was good, but having a college degree was even better. I decided that as soon as I got an opportunity, I was going to apply to Tidewater Community College.

Then there was Lucky. He was putting the full court pressure on me until I agreed to go out on a date with him. He didn't have a car in Virginia so Don Juan dropped him off at the store near my apartment. I met him there to be on the safe side. For him to be a thug, he was very romantic. First, he bought me some flowers and then when we got to the restaurant he pulled out my chair. Very impressive, I must say. Especially since I never had a guy do that for me before. He was really sweet. We talked about life, what we liked to do, the places we've been, and the places we'd like to go. He seemed to have his shit together, but that could very well have been an act.

Lucky didn't look how I remembered. I guess I hadn't looked at him good enough last time I saw him. He was still cute, but in a quirky sort of way. He was kind of cocky. He had a tattoo of a dragon on his neck. He had nice hair and pretty lips. But it was something about his eyes that was kind of strange. They were warm most of the time but every now and then as we talked they would look sort of empty as if there was nothing behind them. But Lucky was really a gentleman. I thought about what Vicki said about me being paranoid.

After dinner, we decided to go and take a walk at the Waterside Mall. It was the first time I had been there in years and it was just as beautiful as I remembered it. The air was filled with the scent of salt water and the night air was stimulating. Holding hands as we watched the boats sail by, we walked along the pier. I was having so much fun I hadn't realized how much time had passed. I didn't want the night to end, but I had to work the next morning. So we left.

On the way home, I asked him if there was anywhere he wanted me to take him.

"Do you think you could give me a ride to Portsmouth? I'll give you gas money," he said, digging his pocket.

"That's not necessary. You've already done enough tonight."

We pulled into a parking lot of this run-down neighborhood in Portsmouth not far from the waterfront. It looked like the projects where K-Dog hangs out.

"Where do you live?"

"I live down the street, but I can walk from here."

"Oh, so you don't want me to know where you live?"

"Somethin' like that. It's no big deal though, right. You did the same thing." That kind of caught me off guard. I guess he called himself playing tick for tack. It was cool. Actually, it was kinda cute. I didn't want to know where he lived anyway.

"Oh no, I totally understand. You can't be too sure about people nowadays," I said as I flashed him a smile.

I thanked him for a pleasant evening with a kiss on the cheek. We planned to see each other again.

I sat back on my bed, staring at the clock on the night table. *Damn, I got to get up in five hours.*

Vicki walked in. "So how was it?" she asked all in my grill.

"It was a date. You know. We ate, talked, and walked it off. Now if you don't mind, I gotta get some sleep."

Chapter Twenty-9

For the next few weeks, Lucky and I became inseparable. After I would get home from work, I would call him. He always came right over. The only day we didn't spend together was Saturday. That's because I would go out and meet up with Nicole and her crew. Sheba and I were still friends but her crew was just too much for me to handle. They were all stuck up and their attitudes irritated the hell out of me.

Most of the time, Lucky was there stalking me. I didn't notice it at first, but he was very possessive. I didn't notice it because he was spoiling me even though we hadn't been intimate yet. He would always make sure no one got to close to me. If they did he would whisper something in their ear. Whatever he said got their attention because they wouldn't say anything else to me.

One Saturday night instead of going out, I decided to stay home. I was flipping through the cable channels when I noticed a shadow at my door. I got up to inspect it, and the doorbell rang. Thinking it was Lucky, I opened it with a big smile. It wasn't him but the smile was still warranted. It was my little cousin, Monique.

"Girl, I heard yo ass was back. What, you can't call nobody?"

"I didn't have your number," I said lying.

"Bullshit."

"You could'a got it from your momma."

"You're right. You caught me. I've just been trying to get used to being back home. Ya'll come in."

Monique and I were always close. When she was a little baby, the only one she would behave for was me. I remember one night my aunt was trying to take some pictures of her, and she kept crying, so my aunt told me to try to get her to sit still. I didn't think she would listen to me either but she did. From that day, I could get her to do anything.

"You remember Laisha don't you? She used to live a couple of doors down from us."

"Little Laisha. Oh my God. I haven't seen you since you were a little youngin', running in and out of our house. Now look at you."

"I know. I moved to D.C. with my father to go to high school. I moved back here after I graduated," Laisha said.

"So now what do you do?"

"I'm doing hair now."

"Good, I need someone to do my hair."

Laisha and Monique were best friends when we lived in Tidewater Park. They would always sit on the front porch and play. Neither Laisha's mother, nor my aunt would let them any further than the porch. They thought the neighborhood was too dangerous.

We sat for hours talking, laughing, and getting to know each other again. They gave me all the gossip. It was like I never left.

I was kneeling down picking up my shoes when I noticed that Monique's feet were swollen.

"Girl, looks like you picked up a little weight," I said.

"A little. Shit, try a lot."

"Well, you better lay off them cheeseburgers," I said teasingly.

"That ain't gonna help. I'm pregnant."

"What? Oh my god. What did your mother say?"

"What can she say? I'm 19 and out of high school."

"So who's the daddy?"

"The guy I been dating from high school."

"Well, I'm happy for you. And if you ever need anything you just let me know."

She told me she was glad to hear me say that because she was taking some night college courses and needed to borrow my car.

Danette Majette

"My dad is gonna buy me a car but he just told me he can't get it until next month and the classes start Tuesday," she said. I told her she could. "Thanks, cuz," she said with one arm around my neck.

We talked a little more then we were interrupted by a knock at the door. When I opened it, Lucky was standing there with this big grin on his face.

"Hey, ma. I missed you today."

"I see. But I told you I was staying in to spend time with Zeta tonight. So why are you here, sweetie?" I said, gritting my teeth.

"I needed to see you," he said with a sad look on his face.

"Alright, come in," I said. I locked the door then led him to the living room. "Lucky, this is my cousin, Monique and her friend, Laisha. Ladies, this is my friend, Lucky."

"I'm more than her friend, I'm her boyfriend."

"Excuse me. You're not my boyfriend until I say you are," I said with an attitude.

"Has she always been this mean?"

"Yep," Monique said in laughter.

The girls left and Lucky and I chilled in my room. He smiled at me as he lit a blunt.

"Ma, hit this," he said, blowing smoke from his nostrils.

"Boy, no. You know I don't smoke weed."

"It's better than smokin' them cigarettes."

"At least they're legal."

"Ma, stop actin' crazy and hit it."

Curious, I took a puff. As soon as I exhaled, I felt my body tingle all over. Then I felt relaxed.

"Ma, don't you think it's time?"

Even though I knew what Lucky was talking about, I smiled and said, "Time for what?"

"You know what."

The thinking part of me thought it was still too soon, while another part of me—and you can guess which part—thought it was just the right time to be taking things to the next level. But once he started kissing my lips and fingertips, I didn't really care if it was too soon, too right or too wrong. It had been a while since someone had made love to me and no matter what, I was going to take a chance.

"So this was the plan, huh, Lucky? Get me high and take advantage of my weakened state." Lucky smiled a smile that said that was exactly the plan.

Lucky kissed my neck softly and then said, "Ma, I would never do that."

Succumbing to temptation, I allowed Lucky to remove my clothes. He explored my body with kisses that filled me with desire. Lucky massaged my nipples with his tongue and slowly moved down to my stomach. After he lingered at my stomach too long, I softly pushed his head down. The heat between my legs had built up to a small fire. I couldn't take it anymore. I needed his tongue to douse the flames. As he began to slide his tongue lightly across my clit, I started gasping for air, my heart raced wildly. Lucky put his tongue inside me. I could feel it snake deep within me. He took it out and slid it across my clit again. And then he put it back inside. After he repeated this a few times, I called out his name and held him tightly as my body began quivering. Lucky came from my middle and took one long lick all the way up to my neck. He sucked my neck as he put just the tip of his manhood in me. I begged for the rest.

"C'mon, Lucky, stop playing with me. Give it to me."

"Let me take my time, Ma. I ain't going no where and neither are you."

"I need to feel you inside me, Lucky. Now, pleaaassse," I begged.

"You 'bout to, ma," he whispered. Lucky pulled back and then slowly put the tip in again. This time though, I raised my hips, grabbed his ass and I pulled him inside me all in one smooth, quick motion. "Damn, girl."

"Mmm, your dick feels soooo good," I moaned.

We made love for hours and fell asleep. I woke Lucky up at around 3 a.m. and asked him to leave.

Shocked, he asked, "Why?"

"I don't want Zeta to see you here in the morning. She's been through a lot over the years. She's seen guys come in and out of my life and I just have to stop the madness and start thinking of her."

"What's that got to do with me? I'm not like the other guys. I'm here to stay."

"I hear what you saying, Lucky, but you have got to know that I have heard that all before. Truth is, I'm not trying to get hurt again. I don't know if this is the real thing and if it isn't I don't want my daughter to see another man in and out of my bed. She saw enough of that in Richmond."

"I understand, ma, and I'ma respect that. He quickly got dressed. I'll see you tomorrow, alright?"

I walked him to the door and then returned to my room to dream. To dream about what could or could not be. *Here I go again.*

Monday morning when I returned to work, Lucky was in the parking lot waiting for me with some roses and a teddy bear.

"Pouring it on a little thick, don't you think," I said, taking the gifts from him.

"Not really. I'm tryin' to show you I'm serious 'bout this thing."

"What thing?"

"You and me."

I wanted to say something smart but I could tell he was speaking from the heart so I tried to give him the benefit of the doubt.

Running late, Harriet drove up and ran inside. I quickly thanked him and followed.

I Shoulda Seen It Comin'

"So who was that?"
"A friend."
"Some friend. Roses and a teddy bear. Looks serious."
"I don't think so. It'll be serious when he buys me a house."
"That's what I'm talking about. Forget the roses."

The restaurant was so busy, I didn't have time to eat. Harriet could see I was on my last leg, so she told me to go home early. When I got home, I had a surprise waiting for me. It was Monique.

She wanted to know if she could stay with me for a while. I asked why, but she was reluctant to talk about it. Not wanting to press the issue, I dropped the subject and just said, "Alright, cuz. No problem."

"Are you still going to school tomorrow?"
"Yeah, if I can still use your car."
"Of course you can."
"Well I guess I better get out of these stankin' clothes."
"Yeah, you do that."

It was good to see she still had a sense of humor even though she was upset.

Chapter Thirty

A few days turned into a few weeks and one houseguest turned into three. Laisha and Monique's boyfriend were living with us too now. It was cool though. We all got along great. Not to mention, I now had live-in babysitters.

As Lucky and I got closer, I started to let my guard down a little. Until one night I came home from work and found the weirdest thing.

"Hey, where is everyone?"

"Zsaset, is that you?"

"Yeah, where are you," I said as I walked into my room.

"I'm down here," Vicki whispered.

"What the fuck are you doing under my bed?"

She took a deep breath then told me Lucky threatened her. Apparently, he was mad because I wasn't home from work yet. I explained to her that I had stopped by my mother's house.

"Well he thinks you're out with someone else."

"Girl, are you kidding me?"

"No. He called here yelling and screaming at me. Then he told me that if you weren't home in fifteen minutes he was gonna come over here and shoot up the place."

The knock on the door sent Vicki right back under the bed. "Girl, get your ass from under the bed."

"Nope, it's him. He ain't gonna kill me."

"You need help, you know that." I left her under the bed and went to open the door. She was right. It was Lucky.

"W'sup, ma."

"Is that all you got to say?"

"What's wrong with you?" he asked trying to hug me.

"Did you tell Vicki you were gonna come over here and shoot her?"

"I was just playin' with her."

"Don't play like that."

Vicki emerged slowly from my room. She stared at him with fear. As soon as he saw her he started to laugh. "I'm sorry, Vicki. You accept my apology?" he said.

It took her a few seconds to respond. "As long as you don't do that shit again," she said, trying to break bad.

"I won't."

I calmed Vicki down as I changed my clothes. Lucky needed a haircut so we went to the barbershop where all the ballers hang out. It was the perfect hangout for them because it was across the street from Norfolk State University. Not only was it the hangout, it was the place hustlers turned good girls into bad ones. And the guys. They may have come to Norfolk State to fulfill their dream of getting a college degree, but only half of them actually did. The rest of them saw the hustler's life and couldn't hold out. So they ended up dropping out to make paper, as they called it. Not thinking about the fact that that paper was only temporary. If they had the sense to stay in school, they would have the kind of paper that would last a lifetime.

I never realized the pull Lucky had in Norfolk until we walked into the barbershop. As soon as his barber saw him, he made the guy already sitting get up.

"Go ahead, ma, and get your eyebrows done."

"I can wait for him to finish with the guy's hair cut."

"Naw, he can wait."

I didn't want to argue with him in front of everyone so I sat down. The barber finished my eyebrows then tended right to Lucky. I felt so ashamed, I couldn't even look at the guy. He couldn't look at me either. I kept a straight face on the outside but on inside I was laughing because his big sloppy ass looked like a little bitch. How do you let a barber put you out of his chair in the middle of getting your hair cut? I would've said, You better make that motherfucker wait. I ain't going nowhere. Shhiiitttt.

The guy slithered back into the chair when the barber signaled for him. Plopping down in the chair beside me, Lucky let it be known that I was his girl. As we sat, I noticed this guy eyeing me. It made me feel uncomfortable.

"Yo, son. You wanna talk to her? Go ahead. You can talk to her."

Trying to figure out what was going on, I looked at Lucky in confusion. Then I turned and looked at the guy. "Lucky, what are you doing?" I asked him.

"I'm sayin' that nigga lookin' like he want to say somethin' to you. Go head, big man, say somethin'."

"I ain't got time for this shit," I hissed.

"Hold on, babe. The man said I can holler at you and Big Daddy don't turn down no pussy," he said in laughter.

Wrong answer. Lucky went right over to him and cranked him in the head with his gun.

"Lucky…"

"Go to the car."

"But…"

"Go to the car."

I could hear Lucky yelling. "Don't chu ever disrespect me like that in front of my girl. You hear me, son," Lucky said. I was too afraid to look back. As a matter of fact, I sped up.

I couldn't hear the response over all the screaming inside the shop. I couldn't believe Lucky did that shit. That proved to be nothing.

Acting as though nothing happened, Lucky got in the car and started a casual conversation. I was so pissed off, I couldn't even look at him. It finally sank in that Vicki was right. Lucky was a loose cannon. I saw little signs of him being crazy, like his possessiveness, quick temper, and Dr. Jeckyl and Mr. Hyde

I Shoulda Seen It Comin'

behavior. But I mistook them for signs of him being crazy about me. I didn't say a word the whole way home. I just wanted to go hide. I had never been so embarrassed in my life. It wasn't like I was Janet Jackson or something. Not to mention, he gave the guy an open invitation to say something to me. All this shit because he wanted to play and flex his power.

By the time we got to my place, everyone was home. "Hey ya'll. Where ya'll been," Vicki asked.

Still heated, I didn't answer, I just went into my room.

"Lucky, what's wrong with her?" Monique asked.

"She mad at me. Don't worry though, she'll be alright." With his tail between his legs, Lucky walked into the room slowly. "I guess you're mad at me, uh?"

"You think? You could've killed him," I said, flopping on my bed.

Lucky told me I was blowing the whole situation out of control. I disagreed.

"What if the police come looking for you?"

Laughing he said, "That nigga ain't callin' 5-0."

"How do you know?"

"'Cause I know. Once they tell him who I am, trust me he ain't gonna say shit."

I wanted to tell him to get the fuck out, but I couldn't. I was falling for him hard. I knew he was running the streets and doing wrong, nevertheless I wanted to be with him. Instead of following my instincts, I followed my heart. I played with fire and I was about to get burned.

"So do you want me to leave? 'Cause if you, do I will," he said, kissing my hand tenderly.

I wish like hell I had been strong enough to say yes. But I didn't.

Instead we made love. And you know how good that make-up sex can be.

Danette Majette

Harriet was handing out checks when I strolled through the door. I lived for payday. I pushed my way through the line and stretched out my hand. "Here you go, Miss Zsaset."

I took my check and went into the dining room. My jaw dropped when I saw how much it was. I had work all that overtime and Uncle Sam took half of it. Stressed, I told Harriet I wasn't feeling well and asked to leave. How the hell was I going to survive off of $535.21? That wasn't enough for me to even pay my car note and insurance. Not to mention rent was due next week. And on top of all that, I had houseguests I had to feed, kids to clothe, and other bills to pay. I needed some money and I needed it quick. I went home to call K-Dog.

K-Dog could tell I wanted something because that was the only time I really called him. After crying the blues about my paycheck, I asked if he had any work that he needed done.

"What, you on some old code shit now?"

"Yeah, well I didn't think it would be a good idea to be talkin'
business over the phone."

"Good girl. I taught you well. Well as a matter of fact, I could use
yo help tomorrow. I need you to see that same guy. He'll give you the details."

I hung up with K-Dog and called Don Juan to find out what he needed me to do. He told me that he needed me to drive to Baltimore, pick up some money from this guy and then take it to New York.

"Why New York?"

"'Cause that's where K-Dog is."

The next day, Don Juan was there bright and early.

"Look, Don, driving to Richmond is one thing but driving to Baltimore and then New York is something totally different."

Seeing the skepticism on my face, Don Juan pulled out a small paper bag. Once I saw the contents, I knew I was on my way to New York.

"Do me a favor, Don. Don't mention this to Lucky." Don agreed not to but I couldn't tell if he would keep his word or not. Lucky had gotten so possessive that he would have told me not to go. I didn't have time for his nonsense. I made arrangements with Monique to watch Zeta, grabbed my purse and proceeded to my car.

"Excuse me. Didn't you forget someone," Vicki asked walking behind me. That's what I liked about Vicki. She was down for anything.

When we got close to Baltimore, I pulled out the directions to the McDonald's where we were supposed to meet Don Juan's friend. We made a few wrong turns before we finally reached our destination. Exhausted, we pulled into the parking lot and waited.

"So this is the infamous North Street," I said looking around.

"What's so special about this street?"

"I don't know. I just know that it's supposed to be pretty dangerous."

"Just great," she said, locking the doors.

Moments later, Don Juan's friend showed up. Dressed in a black hooded sweatshirt and jeans, he swaggered to the car and told us to follow him. We drove for what seemed like eternity before we ended up at an apartment outside the campus of Morgan State University.

"What the hell is going on?" I asked looking out the windows at the slew of SUV's parked in front of us.

"Zsaset, I don't know but I don't like it."

"Me neither."

We sat there for a few minutes then the guy signaled for me to follow him inside the apartment. I entered the apartment then took a look around just to make sure I wasn't being setup.

Danette Majette

Something I learned from watching K-Dog and O.B.. They were always aware of their surroundings when it came to doing business with strangers. After checking things out, I followed the guy into a small bedroom.

This guy was obviously inspired by Rambo movies. There were all kinds of weapons and grenades that looked like military issue lying on the floor.

What the fuck did he hit? An armory, I thought to myself.

"Here," he said, handing me a box. "Tell K-Dog I'll have the rest next week."

"Um...I would prefer if you told him that yourself. I don't get involved in that sort of stuff. I just pick up and deliver."

"You must can handle yourself pretty well, uh."

"Why do you say that?"

"It's not too often a beautiful young woman like you makes this kinda run. I mean, how they know you won't get robbed or somethin'?"

I didn't like his insinuations. Not to mention, he was scaring the hell out of me. So I fired back like I was a ride or die type chick.

"They don't. I don't even know that, but I don't worry about it. See, I'm K-Dog's sister and if anything happens to me, K-Dog would make sure the people responsible pay for it. Get my drift?"

"Yeah, I get your drift."

My bluff worked because the guy cut the conversation short and handed me a Milk Dog bone box wrapped in duck tape.

"What the hell is this?"

"It's the gold and the rest of the work. I wrapped it just in case you get pulled over. That way the dogs won't be able to smell the dope."

"Dope? He didn't say nothin' 'bout dope," I said, inspecting the box.

"Look, man, that's between you and him. I told Don Juan I was gonna send the rest of the work back with you."

I Shoulda Seen It Comin'

"Fine," I said, stomping towards the door. "How do I get back to I-95?"

"Come on I'll show you."

On the highway, I explained to Vicki why she had to do the speed limit. No more, no less. The last thing I needed was to get pulled over with thousands of dollars and dope in my possession. That would be instant jail time and I wasn't jail material. I knew that I was taking an enormous risk with my life, but I felt I had no other choice. I was broke. And being broke ain't no joke.

The ride to New York was quiet. I don't think we spoke two words to each other. I was too scared. The prospect of going to jail made my heart race. So I just prayed to God to get us there safely and without incident. If he did, I promised never to do it again.

We were in New York safe and sound. All I had to do then was call K-Dog and find out where we were going to meet.

"Meet me at Junior's in Brooklyn. You know where that is, don't you?"

"Of course. They have my favorite dessert."

"I know. That's why I told you to meet me there. I figured you could use a piece of strawberry cheesecake."

"See, that's why I love you. You know me like a book."

We ate our meal and shopped at every store in Brooklyn before heading back to Norfolk. This time I drove. It seemed only fair since Vicki drove all the way there. Our trip home was nothing like the way there. Instead we talked, laughed and basically acted a damn fool. We pumped the volume all the way up with the Wu-Tang Clan, Junior Mafia, Biggie, Beenie Man, and Buja Banton.

When we got to Maryland, we decided to stop at a rest area for something to eat. Stretching my arms, I noticed a man in a car watching us. I didn't recognize him, so I kept walking. We feed our faces then prepared to leave the restaurant. I was glad to see that the car I noticed before was gone. I took one last look around then we left.

We had just passed the *Welcome to Salisbury* sign when I noticed the same black Crown Victoria from the rest stop following us. At first, I figured the driver was just going the same way we were, but after making several turns, it was obvious he following us.

"Who do you think it is," Vicki asked.

Irritated by her stupid question, I hissed, "How am I supposed to
know, Vicki?"

"You don't have to get smart. I was just asking a question."

"I'm sorry. I'm just scared," I said, looking in the rear view mirror.

"What are you scared of? We already dropped the money and stuff off." She was right. What was I scared of?

We drove for about an hour and the same car was still behind us. Getting fed up I pulled into a gas station. To my surprise, the car kept going. I was relieved.

"I guess they were just going the same way," I said, watching the car pass.

"Thank, God. I was about to lose it."

"Vicki, you know sometimes you can be real paranoid. I mean to think someone was following us is just down right crazy."

"Oh shut up. You were scared too."

"You got that shit right. I was ready to jump out and fight whoever it was."

We had a big laugh then pulled back out into the traffic. I turned the music back up and we began to sing and act goofy again. All that was short lived when I saw the car behind us again. This time it was clear who it was. The flashing lights were a clear indicator. It was the Highway Patrol.

"Why are they pulling us over?" Vicki asked.

"I don't know. I'm not speeding."

I Shoulda Seen It Comin'

The big burly, red-neck looking dude with a stomach that looked like he was about nine months pregnant and ready to go into labor, walked up and asked me for my driver's license and registration.

"What did I do, officer?"

"Ma'am you were doing 80 in a 55 MPH zone."

"So why didn't you pull me over a long time ago? You've been following me for about an hour and a half now."

He seemed unfazed by my questions. Instead, he looked around in the car.

"Wow, looks like someone's been doing some serious shopping."

"Um…do you think you could just write my ticket so we can be on our way?"

"So where have you ladies been?"

"We were in New York."

"Alrighty… you ladies stay put, I'll be right back."

We sat in the car for fifteen minutes before the officer came back to the car. He looked down at my feet and asked me to put my shoes on and step out of the car.

"Why?" I asked.

"I just need you to come sit in my car for a minute."

If I wasn't scared before I was scared now. I seriously thought he was going to try and kill me or something. I heard so many stories about people pretending to be the police and killing people on the side of the highway. If Vicki hadn't been there I think I would've had a nervous breakdown.

As we walked back to his patrol car, I noticed this big ass dog in the backseat.

"Oh hell naw. I'm not sitting in there. Can't we talk out here?"

"Don't worry, he won't bite."

"Yeah, right."

This dog looked at me like I was his dinner and he wanted me to believe he wouldn't bite. Bullshit.

The officer opened the door and I scooted in. Then he walked back to my car and questioned Vicki. *If that bitch opens her mouth about what we were really doing in New York I'm going to kill her.*

Surprisily, she kept her cool. I guess he didn't get what he wanted from Vicki so he came back to the patrol car. Trying to see if we would slip up, he told me that Vicki told him the real reason we were in New York.

"Oh, she told you we were shopping for my store."

"No, she didn't mention a store."

"Really. That's strange."

See, the fat bastard didn't know that we already rehearsed what we would say if we ever got pulled over.

"Look, officer, we're telling you the truth. If you want I can show you my business license."

I hoped he wouldn't want to see it. He would've had even more questions. Why are you on your way to Norfolk if your store is in Richmond? Shit like that.

Then like the pig he was, he tried reverse psychology on me. "You know a lot of drugs come through these parts. And the drug dealers are getting smart now. They use pretty girls like you to transport them."

"Oh really. That's surprising," I said

"Yeah, we're trying to crack down on them. Say, you wouldn't happen to have any drugs or guns in the car would you?"

"No, I'm not in the habit of riding around with drugs in my car."

Frustrated with his red-necked ass I said, "Hey if it will help speed this process up, you can search my car."

"Well, you know, that would be best. That way we can get you and your friend on your way."

I knew that's what he wanted. Two black girls riding around in a nice car, with the back seat and trunk filled with bags from

I Shoulda Seen It Comin'

every store you can imagine in New York. Yeah, we were definitely drug runners. Funny thing is, he was right.

It didn't take long for the officer to swing into action. He got right on the horn and called for backup. Before I knew it, there were five more patrol cars. They sat on the hoods of their cars and had a big pow wow. Then the officer came back to the car.

After handcuffing Vicki and I, he sat us on the side of the road. Then they started going through my car with a fine-toothed comb. It was like an episode of *COPS*. They opened every bag and looked under the hood. The bastards even took the door panels off.

Pissed because they came up empty, the officer took the cuffs off.

"Thanks for letting us search your car. And just so there are no hard feelings, I'm not even gonna give you a ticket for speeding."

"Thanks, that's really kind of you," I said in a sarcastic tone.

What an ass. He's lucky he carries a gun, I thought to myself.

Staring at him with razor sharp eyes, I took my keys and got back into my car. Vicki followed. This was definitely a sign from God. What if this had happened before we got to New York? We both would've been sitting in jail. You don't have to drop a brick on my head, for me to get it. That was it for me.

Chapter Thirty-1

It took Vicki and I days to recover from our ordeal. I even had to call in and take a couple of days off from work. My stomach was all in one big knot. The food at work would have made it even worst. By the end of the week, we were both feeling better. With all of my bills paid and a pocket full of money left, it was time to go party. I got Vicki and Laisha to go to the club with me for a night out.

It was Friday night and Mr. Magic's was the place to be. When we got there, we met up with Nicole and her crew. We were having a ball. Lucky would come over and make his presence known every now and then, but that didn't stop my flow. He was only doing it to let guys know he was my man. He was so typical.

We danced until we were out of breath. By that time, the bathroom was calling. Of course, I dare not go alone. Women don't go to the restroom by themselves because bitches be hating. So we always had to be ready for them.

The line was ridiculous. But I had to go badly, so I waited.

"Zsaset, you springin' for the Moet tonight," Nicole said.

"What the fuck I look like? An ATM machine? I ain't rollin' in dough, bitch. Get one of these suckers to buy us a bottle."

"Girl, these fake ass niggas ain't buyin' no Moet unless you givin' up some ass."

"So give up some. Shit."

"I might just have to do that," she said in a playful tone.

I was relieved to see I was next for a stall because I knew something was about to happen. *There are too many women up in here,* I thought. My thoughts were interrupted by two girls arguing over a guy they both were seeing. The next thing I knew a bouncer came in and told everyone to clear out.

"I ain't goin' nowhere until I use the bathroom," I said.

"No, you're gonna get out like I told you," the bouncer said, walking up on me.

"Why? We ain't doing nothin'. That's them."

"I don't care who it is. Get out," she said, opening the door for me.

This big oversized bitch meant business. But so did I. I had to go and I was going. Before I could get another word out this ugly bitch snatched me up by the neck and started choking me. I tried to loosen up her grip, but couldn't. That's when Vicki, Nicole, Laisha, and the rest of the crew jumped in. The bitch still didn't budge. It just made her choke me even more. Nothing else was working so Nicole passed me a blade. The next thing I know she was grabbing her face screaming. Blood dripped on her shirt. With all the confusion, I didn't notice I had blood all over me too.

The club was in total chaos. People were screaming and running everywhere like someone had been shot. That's when we made our way out the back door. I was parked on the side so Vicki, Laisha and I got to my car first. Nicole and her crew were all parked in the front and still running to their cars by the time we pulled out of the parking lot.

"Did I slice her face?" I asked not remembering.

"I don't know. I couldn't see. Everything happened so fast," Vicki said.

"I remember Nicole passing me the blade, but I don't remember cutting her. I couldn't see and everything looked like it was moving in slow motion."

"You must've blacked out for a second," Laisha suggested.

"Shit, what if someone tells the police it was me," I said scared.

"All they can say is she was choking you. I doubt if they saw anything else. Shit, we were right beside you and we didn't even see what happened," Vicki said, trying to make me feel at ease.

"Girl, that shit was crazy as hell. She was choking the shit out of you. If you did cut her, it was self-defense. They don't have the right to do that," Laisha said pissed.

Laisha had a point. All I wanted to do was use the restroom. She had no business putting her hands on me.

"Do you think we should go to the police?" Vicki asked.

"Bitch, is you mad or somethin'. You think I'm gonna walk my black ass into a police station in Virginia Beach and confess that I cut someone's face up. Get real. They'll find me guilty before the trial even starts."

It was 2:30 a.m., when we got home and we couldn't wait to wake Monique up and tell her what happened.

"Ya'll bitches must done lost ya'll damn minds wakin' me up."

"We almost lost our freedom tonight,' I said, scooting her over on the bed.

We told her what happened then let her go back to sleep. We were too wired to sleep so we sat up and watched a movie. Halfway through it, Vicki and Laisha feel asleep. I was almost out too, when there was a knock on the door. It was Lucky and he didn't look happy.

"Ma, what chu doin' fighting at the club?"

"I wasn't fighting."

"Then what happened?" he said, looking at me annoyed.

"Lucky, the bouncer tried to choke me to death." Lucky wasn't hearing me. He was still mad.

"I'm tellin' you, Nicole and them gonna get you into some shit, man. Them stupid ass bitches always into somethin'."

His response wasn't what I expected.

"It didn't have anything to do with them."

"Yes it did. You talkin' 'bout me wildin' out. Look at you."

He was right. I was doing what I told him to stop doing. But I was too tired to fight about it. So I told Lucky good night and went to my room and to lay down. I heard Lucky go out the front door as I was falling off to sleep.

The next morning, the phone was ringing off the hook. Seems everyone and their momma wanted to know what happened. I told them I didn't know what they were talking about and left it at that. I had learned one thing over the past few years. Don't trust anyone.

Later that day, Vicki and I met up with Nicole and her girls at the barbershop. We brought a six-pack of Heinekens and compared notes about what went down the night before.

"Zsaset, what did Lucky say?" Nicole asked.

"Nothin' much. He was just pissed. He doesn't want me gettin' into trouble."

"He's one to talk," she said with an attitude.

"What do you mean by that?"

"Nothin'."

"No. What do you mean?" She got quiet. "Do you know something I don't know?"

"I'm just sayin' trouble is his middle name. Now he's tryin' to act like he's some kinda alter boy or something."

I knew that wasn't what she meant, but I also knew she wasn't going to say anything bad about him, even though I knew she didn't like him.

After drinking our last beer, Vicki and I went home.

I assumed Lucky would come over but he didn't which was strange because he always came over, especially on Sundays. I didn't hear from him until I got to work the next morning.

"Hey, ma," he said, sounding down in the dumps.

"Hey."

"What you do yesterday?"

"Nothin' much. Why didn't you come over?"

"I had some business to take care of."

"What kinda of business did you have to take care of that you couldn't even call?"

"Look, don't start with that bullshit," he yelled.

"Who the fuck are you yelling at?" I asked feeling my temperature rise.

"I'm sorry. I'm stressed out and you asking me all these questions like I'm doing somethin'."

"I didn't say you were doing something, but now I have to wonder."

"Wonder about what? I'm always with you. I don't have time to do shit."

I almost believed him. But I knew where there was a will there was a way. It happened to me before and I wasn't going to be ignorant and think it couldn't happen again.

I hung up the phone in the midst of our argument. His sudden attitude change surprised me. In the beginning he was so sweet, but that was slowly fading. Sometimes he would just go off for no reason. I understood his life style was demanding sometimes, but his behavior made me question just what kind of man he really was.

Lucky was there waiting for me for me in the parking lot when I got home. We went inside and went up to my room to talk.

"Ma, I apologize for yelling at you today. I'm just going through somethin'."

"Well tell me what it is. Maybe I can help."

"I wish you could, but you can't. Thanks for trying. See, that's why I love you."

"Oh and here I was thinking it was because of my good stuff."

"That too. Now come over here and put that thang on me," he said falling back on my bed.

"No, you were a bad boy today and bad boys don't get treats."

"Well spank me then."

"You would love that, wouldn't you?"

"I sure would," he said as he kissed me on lips.

I Shoulda Seen It Comin'

Our lovemaking was different that night. I let myself completely trust and believe in him.

Chapter Thirty-2

My mother and and I were celebrating our birthday. Since my mother was turning 50, I thought it would be nice for her to have a surprise party. I invited all of our friends and family to come help us celebrate. I even invited my perfect brother, his perfect wife and their perfect children. I really wanted it to be Ma's day. I also invited Lucky. He had asked me several times about meeting her, but I always came up with an excuse. I wanted to wait for the right time. I figured there was no time like the present.

It was almost 3:00 p.m. and the party was about to begin. I arranged for my mother's sister to take her out shopping first so we could set up. Since I had a large front yard in front of my building, I decided to have a barbeque. We decorated the yard, and I bought the biggest cake I could find. My mother had always been there for me and I just wanted to show her a tenth of love she's shown me.

The kitchen was full of movement with people running in and out with food. I had been preparing this party for over two weeks and I still forgot a few details. Thank God I had Laisha, Monique, and Vicki there to help out.

My mother arrived at three sharp. Boy was she surprised when we all yelled, "Happy Birthday!" She actually thought I was giving myself a party. It felt good seeing her so happy. About half way into the party, Lucky showed up. It was the first time anyone in my family met him. I walked around and introduced him to everyone at the party. After taking a few deep breaths, I introduced him to my mother. He was charming as ever. He even bought my mother a birthday card. When she opened it, there was a hundred dollar bill attached. He was definitely rubbing it on thick.

The party was winding down so I started cleaning up.

After seeing everyone off I went into my room to lie down. Lucky followed.

"So, ma, do you think your mom liked me?"

"I think she did. If she didn't, you would know."

"Well, I liked her. She was cool and so was the rest of your family. It's been a long time since I've been around a family that actually gets along"

"Yeah, we do get along pretty well." I was just about to ask him about his family when the phone rang. It was Nicole.

"Hey, do you think you can give me a ride to the barbershop. My son needs a haircut."

Was this girl crazy? I thought. Not only was I tired. It was my birthday.

"Zsaset, please. He's takin' pictures tomorrow."

My mind was saying no, but my mouth said yes. I was a softy when it came to kids.

"Nicole needs a ride to the barbershop. Her son needs a haircut for his pictures tomorrow. Come go with me," I said, turning to Lucky.

"Why didn't she call his daddy?" he asked sitting up.

"I don't think they talk. Do you know who he is?"

"Yeah, I know Jeter."

"It sounds like you don't like him."

"He's alright. He just thinks he's Scarface 'round this motherfucka. That's all good though. Long as he don't fuck with me." From the way Lucky was talking, I could tell this guy wasn't one of his favorite people.

We picked Nicole up from her apartment and headed to the barbershop. The parking lot was packed. Everybody that was anybody was there. We even had to drive away from the parking lot and park on a side street. As soon as we got close, Nicole let out a deep sigh.

"What's wrong with you?" I asked.

"My baby daddy here," she said, sucking her teeth.

"Is that a problem?"

She told me no but I didn't believe her.

"Can you take him in and get him a haircut because if I go in there, it's gonna be a fight," she said, handing me her son.

"I can't believe he would fight with you in front of his son and all these people."

"Girl, you don't know him."

"Look, Zsaset, I don't want you to get into no shit trying to help her ass out. 'Cause if the nigga lunch out on you, then I'ma have to come handle that shit."

"Lucky, chill. I ain't gonna say nuthin' to the nigga. It ain't gone be no shit. I'll be right back."

To avoid a scene, I took her son in the barbershop while she and Lucky waited outside. As soon as I walked in, it was obvious who her son's father was.

"Why chu have me son?" he said, taking the baby out of my hands.

"Oh, I brought him to get a haircut."

"Who are you?"

"I'm Zsaset. I'm Nicole's friend."

"Me not seen chu before." I tried to explain to him that I had just moved back into town, but he didn't seem to care about that. "Where the biaatch at?" he said, looking out the window.

"If you're talking about Nicole, she's waiting outside."

"Tell her be gone when me reach outside."

"Excuse me?"

"I want her be gone when me reach outside, or me gone kill her ass dead. Me hate that bitch."

I Shoulda Seen It Comin'

"Go tell her now."

Before I could get out the door good, he was yelling and waving his gun. I couldn't believe he was acting like that in front of his own child. There was absolutely no excuse for that shit. I don't care how much you despise your child's mother. To say you're gonna kill her in front of your child is wrong. It didn't take me any time to get across the parking lot to tell her.

"Nicole your baby daddy is spazzing out in the barbershop and he took the baby out of my arms. You didn't tell me this nigga was a straight up lunchbox."

"What is he doing?" she asked unfazed.

"It's not what he's doing, it's what he's gonna do if you don't leave before he comes out."

"What?"

"He said he's gonna kill you if you don't leave by the time he comes out. He even pulled out his gun. What a nut case."

"Girl, he ain't gonna do shit. He's always running off at the mouth."

"Nicole, it didn't sound like he was playing."

"Even if he wasn't playing, he don't scare me."

"Well, he sure scares the hell out of me. So let's go."

"Ma, you ain't got to be scared of that bama ass nigga. Look, Nicole, we ain't got time for all this shit. We bought you up here as a favor. If ya'll want to beef, ya'll gonna have to do it on ya'll own time. Let's go, ma," Lucky said in anger.

Just as we were about to leave, Jeter came out of the barbershop holding the baby. "Didn't me tell chu to leave?"

"I'm leaving, bitch," Nicole said, spitting at Jeter.

"What chu call me?" Jeter asked pointing his gun at Nicole.

"You heard me. Fuck you, faggot ass nigga."

Why did she have to say that? The next thing I knew Jeter was busting off shots everywhere. He had the gun in one hand

and the baby in the other. Scared, I ran to the car. Nicole followed. When we got to the car I felt like shooting Nicole's ass. "I told you he wasn't playing. What if he had shot you or worse shot your son. It's obvious he doesn't give a damn about you or your son." I wanted to get the hell out of there but Lucky wasn't in the car yet. Moments later, he entered the car with his gun in his in hand. "Lucky, what are you doing?" I asked looking in the back seat of the car.

"Just making sure he doesn't try anything," he yelled pulling out his 9mm.

"He's just runnin' off at the mouth. He ain't gonna shoot nobody," Nicole said.

"You know what, bitch, shut the hell up. It's because of your stupid ass he shootin' and shit. I swear to God if he had hurt my girl, you and him would've both been in body bags."

Surprisily, Nicole didn't say anything back. She did all that talking to Jeter, but when Lucky said something she just kept quiet. Why was she scared of Lucky, but not her crazy ass baby daddy?

We dropped her off and headed to my apartment. I needed to rest my nerves. All the drama had me chain smoking.

"I don't want you hangin' 'round her no more. She's a fucking idiot," Lucky said, securing his gun in his pants.

"What about him? He was the one shooting," I said.

"I don't give a fuck about him. He's gonna get his. You just stay away from her."

"Lucky, first of all, don't be yelling at me. Second, you don't tell me who the fuck to see or not see. You got that?"

"What did you just say? What did you say," he said with his hands around my neck choking me. I was so shocked I couldn't even speak. My eyes widened, as his grip got stronger and stronger. My body was paralyzed with fear. This was the first time he had ever done anything like that and it scared me. I didn't want to admit it, but I knew after that, things would never be the same between us.

I Shoulda Seen It Comin'

The drive home was quiet except for the sounds of Faith Evan's *Soon As I Get Home* playing on the radio. He let me out in front of my apartment then pulled off in his rental car and left. Still shaking, I sat there and tried to figure out what had just happened. This was our first fight and I didn't know how to handle it. It wasn't like I had never yelled back at him before, so why did he go off this time? What was going on? I soon found out.

About three days had passed before Lucky called. When he did, he apologized for choking me.

"Ma, you don't understand. I was trying to protect you and you took her side."

"I wasn't taking sides. I just said don't tell me who to be friends with."

"Even when I'm telling you some good shit, you don't wanna listen. That bitch is trouble but you don't see that."

"It seemed like he was more trouble than Nicole was. At least she didn't choke the shit out of me."

"Look, I'll be over later so we can sit down and talk about this."

"Alright."

I hung up the receiver and sat on the couch. I just felt something wasn't right about Lucky but I couldn't put my hands on it. He would disappear for days without even a phone call and then he would have these crazy mood swings. I was determined to find out why when he got there. But someone beat him to it.

I was in the middle of watching television with Monique, Laisha, and Vicki when the phone rang.

"Hi, can I speak to Daset?"

"You have the wrong number," I said.

Seconds later the mystery woman called back. "Hi, my name is Tammy. I'm looking for someone named Daset, or Gaset."

"Do you mean Zsaset?"

"Yeah, I think that's it."

"This is she."

"Zsaset, do you know a guy named Lucky?"

"Yes, that's my boyfriend."

She let out a snicker. "How long have you been seeing him?"

"For a couple of months now. Why do you want to know?" I asked curious.

"Because he's my boyfriend. We've been together for three years."

I almost choked. "What? Is this a joke?" I asked crushed.

"No. I assure you it's not."

"How did you find out about me?" I said, holding back my tears.

"Well for one, I overheard him talking to you one night so I asked him who you were. He gave me some song and dance about you being a runner. Then some of my girlfriends told me that he was seeing some girl from Norfolk, so I did a little investigating. I went into his phone one night while he was sleep and I saw this number in it a couple of times. So I decided to call. I'm sorry. I'm not trying to start anything with you but I'm tired of this shit."

"I can't deal with this right now. When you see him, tell him I said lose my number," I said.

"You know what, the bastard's walking in the house right now," the woman said.

"Oh, he is? Put him on the phone," I said ready to explode.

"Here, someone wants to talk to you."

"Speak," Lucky said sure it was one of his boys.

"Yeah, I guess you forgot to mention to me you had a girlfriend, uh. You ain't shit. Don't ever call me or come over here....."

Before I could finish my sentence, I heard a loud whomp and then the girl started screaming in agony. He was beating her relentlessly. Then the phone went dead. My knees began to shake and I dropped the phone.

"Zsaset, what's wrong," Vicki said.

"That was Lucky's girlfriend."

"What girlfriend?" Laisha and Monique said in unison.

"That was his girlfriend. She said she's been with him for three years."

"What? What the fuck? Niggas ain't shit these days," Laisha said.

"Worse than that, I just heard him beat her ass. He was in the wrong but he beat her ass." I was starting to think Lucky really had some mental health issues. He would act strange sometimes but I would've never thought he had another girlfriend. He was acting like it was all about me, but it wasn't.

My heart raced as I tried to comprehend what the woman told me. How could he do this to me? My heartache soon turned into anger.

"When I think about all the times I would tell him about the other men in my life and how bad they treated me, all he would say is he's gonna be different. That was a bunch of bull."

"Zsaset, guys worm their way into your life with all that talk about forever. It just gets appealing to you," Vicki said.

"You're right. It was all part of the game. And he played it well. That's okay though I'm going to play a little game of my own now."

"What you talking about?" Monique said as if she was worried.

"Nothing. I'm just blowing off steam."

"Just be glad you left him alone when you did. Look how he beat that girl up. That could've been you. I'm telling you that boy ain't wrapped too tight."

I went into my room, buried my face in my pillow and cried. My relationship with Lucky was one big joke. But I had no one to blame but myself. When I was finally able to get control of my emotions, I started shredding anything that reminded of Lucky. My heart was bruised and I never though it would heal.

The next day, Lucky called me twenty times, but I wouldn't accept any of his calls. After a couple of days he stopped. I guess he got the message that I didn't want to be bothered with him. I was too depressed and angry about what had happened. I couldn't stop thinking of how dumb I was for falling for Lucky's lies. I thought he really cared for me. I didn't deserve to be treated like that. I gave my heart and soul to him and him only. He just couldn't do the same.

Chapter Thirty-3

For weeks, I I had no life. The weather was cold and I was lonely. Sitting in my room just reminded me of Lucky. With nothing else to do, I threw myself into my work. I wouldn't even go out because I didn't want to run into him. I was scared of what I might do to him if I were to come face to face with the snake. Nevertheless, I needed to move on.

One Saturday night while in my room looking at television, Nicole, Laisha, and Vicki came in and told me to get up.

"Girl put some clothes on. We goin' out to that new club. Monique said she'll watch Zeta," Laisha said.

"Yeah, we tired of watchin' you walk around here like you in a daze," Vicki said.

"No, ya'll go head. I'm not in the mood," I said.

"Well if you keep sitting in here like this you ain't gonna never be in the mood. Now put your clothes on, we're going out, "Laisha said with authority.

After realizing they weren't going to take no for an answer, I got dressed. When we got to the club, I went to the bar and ordered a Remy and Coke. It was good to see all the new faces. This club was hot. And after a few more drinks, I was on the dance floor. It was like I didn't have a care in the world. But all that ended when I saw Lucky.

"Zsaset, be cool," Laisha said.

"Girl, I'm cool as ice. I ain't gonna let him get to me. As a matter of fact, I'm gonna go over and talk to his friend, Mike."

Mike was a ladies man. He was fine as wine and had a body of a God. That's why Lucky never let me talk to him for long period of time. Whenever Mike would come over, Lucky would make him sit in the car.

"Hey, Zsaset. What's up, ma?" Mike said smiling.

"Please don't call me that."

"Oh yeah, I forgot. Ya'll not back together yet."

"No, we're never getting back together. So I can talk to you now," I said flirting.

"I kinda figured he told you not to talk me. He always do that shit. I can't help it if I'm the man."

"No, baby, he was the man. Walking 'round here with two girls."

"I know. He almost beat her to death for callin' you too."

"What?"

"Yeah. He broke her arm and her jaw. And her crazy ass is still with him."

"Couldn't be me." I said, but I was hurt that he was still with Tammy.

"I hear ya. That bitch must got low self-esteem or somethin'. So what about you? You seein' anyone?" he asked staring at my breasts.

"No way. I'm staying single for the rest of my life."

"You say that now, but somebody gonna change that." From the way Mike was looking at me, I could tell he was talking about himself. Not trying to go that route, I excused myself.

"Before you leave, you wanna hit this blunt?"

I was about to decline his offer when I noticed Lucky watching me from the bar. "Yeah sure." After taking a couple of pulls, Mike ordered me another drink.

"You know I've always had a crush on you."

I couldn't believe what he was saying. "I thought you were Lucky's friend."

"Baby, in this game you don't have no friends. Anyway, I just thought I'd tell you how I feel now that ya'll not together no more. That's all. I mean I wouldn't try anythin' now unless you wanted me to."

"Naw, I don't think that would be a good idea."

"That's cool. We can be friends though, right?"

"Yeah. We can be friends."

For the rest of night, Mike and I talked as if we were the best of friends. He was like a breath of fresh air.
"I see someone's coming out of their shell," Vicki said.
"You got that right. I'm having fun. Thanks for making me come out tonight. I needed this."
"I know something else you need too," Vicki said with a mischievous grin.
"What?"
"A big stiff dick. Remember, the way to get over one man is to get under another one."
I can't believe she just said that. She's really fucked up or she's been hanging 'round Nicole too much.
"It would be nice to be with someone, but I'm not ready for a relationship yet."
"Who says you have to have a relationship? Haven't you ever heard of recreational sex?"
"Girl, please. You're talking to an old head."

After I finished talking to Vicki, I went back over to where Mike was standing and continued to talk. Glancing around the club, I noticed some girls gritting on me. I guess they are some of Mike's admirers. *Too bad, bitches, he's talking to me right now,* I thought to myself.

Even Lucky was glaring at me like he was pissed, but I didn't care. As a matter of fact, I took it one step further by asking Mike back to my place.
"Are you sure?" he asked shocked.
"Yeah, I have some Remy at the house."
"Alright."
On the way out, I shot Lucky a sneaky smile and left.

When we got home, I made us all drinks and Mike lit up another blunt. We were having such a good time that I almost forgot about the past few weeks. The girls were tired so they went to bed.

"So I guess you're ready to go to bed too?" Mike said, putting out his blunt.

"Not really. Why, do you have to leave?"

"Naw, I'm cool. I don't have anyone at home waitin' on me," he said with a laugh.

"Oh so you got jokes, uh," I said, squinting my eyes.

"Naw, I'm being serious."

"Come on, let's go to my room."

When we got into my room, I lit a candle and sat on the bed.

"Aren't you scared Lucky's gonna come over here? You know he saw me leave with you," Mike said.

"He better not come over here after what he did to me," I said, feeling my temperature rise.

"Exactly what happened?" Mike asked curiously.

"I don't want to talk about it."

"Well, what do you want to do?"

"If you come a little closer I'll show you," I said, pulling him closer.

That's when our lips met. As he unbuttoned my shirt, a tingling sensation ran through my body. I imagined I was being touched for the first time. He slowly removed my clothes and began to kiss me all over. When he started kissing between my legs I started to moan softly.

After our desires exploded, I cradled in his arms. Holding each other, I feared that I had just made the biggest mistake of my life. I couldn't even explain why I did it. I guess deep down, I was still hurt and I wanted to teach Lucky a lesson. But as fate would have it, I was the one about to learn a lesson.

The next morning, Mike woke up and began to get dressed. Before he left, he sat down on the bed next to me.

"Do you feel guilty?" he asked.

"Yeah, a little. How about you?"

I Shoulda Seen It Comin'

"Yeah. We could blame it on the alcohol, but that would be a cop out. The truth is, I wanted you. I ain't gonna lie."

"I wanted you too, I just don't know if I wanted you for the right reasons," I said, ashamed of my actions.

"So where do we go from here?" he asked.

"I'm not sure. Can you just give me some time to sort this out?"

"Yeah, as long as you promise me you'll call me," he said with a smile that made me melt.

"I promise."

I lay in the bed wondering what was going to happen when Lucky found out we slept together. Why did I even care? Our whole relationship was a lie. I guess you could say we never really had a relationship.

When I finally got out of bed, everyone was waiting to get a play by play of last night's action.

"Hey, girl, how was it?" Laisha said.

"It was okay."

"Yeah, right. That nigga too fine to be givin' it out just okay," Laisha said, slapping them all high-fives.

"Ya'll got issues, you know that," I said.

"We know but you're gonna have them after psycho finds out," Vicki said whining.

"Fuck him," I said, playing it off.

"That's what your mouth say. But you know he's gonna go crazy. I just hope I'm not around when he does. His crazy ass will probably try to take us all out," Monique said joking.

We all laughed about it for a while, but then I found myself starting to think about it. Lucky was not the most stable person in the world. What if he did try to hurt me? No, he wouldn't. At least that's what I thought.

The day was so nice. Monique, Laisha, Vicki, and Zeta wanted to take full advantage of the weather so they decided to go to the waterfront and eat lunch. I wasn't in the mood to be around a crowd so I stayed home. Just as I was about to cook myself something to eat, the phone rang. It was Lucky. My heart started to pound like it was going to jump out of my chest. I knew from the sound of his voice that he knew about Mike but he tried to act like he didn't.

"Hey. Can I come over? I need to bring you somethin'."

"Bring me what? Look I really don't have anything to say to you."

"It's business. K-Dog told me to bring you somethin'."

"He didn't mention anything to me about it."

"I know he just called me. Look, it won't take long."

I had a feeling Lucky was using K-Dog as an excuse to come over. I hadn't told him about what happened because I knew they did business together. I thought that would make things awkward between them. The truth is I didn't want K-Dog to know what a fool I was.

Lucky showed up about an hour later with flowers in his hand. I knew he had something up his sleeves.

"Hey, ma. Where everybody at?"

"They went to the waterfront."

"How long they been gone?" he said, peeking out the window.

"They just left. Why?"

"I'm just asking. Look, first of all I want to apologize for lyin' and deceivin' you. I know that I'll never have another chance with you, but I just want us to at least be civil to each other."

"I think I've been very civilized towards you."

Just as I said that he went into my bedroom and turned the television up. He returned to the living room moments later and did the same thing.

"What are you doing? You got the volume up too high."

"Ma, sit down."

"No, I want you to leave."

I Shoulda Seen It Comin'

His behavior was very unusual. In all the months we were together, he never once touched my television. He always had me do it. On top of that, he had the volume turned up as far as it could go.

"Ma, I'm not gonna ask you again to sit down," he said with a demented look.

I was convinced the only way he was going to leave is if I let him say his peace. So I sat down. "Lucky, what do you want to talk about?"

"To be honest with you I don't want to talk. I just want you to shoot me in the head," he said as he pulled his gun out of his waist and placed it in my hand.

"Look, stop acting stupid," I said as I laid the gun on the coffee table.

"Look just leave. I don't have time for this."

"Really."

"Yeah, really."

"Oh you don't have time to talk to me, but you have time to fuck my man. Is that how this shit works?"

That's when I saw the real Lucky. He smacked me right across my face with the butt of the gun. I was so shocked I couldn't move. I just stood there while blood trickled from my nose and mouth. *If I had known you were gonna pull this shit, I would've shot your ass.*

"Did you really think I was gonna let you get away with humiliating me? Yeah, that's right. I know all about last night, you sleazy bitch. You know I have killed...I don't know maybe twenty people in my life and I've never been to jail for any of them. But you know...I think...I think you're my punishment." He scratched his head. "Falling in love with you was my punishment."

That's when he hit me again. I could have fought back, but I didn't. I was paralyzed and numb with fear. Instead, I just pleaded with him to stop, but my pleas fell on deaf ears.

I screamed as he beat and called me every name in the book. This lasted for thirty minutes. Just when he was about to smash me in the head again with his gun, the phone rang. I was in so much pain I couldn't even think straight so I didn't answer it. But Lucky did. He thought for sure it was Mike, but it was Vicki. Frustrated, he threw me the phone.

"Tell her you're about to die, bitch. Tell her!"

I was so out of it, I dropped the phone and started screaming. That didn't do any good. He had the volume turned up on the television so no one could hear me. I couldn't believe this was happening. He made me feel like I deserved to be hit when the truth is no woman deserves to be hit by a man—ever.

Not ready to die, I tried to talk some sense into him. But as soon as I said my first word, he hit me with the gun across my leg. The pain was like someone had stabbed me with a knife. Then he took me into his arms and told me he loved me.

"If you love me then why are you doing this?" I said spitting blood out of my mouth.

"Because you cheated on me."

I seriously was about to lose it, but I had to keep in mind he was the one holding the gun. He struck me again and again until he got tired. Then he pointed the gun at me and fired two shots. Miraculously, I rushed him before they hit me. Pissed that he had missed and that I still was standing after enduring his beating, he aimed the gun at my forehead and pulled the trigger again. For the second time in my life, the Lord spared me that day because the gun jammed. He slammed it on the table in an attempt to unjam it, but it didn't work.

Frustrated, he punched me in the face so hard, the force knocked me to the ground. After kicking me until I almost passed out, he pulled me by my feet into the bathroom.

"Look what you made me do. Look at what you made me do to my shirt. It's all fucked up. I got blood all over it."

I Shoulda Seen It Comin'

Lucky was certifiably insane. He had beaten me to a pulp, then had the nerve to blame me for his shirt being ruined. What a psycho.

I sat on the bathroom floor for what seemed like forever, Lucky finally let me go lie on my bed.
"Ma, are you hungry?" Lucky asked trying to redeem himself.
"No."
"Yes you are. I hear your stomach growling," he yelled at the top of his voice.
Scared he might flip out on me again, I said yes and then handed him the phone to order a pizza. When the pizza man arrived, Lucky kissed me on the forehead and told me he would be right back. I thought I was dreaming. How the hell could I allow myself to fall for this guy? I knew he had a temper, but I never thought he would ever do anything like this to me. It made me wonder. Is that the reason why he can't keep a girlfriend? Was he on the drugs he sold? I mean, what. My thoughts were interrupted when Lucky threw the pizza on the bed.
"Eat. Then hurry up and clean up before someone comes home."
"It doesn't matter how much I clean myself up they're gonna see the bruises."
"You're right. So you better think of somethin' to tell them."
"What?"
"You heard me. Now I'ma leave and you better do what I told you. When I come back we're gonna forget all this shit ever happened. We're gonna be a family again. And I swear on my parents if you call the police, I'm gonna kill all of ya'll. See you later. Remember, I love you," he said as he walked out.

About fifteen minutes later Vicki, Laisha, Monique, and Zeta came running in. They started screaming and crying as soon as they saw me.

"Mommy, Mommy. You're bleeding. You're bleeding," Zeta screamed.

"I'm alright, Zeta Beta. I'm all right. Monique can you take Zeta to my mom's house. Don't tell her what's going on though. She'll get all worried."

Reluctantly she left and took Zeta with her.

"I'll be right back."

While she was gone, I told Vicki and Laisha what happened. And I swore them to secrecy.

"He said he would kill all of us if I told anyone."

"So what are you gonna do? He said he was coming back didn't he," Vicki asked.

"I say we fuck his ass up when he gets here," Laisha said with eyes red and swollen from crying.

"We can't. He might hurt Zeta or my mom or one of you for that matter. Just play along with me. I'm just gonna act like nothing is wrong until I come up with a way to get him out of my life. Maybe in a few days, he'll move on to someone else."

"Zsaset, you have to call the police. What if he does this to someone else? They might not be so lucky," Vicki said with concern.

"Vicki, I don't even know his real name. Even if I did, he would be out before we knew it. Then what? I would be looking over my shoulder every time I went out of this house. Just let me do this my way."

"Okay well at least go to the hospital."

"No. I'm all right. I'm just sore."

I pleaded with them to go along with me, and they agreed against their better judgment. Finally strong enough to get up, I went into the bathroom to look at my face. I couldn't believe how I looked. Both of my eyes were blacked and my nose looked like it was broke. My legs were all black and blue. And it looked like a few veins were broken. There was no way I was going to go to the hospital looking the way I did. I would've been too embarrassed. I got the girls to take some pictures of me. Then I cleaned myself up and got in my bed. Scared for me, Vicki and Laisha laid next to me.

"Zsaset you need to call K-Dog," Vicki said.

"I know but I don't want him to do something stupid and get into trouble. He has a baby on the way. Don't worry, I'll take care of this myself."

"What are you gonna do?"

"I don't know, but he's not gonna get away with this. If I knew that he was gonna beat me up, I would've shot him in the head."

"What are you talkin' 'bout," Laisha asked.

"Before he starting beating me up, he handed me his gun and told me to shoot him in the head."

"Zsaset, do you know how lucky you are?"

"I know. Oh, he shot at me too. I didn't tell you about that."

"Why not?" Monique said.

"I don't know. My mind is so fucked up right now. I can't even think. Hey, help me look for the shells. He was shooting in the living room somewhere."

We found the casings and put them away. For the rest of the day, all I could do was thank God for sparing my life and giving me a second chance. After all, I brought this whole situation on myself. I should'a seen it comin'. All the signs were there and I ignored them. My knight and shining amour turned out to be my worst nightmare.

Chapter Thirty-4

The next two days were painful. My body ached and my face was swollen and discolored. I could barely walk because of the bruising on my legs. My nose was crooked from the broken bones.

Lucky came over on the regular like nothing had happened. He would bring me food and lie in the bed with me like old times. It was sickening. I kept it together though. That's more than I can say for Laisha, Monique, and Vicki. They would give him deathly stares when he wasn't looking and we would all curse him out when he left.

After a few days, I finally felt well enough to go back to work. Unfortunately, Harriet couldn't hold my job for me. Upper management told her she had to let me go because I hadn't brought in a doctor's note. That's hard to do when you haven't seen a doctor. With no money and bills to pay, I had no choice but to call K-Dog and tell him what happened. He was so pissed, he got right on Highway 64 and headed to Virginia Beach. When he got there and saw my face, he punched a hole in the wall.

"Where's that punk ass mothafucka?"

"I don't know but you can't say anything to him. He said he would kill all of us."

"He ain't gonna get the chance to."

"K-Dog, please let me handle this. You gotta stay away from this kind shit, now that you're gonna be a daddy. I swear, after a few days he'll forget all about me."

"I'ma let you handle it for now. But if he lays another hand on you, I'ma kill his ass."

"Deal."

Before leaving he gave me enough money to live off of for a while, then kissed me goodbye.

I Shoulda Seen It Comin'

The following Friday, Monique and I went out to lunch at Ruby Tuesday's. I had fun, but my body still ached. It was my heart that hurt the most.

"Girl, you alright?"

"Yeah. My body just feels like I've been hit by a Mack truck."

"It'll get better soon. You just need to concentrate on getting this motherfucker out of your life."

"I know. Do you know he hit me again last night?"

"What the fuck is the matter with him?"

"He bugged out because he had been coming up to my job for the past couple of days sitting in the parking lot waiting to see if I was showing up for work. I had never told him I lost my job."

"He bugged out because you didn't tell him you got fired?"

"Yeah, he started screamin' saying I was spending the day with a nigga. First he smacked me so hard across my face, it felt like I got hit with a two by four. But I was stubborn and I hardly flinched and just gritted on him. That shit made him made and he started pounding me with his fists. I couldn't breathe he was hitting me so hard..."

Monique interrupted, "Zsaset, how long are you gonna put up with this shit?"

"I don't know. I don't know what to do."

"It's simple. Call the police."

"Monique, he'll be out before the ink dries."

"So what! Place a restraining order against him."

"Do you think he's gonna let a piece of paper stop him from getting to me or someone else I care about? I'm such a loser."

"You're not a loser."

"Then why does shit keep happening to me? It's like I'm a magnet for trouble. I keep getting involved with these guys that cheat on me, never thinking of the consequences. Now I've put everyone I love in danger. Not to mention, I still have this mental case on my hands."

"First of all, you're not the first woman to get cheated on and you won't be the last. You just need to stand up to this asshole. I guarantee you he'll think twice about fucking with you again. Fuck the dumb shit. The next time he hits you, fight back. I mean fuck his ass up good. Put them Marine ass-kicking skills to work. You just get the party started and the whole family will jump in, we got your back. You have to make the first move though. Not unless you want to walk around with dark shades on for the rest of your life."

Her words struck a cord. But I was still a poster child for abuse. Instead of dealing with reality, I always had these dreams of what love was supposed to be. The problem was I never waited patiently for love. When you're desperately seeking it, you'll take any man who shows you just the slightest bit of attention. But how do you know the difference between the good and the bad? It made me not believe in love anymore at all.

A few days after our heart to heart, Lucky hit me again. It started because Mike had heard through the grapevine what Lucky had done to me. He called to check on me. When the telephone rang, somehow I knew that I shouldn't answer it. I tried to distract Lucky but he wasn't going for it. After the phone rang about three times, Lucky picked it up.

"Hello."

I guess Mike ain't catch Lucky's voice. "Zsaset home?" Lucky laughed. "Yeah, man, who is this?"

"This Mike."

"Oh yeah. Hold on, Mike." Lucky got that look on his face. "Zsaset, Mike is on the phone." Lucky said it in the kindest voice he could muster but the look on his face betrayed his voice. I hesitated. Lucky yelled at the top of his lungs. "Come get the fuckin' phone, bitch." I slowly walked towards Lucky and the phone trying to think how I was going to get out of this situation. When I got to the phone, Lucky lifted the receiver high above my head and came down full force, crashing it into my head as hard as he could. I saw stars but I stayed on my feet and I swung back drawing some of his blood for a change.

"What the fuck? I'ma kill you this time, bitch."

"I don't think so," I said, swinging the baseball bat I kept in my room. Yeah, I got smart and bought a steel baseball bat. I was going to be ready when he hit me again. I swung the bat and cranked his knee. He fell to the ground shrieking like a little bitch. Like the true soldiers they were Laisha, and Monique came running into aid. Vicki's scared ass stood in the corner crying. Sufficed to say, we whipped his ass good.

"I'ma kill all ya'll," he screamed in agony.

"Shut the fuck up. That was the last time you gonna put your hands on me you woman-beating asshole."

"Bet you didn't see that coming did you?" Laisha said with laughter.

"Alright. Alright. You got me. But now I got you," he said as he
reached for his gun.

"Not," I said. His stupid ass didn't realize it, but when he went to the bathroom, I emptied his gun. "I'll take that," I said as I took the gun and smacked him across his face with it. Monique stood over him with the bat.

"I want you to get your sorry ass out of here. If you ever come near my family or me again, I will not hesitate to put one in your ass. You understand me! Now get out!"

Just for the hell of it, I kicked him in the ass on the way out.

That night we went to a hotel just in case he came back. I knew he wasn't going to let us get away with making a fool out of him like that. It was only a matter of time before he retaliated. Little did I know, it would be so soon.

After staying in the hotel for a few days, I felt it was safe enough for us to go back home because there had been no sign of Lucky. The word on the streets was he had left town. Never believe gossip. It can get you in a world of trouble.

Danette Majette

It didn't take long for the word to get out about what I did to Lucky. And when it did, my phone rang off the hook. Not in the mood to talk about it, I didn't take any of the calls. That left people coming up with their own scenarios of what happened. There were all kinds of stories floating around. Some people were saying we killed him. Then there were people that said he had killed me.

One day, riding past the barbershop, I noticed a lot of commotion going on. *Some one must have gotten shot over who had the chair next,* I said sarcastically to myself. I pulled into the parking lot and got out of my car. The pandemonium was Lucky and Mike fighting. I ran up screaming but someone held me back. The loud explosion of a gunshot went off then Mike fell to the ground. I wanted to run to his side, but my feet wouldn't move. I just stood there petrified.

Blood was everywhere. Mike laid on the ground moaning until he lost consciousness. I could hear the sound of police sirens from a distance. As the sounds got closer, people scattered. I watched from a distance as the paramedics arrived and immediately began working on Mike, but it was too late. He was dead. My heart ached and ached. My stupidity caused Mike his life.

Mike's killing was on every news channel that night. The police speculated that it was drug related, but I knew better. It was because of me. And it was Lucky's way of telling me I was next.

That night, I couldn't sleep thinking about how Mike lost his life. I couldn't help but wonder who would be next. It was apparent Lucky was willing to kill anyone or anything associated with me. And it was all because he lost the one thing he held near and dear to his heart. The control and power he had over me. That made him angry. That's a real blow to man like him.

Several days later, Mike's parent held a memorial service for him so his friends in Norfolk could say good-bye. The funeral was going to be in New York later that week. I couldn't believe

I Shoulda Seen It Comin'

they even considered doing something like that. I would have taken my son home and said fuck all ya'll. Especially since no one helped the police solve his case. There were about fifty people outside when Lucky shot Mike and no one would tell the police a thing, including me. I felt like shit about it.

The service was at a church on St. Paul's Blvd. near downtown Norfolk. The girls were in short dresses and overly applied make-up, while the guys, mostly his friends in the drug game, came pimped out in their minks with music blasting from their cars. It looked more like a circus than a memorial service.

Armed with Lucky's 9mm and disguised in a blond wig, I sat in the back of the chapel. My heart ached as his parent's wept uncontrollably. I couldn't imagine what they were going through. How do you survive burying your child? Making my way to the front of the chapel, I leaned in the casket and said good-bye.

Just as I was about to leave, his mother approached me and asked me how I knew her son. Stunned by her question, I stood there with a blank expression. "I actually didn't know him that well. I met him through a mutual friend." As I talked to Mike's mom I could see where Mike got his good looks. He was the spitting image of his mother. I could see that her beauty was striking even through her swollen eyes and grief-stricken expression.

"That's nice. I was surprised to see how many people came to show their respects today."

Not sure what to say I just looked around and said, "Yes ma'am. It was a nice."

"You know, Mike was our only child."

"Really, I didn't know that."

"Oh, how could you, baby? You said you barely knew him. You know I didn't approve of his lifestyle but he thought it was the only way for him to provide for his daughter," she said looking down at Mike's lifeless body.

"He had a daughter?" I asked stunned.

"Yes. She's only eight years old. She lives in upstate New York with her mother. When we told her the news, she was devastated."

"I'm sure she was," I said with tear-filled eyes. I was sure Mike's mother could see the guilt written all over my face, so I tried to excuse myself but she grabbed my arm before I could take a step.

"Wait. You know something about my son's death, don't you?"

"No. I'm sorry I don't. Like I told you before, I barely knew him."

She looked deeply into my eyes. Pleading like only a mother can, she said, "Please if you know anything, anything at all, would you please tell me? I'm not gonna be able to rest until I know what happened to my only son."

"I understand you want justice for your son, but I can't help you. I can tell you that whoever did this will spend the rest of their life behind bars when the police catches them. Just have faith in God and the police. You'll see. It will all work out. Trust me."

My days and nights were consumed with thoughts on how to make Lucky pay for what he did to Mike and me. He vanished again after killing Mike but I knew he would resurface sooner or later. After all, he still had me to deal with. When he did resurface, I started following him until I could come up with the perfect plan to get rid of him.

One day while at the nail salon down the street from the barbershop, I overheard two girls talking about the shooting.

"It don't make no sense how Lucky shot Mike in broad daylight, and the police ain't doin' nothin' 'bout it," said her friend.

"What can they do? Ain't nobody gonna tell them nothin'. Besides who they gonna look for? They don't even know his real name or where he's from. It's like he don't even exist."

"You got a point."

I Shoulda Seen It Comin'

"Hey, did you hear about the girl he beat up in Portsmouth."

"Yeah, girl. He beat her up because she called that other girl he was talking to and told her she was his girlfriend too. So to get back at him, the other girl slept with his man, Mike. So he beat her up too."

"Someone needs to beat his ass."

"Can't get mad at him. It's their fault. They shouldn't have got involved with his crazy ass in the first place."

Without getting my nails done, I walked out of the salon. It's so easy for people to judge others. How dare those bitches say it was my fault for almost getting killed? It's not like I did a background check before I slept with him. Besides, a man shouldn't put his hands on a woman no matter what the reason is.

They were right about one thing though. The police would never catch Lucky. Even if they did, he would just get off because the witnesses would probably just disappear. There's nothing worse than a snitch. Sure the police will try to protect you. But who wants to take that chance? Sometimes they'll go as far as saying, "We give you our word." Asking a man to give you his word is like asking him to lie to you.

Because the shooting was at barbershop near a high school and college, the cops needed to solve it fast to put everyone's mind at ease. They were under enormous pressure from the schools and the mayor's office. Not only did the schools see a decline in admissions for the next school year, they were losing a lot of donations from the private sector, which meant the city had to make up the slack. With the city backing them, the police were able to pull out all the stops where this case was concerned. I figured with the police on his ass like that, Lucky wouldn't be dumb enough to step foot back into town, but he did. So I figured I had better put my plan into action soon before he left again without justice being served.

Danette Majette

One night while following Lucky, I heard a news bulletin. It said a New York man was wanted for questioning in connection with Mike's death. "Suspect is armed and dangerous and said to frequent the Portsmouth area." *Dangerous ain't the word for that fool,* I thought.
  The bulletin also mentioned the suspect was out on parole. That's it. The police would never make the murder charge stick without witnesses. But if they caught him doing something illegal while he's out on parole, they would have to react. I had to make a move and I had to make a move quick.

  Reluctantly, I told Monique what I was planning to do.
  "Are you on somethin'? I mean have you totally lost it? Look, just let the police handle it."
  "First of all, no one in their right mind will ever testify against him.
I'm telling you Lucky will be back out on the streets by dawn."
  "Maybe so. But that still doesn't mean you need to be runnin' 'round here like Charles Bronson playin' vigilante."
  "I'm not trying to be a vigilante. I just want to make sure he doesn't bother me again. You know as well as I do, it's only a matter of time before he tries to get back at me."
  "He hasn't tried anything yet. So just let sleeping dogs lie," she said.

  Not taking her advice, I set out to meet with Krazy Kincaid. Kincaid made a name in the streets for himself when he was eighteen years old. He started off a dime boy for Boo-Legs Larry back in the 70's then moved his way up. He was into everything from selling drugs and firearms to prostitution. Kincaid was considered one of the smartest hustlers out there. Whenever he would get caught doing something he would just act crazy and get sent to a mental intuition for a year or two.

I Shoulda Seen It Comin'

I met Kincaid in an alley in the back of his house on Hanson Avenue.

"Ain't chu Lucky's girl?" he asked.

"Not anymore," I said, shooting him a nasty look. "Anyway I was wondering if you could help me with something."

"What can Krazy help you out of...I mean help you with," he said undressing me with his eyes.

I told Kincaid what I needed, without getting into details.

"I think I can manage that. It's gonna cost chu," he said rubbing his fingers together.

I fumbled threw my purse and pulled out a bundle of money. "Is this enough?"

"Little lady where you get all that money from?"

"Don't worry about that. Just get me what I need."

Krazy Kincaid walked away with the money in hand. *Damn, should I trust that fool?* I guess it was a little too late to be wondering. He already had my money.

Later that night, I met Krazy Kincaid back in the alley. This nigga was crazy. When I told him what I was planning, I was sure he was gonna laugh at me. But he didn't. He got me what I needed. Krazy Kincaid put the package in the truck I rented under an alias and walked away.

"Good luck," he said as if I were asking for a death wish.

"Thanks," I replied before pulling off.

I immediately drove to the weed spot and waited for Lucky. I wasn't surprised to see he was alone. Because of the shooting and all the media attention no one wanted to be around him. It was already indictment time and niggas were trying to keep a low key.

As Lucky pulled out of the parking lot he looked back to see if anyone was following him. He was so busy looking for the police he didn't even think that someone else could be on his ass. This made it easy for me to follow him without him noticing.

Lucky headed across the bridge into Portsmouth unaware I was right behind him. He made several stops before he finally reached his destination, a dark abandoned warehouse. Lucky turned into an alley and walked around to the front. I knew I only had a few minutes to do what I had to do then call the police, so I sprinted to the car. When I got to the driver's side door, I noticed it was unlocked. Thank God. That was one small detail I forgot. I made sure the coast was clear, kneeled down then placed the package in the back seat. Just as I was about to go back to my car, I heard a voice. It was Lucky. *Shit, how am I gonna get out of this one?*

"So what, you followin' me now?"

"Actually, I saw you pull into this alley, so I decided to stop. I haven't seen you in a while… and I thought maybe we could talk and kinda squash the beef between us."

"Now what would you have to talk to me about?" he said, folding his arms.

"I don't know, I guess I wanted to know why you did what you did to me and why you killed…"

"I killed Mike because of you, bitch. You fucked with my head so I just thought I would fuck with yours."

"How did I fuck with your head? You were the one cheating."

"What do you call sleepin' with my man, uh? What do you call that?" he asked snapping. I stood there with nothing to say. "You know what, it don't fuckin' matter. It's all water under the bridge now. Now get the fuck away from my car," he said, pushing me aside. He began to inspect his car. "What's this?" he said.

Without wavering, I tried to run, but I tripped over his boots.

"Get up. What the fuck is in the box?" he said, pointing his 9mm at me.

"I don't know," I said dumbfounded.

"We'll just see 'bout that."

He became enraged when he opened the box and saw the kilo of crack. It was the same look he had in his eyes when he nearly beat me to death. It was like he was burning a hole through my soul.

"You tryin' to set me up," he said as he slapped me across the face with the butt of the gun."

Not again, I thought.

"I don't know what you're talking about," I said as I held my hands up to protect my face from another blow.

"Oh sure you do. You were gonna try to set up mean old Lucky. Ain't that a bitch," he said as he exploded into a loud ball of laughter.

Looking at me with utter disgust he said, "I guess you didn't learn yo lesson the first time. I told you about fuckin' with me. Well this time I'ma make sure I kill yo stupid ass."

When he said that, thoughts of the day he beat me up and killed Mike ran through my mind. So with every ounce of strength I had, I kicked him in the groin. As he fell over in pain, he dropped the gun. That's when I kicked him again. I grabbed the gun from him and aimed it straight at his head.

"You know I should shoot you, right? But I'm not. I'm not gonna stoop to your level. Instead you know what I'm gonna do?"

"What," he said in agony.

"I'm gonna call the police and when they lock you up, I'm gonna collect the reward money," I said.

"Fuck you, bitch."

"No, no, Lucky. Fuck you."

Scared he might try something I stood in the alley yelling trying to get someone's attention. But no one was around. The alley was deserted.

"Get up real slow," I said as I aimed the gun towards him.

"Where are we going?"

"I need to get to my phone so I can call the police. Then they can put your sorry ass away."

"Do you really think that's gonna happen? I'll be out by tomorrow morning. And as soon as I do, I'm gonna kill you and anyone who knows you."

Danette Majette

I knew he meant every word that he was saying and I knew he was right about getting out. And it angered me. What if the cops did let him go? There would be no justice for me or Mike. It was like playing chess. I was trying to plan my next move that would keep him from yelling checkmate. But as usual, he was always one step ahead of me.

Seeing that I didn't know what the hell I was doing, he tried to rush me for the gun. Without even thinking twice, I shot off two rounds right into the side of his head. I watched the blood gush as the holes simmered with smoke. With his cold, hard eyes still fixated on me, I tried to find a pulse. But there wasn't one. The deviant that almost beat me to death, killed his own friend and countless others was dead.

I did what I thought I would never do. I had killed a man. Trying to regain my composure, I stepped back and took a moment to think. It was very important that I keep my cool even though I was freaking out. What was I going to do now? I couldn't just leave him there. Then it hit me.

With blood all over my clothes and hands, I patted him down and took his money and jewelry. *I'll make it look like a robbery.* If the police thought it was a drug related robbery, they probably wouldn't even waste their time looking for the killer. If you think about it, I was doing the police a favor getting this piece of shit off the streets. More importantly, I saved the taxpayers a lot of money.

After tucking away the money and jewelry, I heard sirens so I ran back to my car and sped off. About two blocks down the street, I looked in my rear view mirror and saw a cruiser behind me. This was it. I was caught. Lucky had terrorized the streets for years and he was going to get off scott free. Meanwhile, I was about to go to jail for the rest of my life. Ain't that a bitch?

The lights of the police cruiser behind me woke me from my trance. As I was pulling over, my whole life flashed in front of me. All the things I did right, and the things I did wrong. But it was too late to dwell on all that. I had to prepare myself for what was about to happen.

"Ma'am can I see your license and registration please?" Confused, I opened my glove compartment. "Do you know why I stopped you?" the officer asked looking inside the truck.

"Yes," I said in a faint voice.

"Well you really shouldn't be driving around with your brake light out. Someone could run into you, especially if it's raining."

Convinced I was out of the woods, I handed him my license and registration. He retrieved it, and then walked back to his cruiser. When he returned, he asked me to put my hands where he could see them and step out of the car.

"What's the problem, officer?" I asked baffled.

"I don't know. You tell me. You can start by explaining where this blood came from," he said as he held my registration in front of my face.

In all the confusion, I forgot to wipe the blood off my hands.

Chapter Thirty-5

With the one call I was given, I called Monique. I asked her to call K-Dog so he could hire a lawyer to represent me. He had a friend who was a lawyer and fortunately for me he lived in Virginia Beach.

I felt a bit of confidence and a small sense of relief when Michael Muhammed walked towards my cell. He was already debating with the guard on my behalf.

"I'm not comfortable with my client being in this facility. This place is dirty and rat infested, I'm sure."

"Sir, you gone have to talk with the Facility Manager about that."

"Yeah well write down his name for me. This is crazy. This place isn't fit for human inhabitance."

After the guard walked away, Michael whispered to me, "They're not gonna let you out of here tonight but I'm not gonna let this be easy for them. Unfortunately, Zsaset, you're going to have to spend the night here tonight. You're arraignment isn't until tomorrow morning. Don't worry. I'll have you home by tomorrow afternoon."

"I don't think I can stay here tonight." I looked around the interrogation room. "I'm scared," I said in a shaky, babyish voice.

"I know, but there's nothing I can do tonight. Look, just try to get some sleep. Everything will be straightened out tomorrow," he said.

"Do you think I'm gonna go to jail?"

"Not if I can help it. This Lucky guy was a real piece of work. There's no way any jury will ever convict you for protecting yourself," he said. "I'll see you tomorrow." Michael called for the guard. As he began to walk away, I wanted to beg him to stay with me even though deep down I knew that was ridiculous. He was my lawyer not my father. He looked so confident and strong. He wore a tailored charcoal grey suit. He was slightly grey and he walked with an arrogant pimp that said *I run shit.* He argued with the jail officials as he walked. I don't think I had ever really witnessed a man like him before. As he disappeared through the door at the end of my cell block, I could still hear his voice and I thought to myself maybe if I had a father like that I wouldn't be in this predicament right now. But deep down I knew black men like Michael were rare. I didn't have a father like him and no one I knew had a father like him so it wasn't any use in me feeling sorry for myself or using that as an excuse for my problems.

    I didn't sleep a wink that night. Instead I sat on my bed against the damp clammy walls of my cell and listened to rattling pipes that were obviously in need of repairs. I felt like I was being suffocated. As I sat and looked around the barely lit holding cell, I did some soul searching. I had given my heart to men who let me down over and over again, undermining my self-confidence.

    Before I knew it, it was morning and Michael was walking into my cell.
"What happened?" I said almost afraid to hear his response.
"The judge granted you bail since this is your first offense."
"Thank you," I yelled as I hugged him tight.
"Thank your brother. He paid your bail."
When I asked him how much it was, he shook his head and told me I didn't want know.
"It was that much."
"Yeah, it was that much. Look, go home, get some rest and remember, don't talk to anyone about your case. I'll be in touch."

    At my preliminary hearing, I pleaded not guilty. My defense was self-defense, but the prosecutor trying my case was a real hard ass. Word was that he was in line for a promotion to District Attorney and he wanted to make an example out of me. He had one agenda and one agenda only. That was to convince the people of Portsmouth that he was ridding the city of violence. When in actuality, crime was at its all time high.

My case was turned over to the grand jury for a hearing. After hours of testimony, they found there was enough evidence to send me to trial. I couldn't believe it. After hearing what a monster Lucky was, I was sure they would drop the charges against me. But they didn't. Seems Lucky was haunting me even from his grave. Not only was he making me suffer, he was making my family suffer as well. *Bastard.*

Two months later and 30 pounds lighter, my trial started. The courtroom was packed with my family and friends. My mother, Monique's mother, my brother and his family were all there. Deonte, looking sympathetic, and his girlfriend, along with her mother, Ida, had come. All of my girls were there to show their support—Brina, Nicole, Sheba, Londa, Vicki, Clova, Rachel, Convict Kim, Laisha and of course, my cousin, Monique. You know Lina's nosy ass wouldn't have missed my trial for the world. But I was most surprised to see Pit's girl, Kim, smiling at me from the back of the courtroom. *Guess the bitch rolled over on him after all. But what the hell is she doing here?*

I continued to look around when I noticed my crew from The Foot Locker and Captain D's. K-Dog, O.B., Quan and their crew, despite being uncomfortable in a court of law, had all come to show their love. The families of Lucky's victims had all come as well. There were people there I didn't even know. They were all there to show their support. The lead up to the trial had gotten a lot of news coverage. So I had support from a lot of women's groups that fought against domestic violence and for women's rights. There were hundreds of people outside with signs that read

"Free Zsaset and We want justice for Zsaset." Their support and compassion touched me.

After the prosecutor, a man named Warren Moffet, made his opening statement, I wanted to go over and spit in his face. Warren was your basic white racist who didn't give a damn about black people. He painted us all with the same brush and his goal was to lock up as many niggas as possible. The actual specifics of the case meant nothing to him. The county put Warren on the case because his conviction record was almost perfect. He portrayed Lucky as the victim of a horrendous crime and a man who provided for his family by working hard at the Ford Plant. *Who the hell was he talking about*, I thought to myself. First of all, this nigga was slinging dope from Portsmouth to New York. Second, did he notice the families of his victims sitting behind me still grieving? Third, did he see the photos of my face after the asshole almost beat me to death? What the hell was he thinking? No one was going to buy that choirboy shit.

One thing I had on my side, I hoped, was that the judge was a woman, a white woman, but a woman nonetheless. I could only pray that she could sympathize with a young black woman in a situation where she felt helpless and had to make a deadly choice.

Witness after witness took the stand in my defense. As each witness spoke, I would glance at the jury. Many of their faces didn't soften as people talked about how awful Lucky was. Monique, Laisha and Vicki testified about how Lucky beat my ass regularly. Warren was particularly hard on Monique for some reason.

"Ms. Jones, what is your relationship to the defendant?"
"Cousin."
"Speak up, Ms. Jones, so the jury can hear you."
"Cousin. I'm her cousin," Monique said and then roller her eyes at Warren.
"Oh, you're her cousin."
"That's what I said," Monique said with sass.

"So you would do anything to help your cousin out of a tough situation?"

"Look don't play games with me – Lucky was a crazy asshole and everyone in this courtroom will tell you the same thing."

Warren kept the pressure on everyone and the jury seemed to be buying the game he was playing. That's when I decided I needed to testify.

"Zsaset, that prosecutor will tear you apart," Michael said advising against it.

"I don't care. I need the jury to hear my side of the story. He was gonna kill me. They need to know that."

"I understand that, but it's your word against his. And since he's not here to defend himself, I'm telling you this is a suicidal move. I can't allow it."

"Well, it's not your choice. This is my life we're talking about." Mad, I stormed out the courtroom.

"Fine. But don't say I didn't warn you," he yelled as the doors to the courtroom closed behind me.

I couldn't sleep that night. I couldn't fathom the thought of going to jail for the rest of my life. What about my kids? Who was going to take care of them? I had no answers, only questions, so I turned to the only person I knew who had them. God. I prayed all night that he would make this nightmare go away.

The next day, before I sat at the defense table, my mother handed me a small piece of paper. It was a scripture from St. John. "Let not your heart be troubled: ye believe in God, believe also in me."

I turned around and smiled at her. She always knew what I needed even when I didn't.

With my family and my girls sitting behind me in the packed courtroom, my lawyer leaned over and asked if I still wanted to testify. I thought about it for several minutes, then I told him "No."

I could see the relief on his face as he stood up and told the judge he rested his case. After compelling closing arguments from both sides, the jury deliberated.

"Well this is it." He grabbed my hand. "It's in their hands now."

"Do you think they're gonna convict me?" I asked watching the last juror leave the box.

"Not a chance," Michael said with confidence. "Why don't you go home? I'll call you when the jury returns with their not guilty verdict," he said smiling. If Michael said it then it must be true.

"Alright. I could use a little rest. I was up all night."

"I'll call you when I hear something."

After eight hours of deliberation the jury returned. I didn't know if it was a good thing or a bad thing that they returned so early. I couldn't call it but I kept replaying Michael's words from earlier in my head. They put me at ease.

"Will the defendant please rise?" said the Judge. Slowly rising out of my seat, I turned and faced the jury "Mr. Foreman, has the jury reached a verdict in the case of Zsaset Jones vs. the state of Virginia?

"Yes, we have, your honor." The foreman had a look on his face that I now know was a sign. I ignored it and tried to focus on Michael's words to me earlier. I tried to make eye contact with the foreman but he looked straight ahead at the judge.

"What say you," said the judge.

When the foreman read the verdict I couldn't believe it.

"We the jury hereby find the defendant, Zsaset Jones, guilty of 1st degree murder."

The courtroom went into an uproar. My mind began to slowly leave, as I floated outside of myself. I felt like I was in a dream. Michael was yelling something at the judge. All of the

259

noise became very distant. It seemed very far away from me. I could hear this far off screaming. I think it was my mother but maybe not. When the deputies grabbed my arms, put them behind my back and began cuffing my hands, I heard a loud pop that surged me back fast from wherever I had started drifting to.

    I didn't understand what was happening until I heard someone say, "She's got a gun!" I heard three more shots, and watched helplessly as the deputy cuffing me fell to the floor from a gunshot to his neck. For some reason, I did not think to duck. Instead, I turned around to see who was doing the shooting.

    "I'm gonna kill you, bitch! You got him sent to jail and they killed him! Now I'ma kill your ass!" It was Kim, and she had a deranged look in her eyes.

    It was all happening so fast that I couldn't think. Then I felt a burning sensation in my chest. I could hear my mother and Deonte screaming, "No!"

    I looked down and saw the blood spilling out onto my starched, white shirt. I thought of Ryan and Zeta and my whole pathetic life flashed before my eyes. I was beginning to feel weaker and weaker. I dropped to my knees and looked up at everyone and mouthed the words, "I'm sorry." As I drifted into unconsciousness, my last thoughts were, *Damn, I should'a seen it comin'*.

Thank you for reading. Please be sure to check out these other titles from Nvision Publishing and Life Changing Books!

Before I Let Go
By Darren Coleman

A Life To Remember
By Azarel

Don't Ever Wonder
By Darren Coleman

Bruised
By Azarel

Do Or Die
By Darren Coleman
A novel by D

Double Life
by Tyrone Wallace

No Way Out
By Zach Tate

Lost & Turned Out
By Zach Tate

Coming Soon

Teenage Bluez

Secrets of A Housewife

Crocodile Tears

Nvision Publishing Order Form

No Way Out

Lost & Turned Out

Do Or Die

 Before I Let Go

 Don't Ever Wonder

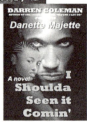 I Shoulda' Seen It Comin'

Add $3.95 for shipping via U.S. Priority Mail. Total of 18.95 per book for orders being shipped directly to prisons Nvision Publishing deducts 25%. Cost are as follows, $11.25 plus shipping for a total of $15.20. Make money order payable to Nvision Publishing. Only certified or government issued checks.

Send to:
Nvision Publishing/Order P.O. Box 274
Lanham Severn Road, Lanham, MD 20703

Purchaser Information

Name_____ Register #_____
(Applies if incarcerated)

Address_____

City_____ State/Zip_____

Which Books_____ # of books_____

Total enclosed $_____

Life Changing Books Order Form

A Life to Remember	Double Life	Bruised by Azarel	I Shoulda Seen it Comin'
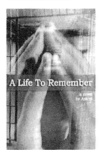			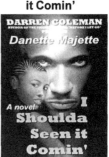

Add $3.95 for shipping via U.S. Priority Mail. Total of 18.95 per book for orders being shipped directly to prisons Life Changing Books deducts 25%. Cost are as follows, $11.25 plus shipping for a total of $15.20.

Make money order payable to Life Changing Books. Only certified or government issued checks.

Send to:
Life Changing Books/Orders P.O. Box 423
Brandywine, MD 20613

Purchaser Information

Name_____

Register #_____
 (Applies if incarcerated)

Address_____

City_____ State/Zip_____

Which Books_____

_____# of books_____

Total enclosed $_____

About the Author
Danette Majette, the interview

I recently sat down with Danette Majette, find out what her purpose was for writing the book.

D: So Danette, we both know you've been waiting for this day for some time, how does it feel to become a published author?
Danette: Oh my God it feels so good. I'm really excited the hard work has paid off.
D: Tell the readers a little about your purpose for writing this book?
Danette: I just wanted share some of the experiences that me and some of my friends went through growing up, and hopefully provide some lessons that young women can learn about getting caught up with bad boys, loving someone who doesn't love you, chasing after material things and most of all, playing games where there is *everything* to lose.
D: I feel you. So you're coming with some depth. I notice you repped the Tidewater area and the 804, Richmond.
Danette: Yeah, people sleep on V.A. Where I came from, Virginia was definitely not for lovers. It was rough.
D: I think you did a great job, any words for your fans about your future projects?
Danette: Yeah, the second book is almost finished and I definitely plan on taking it to the next level. To my readers, thanks so much for the support. Spread the word for me and please tell some folks to buy, not borrow... a girl is trying to come up. I love ya'll.

For more of the interview hit the Nvision Publishing, Life Changing Books website. Click on *I Shoulda Seen It Comin'*.

For info on availability of this title go to
info@nvisionpublishing